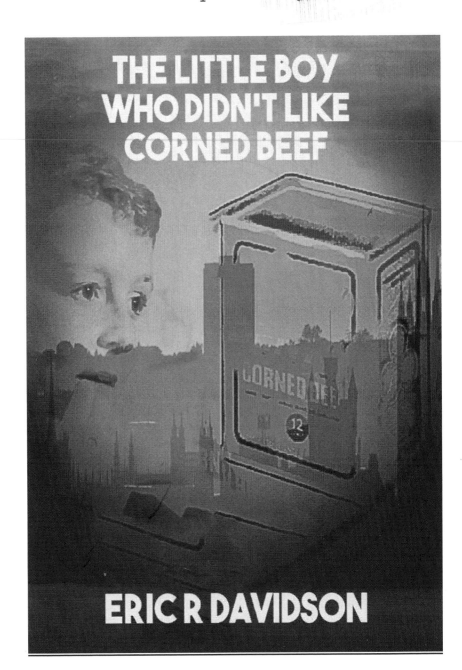

The Author Thanks:

Firstly, my thanks to my wife, Heather, for proof-reading this book and identifying changes that were required to the grammar, spelling and general flow of the story.

Secondly, my thanks to my son, Adam, who also proof-read the book but, more importantly, designed the cover. Given the title of the book, I was mightily impressed with how quickly he came up with the idea for this cover.

Although all the information, on the typhoid epidemic in Aberdeen, is readily available from the newspapers of the day, I do offer my thanks to Richard North, who wrote a narrative, on the subject, in January 2017, taking his information from *The Times* rather than the local papers. Richard provided one or two facts I had not picked up from the *Evening Express.*

The real timeline of events during the typhoid epidemic may not agree exactly with the one shown in the book. However, this is a work of fiction after all and I felt the story flowed better as a result of the few changes I made.

I should also note, at this point, that most of what Doctor Ian MacQueen says in this book was paraphrased from comments he made to the Press. The opinions expressed were certainly his own and I have not tried to put words in his mouth, simply to enhance the story in any way.

As usual, my thanks to The Diced Cap, my bible for all things related to the history of the police in Aberdeen.

I also offer thanks to those people who shared personal memories of how life was for them, back in 1964. For me, it was a time of longer school holidays and sunny days. I seem to remember programmes on the television during the day, which of course was not normal for those days. However, similar to today, most of the programmes were not very good.

I should also mention that I publish this while in the grip of the coronavirus. Much of what the world is being asked to do now can be seen in the action taken during the typhoid epidemic all those years ago.

Finally, I'd like to thank everyone who reads my books. Hope you enjoy this one as much. I have always wanted to write a story that involved the typhoid epidemic in some way; I only hope I've managed to come up with a story that does the idea proud.

Eric R Davidson – Aberdeen – April 2020

Other Books by Eric R. Davidson

1906 – September

1906 – October

1906 – November

1908 – Summer

1908 – Christmas

MILO: The Varga File

MILO: The Assassin File

MILO: The Election File

One Less For Dinner

Inspector Fraser's First Case (A Short Story)

1 1

It was out there.

It had been out there for a while.

For at least the last fourteen days it had been passing from one person to another, slowly spreading throughout the city, with even those who had become infected not realising anything was amiss.

It would eventually affect hundreds of people but, for the moment, only a handful were starting to suspect that something very serious might be about to surface.

The incubation period concealed the problem; at least for now.

It would not remain concealed for long. And when the incubation period ended and the numbers infected started to rise, everyone in the city would then be affected to one degree or another.

And it all started in the middle of May, 1964.

It all started with less than a dozen people being taken to hospital.

Over the next few weeks, it would develop into the biggest medical crisis the city of Aberdeen had faced in decades, possibly centuries.

And in the aftermath of it all, in some ways, things would never go back to the way they were.

*

It was Saturday, 16th May, 1964.

Detective Chief Inspector Graeme Ogston was in his element. For one thing he wasn't at work, something guaranteed to always put a smile on Ogston's face. For another, the sun was shining and the air warm, not something the north-east of Scotland always enjoyed.

Yes, it was a day to feel good and Ogston had more reasons than most, for his spirits being high. He was at Pittodrie and Aberdeen were leading, in a Summer Cup match, against Dundee.

He had a pie in one hand and a newly poured coffee in the other. Ogston always took a flask of coffee with him to every game he was able to attend. However, the pie was always bought from the stall at the Merkland Road entrance. It involved queuing, but Ogston felt the pie was worth the effort.

No one could enjoy watching a game of football without having a pie at some point of the match.

There were 9,000 other souls at Pittodrie that day and most of them had a smile on their face, a bit of a rarity for those who regularly followed Aberdeen Football Club.

Ogston was there on his own, offering his usual words of encouragement to the team and general abuse towards the referee. Truly, the men in black had been put on this planet to allow mere mortals to let off steam. And let off steam they did.

The game finished in a 3-1 victory for Aberdeen and kept them on track for winning their group.

Ogston left the ground and made his way to the queue of buses waiting just around the corner. He lived above Telemech, on Marischal Street, and any bus that took him to the Castlegate would suit him.

He climbed aboard and went upstairs, sitting at the back, where he'd always liked to sit since childhood. Once full, the conductor pressed the bell and the journey began. There was a general sense of wellbeing amongst the fans that day, with the football banter carrying on for the whole length of King Street.

In Ogston's mind it was as much part of the game as the match itself and he loved the humour that shone through in much of what was being said. The bus turned in to the Castlegate and Ogston hurried downstairs and jumped off.

He walked the relatively short distance to his flat. He lived on the first floor. He had been there for four years and liked the fact he was so close to work. From bed to desk was a little under five minutes: no one could complain about that.

Ogston let himself into the flat and immediately switched on the radio so that he could catch up on the other scores from the day. Half-time scores had been provided at Pittodrie, but only through a board at the back of the gasworks terrace, where metal numbers would be hung, to indicate the scores at other grounds.

However, the information meant nothing, unless a programme had been purchased. On the back of the programme would be the other fixtures and each match would be assigned a letter of the alphabet. The half-time board would only have that letter of the alphabet, so without the programme no one had any idea as to which match the numbers referred to.

There was also the little matter of not being able to read the board from many parts of the ground. Ogston had had neither programme nor view of the board, so now that he was home, he was able to check all the full-time scores. Graeme Ogston had always liked his football; it was the making of a Saturday afternoon.

Having brought himself up to date, with all the football news, Ogston then set about cooking himself something to eat. He was reasonably proficient in the kitchen and enjoyed his food too much to ever starve.

If Graeme Ogston were being brutally honest with himself, he'd have admitted to not being the greatest fan of living on his own. Although the thought of marriage had never been uppermost in his mind, the thought of growing old entirely on his own, did not appeal. He had had girlfriends over the years. Nothing had ever come of any of his relationships, often his job had got in the way. Not that he would ever have used the job as an excuse for his relative lack of success with the ladies.

No, that was entirely down to him.

Ogston had reached that point in his life, where he'd become set in his ways. Perhaps *too* set in his ways. There possibly was no longer space for romance. He was comfortable with his lifestyle and tried to keep all thoughts of growing old at arm's length.

In some respects, Graeme Ogston had been unlucky to be born at the wrong time. At just eighteen, he had been called up to fight for King and country. After a period of training in the south of England, he had found himself, in 1940, on his way to Norway.

He had just turned nineteen and now his country expected him to be a killer. He had been given a gun and trained in how to use it. While a man of his age ought to have been at the dances, chatting up the girls, he was on his way to war.

However, for Graeme Ogston, it would be a very short war. In only his second contact with the enemy, he was seriously wounded and shipped back to Britain. He had spent a year convalescing in a hospital in the south of Scotland, before being told that he would never fight for his country again unless the Germans invaded Britain, at which time everyone would be called to action.

Ogston had been hit by two bullets. The first had smashed his left shoulder, leaving his left arm functioning to only fifty per cent of its normal mobility. The second bullet had done permanent damage to his right leg. For the rest of his life, Graeme Ogston would walk with a limp.

Graeme Ogston had arrived back in Aberdeen in late 1941. Keen to still play an active, uniformed, part in the war, Ogston joined Aberdeen City Police.

Now, twenty-three years later, he was Detective Chief Inspector Ogston and living with the possibility that he would have to retire within the next ten years. He didn't like to think about retirement as that meant accepting he was getting older.

Walking with a slight limp, had never affected his duties as a police officer and being right-handed, his weak left arm had never been a problem either. Over time, Ogston had come to ignore both disabilities, seeking to push the positives of what he could offer the police force rather than dwell on the negatives.

His general fitness had always been tip-top. His mind was sharp and his eyesight keen. Ogston noticed things that other police officers didn't and he had a way with people that rarely ruffled feathers. Whether interviewing a petty criminal, or speaking to the Chief Constable, Graeme Ogston was accepted for what he was.

Colleagues rarely criticised Graeme Ogston and few had had issues with the promotions that had come his way. He was now, effectively, the man running the CID, in Aberdeen. A position he took very seriously.

Ogston took a piece of fish from the fridge. A refrigerator had been his latest purchase. His mother had told him it was a waste of money. To her, there would never be anything wrong with a well-stocked larder, even though the larder was always more successful in the cold of winter.

To go with the fish, Ogston cooked some chips. He cut up the potatoes and put the pieces in a basket, while the oil heated in a pan on the cooker. Ogston was not a fan of making chips; he could see the danger in it. However, it was a means to an end; if he wanted chips then he'd just have to make them.

He plunged the basket into the hot oil and it bubbled up furiously. There were many tales of fires being caused by chip pans, especially amongst drunks coming home from the pub and deciding a nice plate of chips would be a good idea. They'd heat the oil, fall asleep and in some cases, never wake up again.

Once the meal was ready, he sat at the kitchen table and ate the food, washing it down with a bottle of beer. He then washed the dishes, put them away and went through to the living room to watch some television.

By nature, Graeme Ogston was a very tidy person. He hated mess of any kind. Wherever he went and in whatever he did, Ogston created order around him and took unkindly to anyone who did not buy in to his tidiness.

Both at home and work, everything was in its rightful place and woe betide anyone who borrowed an item and didn't put it back where they'd found it.

Ogston settled down to an evening's television; he had The Saint and Morecombe and Wise to watch, which would pass most of the time. He also had one more bottle of beer to drink; another Saturday treat.

Much as his eyes might have been on the television screen, Ogston's mind wasn't really focused on what he was watching. His mind was pre-occupied with thoughts of his father, who had died a few days earlier.

The coming week would bring the funeral; an event which Graeme was not looking forward to in the slightest.

If truth be known, Graeme Ogston was only going to be at his father's funeral to offer support to his mother. Father and son had never been close. Graeme had always felt that his father had resented the fact his son had been wounded so early in the war.

Ogston Senior had always thought that his son had, literally, limped out of the war. Being a police officer was not the same.

Having played a full part in the First World War, Ogston Senior had known what it was like to fight for his country. He had felt lucky to have survived all those years of carnage. Now, as the world erupted into war yet again, he had got his son back almost before he'd gone away.

As a result, Ogston Senior never really accepted his son's return. There was always to be a distance between them. Graeme had tried bridging the gap, but soon learned to give up. His father had shown no interest in building bridges; no interest in repairing his relationship with his son.

Graeme had, therefore, gone his own way in life.

The police had provided early accommodation so he hadn't need to live with his parents on his return from his convalescence. Due to his father's rather off-hand attitude towards him, Graeme stopped visiting on a regular basis. Even his mother learned to live with the problems between father and son.

It hurt her deeply, but nothing she said seemed to have any effect on either of them.

Time passed and Graeme stopped going to the house altogether for a while. He maintained contact with his mother through lunches in the city centre. She'd plead with her son to patch things up with his father but, to Graeme, his father was the problem and he would have to make the first move.

That move had finally been made two months ago, when a father who now knew he was dying, got in touch with his son through writing a lengthy letter.

Graeme visited his parents at once. His father had lung cancer. He was already in a bad way, with a cough that threatened to turn him inside out. Father and son met three times more before death separated them forever.

Thankfully, Graeme's mother was a strong woman. She had lost a husband, but was determined to enjoy what was left of her own life. She had never smoked, but she had lived most of her life in a smoke-filled environment. Perhaps her own lungs had been damaged in the process?

She gave no thought to such things. She felt fine and saw no reason why she should not enjoy a number of years ahead. She had been greatly heartened by the fact that Graeme had started visiting again on a regular basis and that they would both be able to think of happier days, when attending the funeral.

Graeme hadn't been so sure that he'd be able to forget all the bad days, but he vowed to at least try.

*

As Graeme Ogston sat in his flat that night, pondering on missed opportunities in the relationship he'd had with his father, two medical students were being admitted to Aberdeen Royal Infirmary at Foresterhill. They were both suffering from stomach pains and diarrhoea and irrespective of any medical treatment they might have been receiving, their condition was getting worse and the doctors were worried.

A decision had been taken to monitor the students, but it hadn't gone unnoticed that other patients were being admitted with similar symptoms and they'd need to be monitored as well.

Though no one would openly say anything, there was a general sense of concern permeating the medical staff at Foresterhill and a feeling that this might just be the start of something major.

*

The next day was warm and sunny, yet again. It was a day for going to church, for those who were in anyway religious. For those who were not religious, it was simply a day of leisure, often the only one available to them.

Ron Smith was one of those enjoying a day of leisure with his wife and family. Ron worked for Aberdeen Journals, having been a journalist with the *Evening Express* since 1959.

Ron's wife, Doreen, had provided him with two children; Derek was now seven and Barbara, five. Doreen had gone through a difficult pregnancy with Barbara and had been told it would be dangerous for her to have any more children. Ron had then taken responsibility for Doreen's well-being, by having a vasectomy.

There would be no mistakes that might lead to another dangerous pregnancy.

Ron Smith was now thirty-seven. Prior to getting a job with the *Evening Express*, he had worked for rural papers covering stories as important as missing sheep and the occasional award, won by some farmer's wife for the scones she'd baked.

He had longed to write proper articles, so when he saw the advert for the *Evening Express* he had completed and sent his application before the day was out.

Ron had never moved the family to Aberdeen, however. They had a lovely cottage, just outside Ellon and there seemed no need for them to move. Sixteen miles was no distance to drive, even in the dead of winter.

That particular Sunday, Ron had decided to take the kids into the country for a picnic. There had been much excitement in the house as sandwiches were made and juice poured into flasks. Ron and Doreen were very happy together and liked to think their children would grow up with happy, childhood memories.

It was just after half past ten when they set off on their picnic.

*

Graeme Ogston was also out and about that Sunday. He had decided to visit his mother and make sure she was organised for the following Tuesday, which would be the day of his father's funeral.

Rose Ogston lived on Gordon Road in Mannofield. She had moved there, with her husband Archie, in 1937 when Graeme had been sixteen years old. Archie had worked in a bank and destined to be managing his own branch by the end of the war.

Gordon Road was a quiet, well-appointed street, in the Mannofield area of Aberdeen. Many of the residents had been there as long as Rose, so she got all the support she'd needed in the aftermath of her husband's death.

As Graeme got out of the car that day, he noticed a young woman walking in his direction. Even from a distance he liked what he saw and he deliberately took his time in locking the car door, giving her time to get closer.

It was only once she had walked right up to him that he realised it was Alison Young, daughter to his parents' neighbours who lived across the driveway.

Alison was ten years younger than Graeme. However, even as an eight-year-old, she remembered Graeme going off to join the army. She had always thought that the boy next door had been very handsome and ever so well mannered.

However, over the years, they had seen little of each other. With Graeme rarely going to Mannofield, there had been few opportunities for them to cross paths. In fact, this would be the first chance they'd had to speak to each other in years.

Alison's first impressions of Graeme was that he had retained his good looks.

As for Graeme, he still carried memories of that annoying little girl next door; the one who had been put out the back in her pram because she wouldn't stop crying as a baby. It was hard for him to accept that that baby was now a very attractive, grown woman.

Alison had been smiling as she had approached, but a solemn expression now crossed her face.

"I was so sorry to hear about your father," she said. "I didn't know him that well, but it's sad all the same."

"I don't think I knew him that well either," said Graeme. "Anyway, it's all about Mum now."

Those last words were accompanied with a glance towards the house. He felt sure his mother would be lurking behind the lace curtains, watching all that was going on outside. She'd be curious to know what Graeme and Alison were talking about. He expected a grilling once he got into the house.

Alison's parents were also in their mid-sixties. Her father was in perfect health for a man of his age, but her mother had developed various problems, for which there had been a constant need for pills. Their family circle was tighter and happier.

"Mum will probably stay at home, on Tuesday," Alison then said, "but Dad and I will be at the funeral."

Graeme found himself smiling, as if he had just heard the best news in the world.

"Thank you. How's life treating you these days?" he then asked, trying to keep the question as casual as possible. He was really fishing to find out if she was in a relationship, but daren't be so bold as to ask outright.

"Still in nursing and still too busy to have a real life."

"Just like being a police officer," added Graeme.

"Indeed. We are at the mercy of the job all the time."

Alison sounded quite down, as if she weren't entirely happy with the way her life was developing. On impulse, Graeme suggested they might meet for a coffee, or even lunch, someday.

Alison thought that would be an excellent idea. Graeme then asked if she might want a lift back into town. Alison thought that, too, was an excellent idea. They agreed to meet again at five.

*

Alison was still smiling as she closed the door and took her coat off. She was still thinking about Graeme, when her mother appeared from the living room with a smile on her face.

"Well, what was Graeme saying?"

"We were just talking," replied Alison, "about the funeral, if you must know."

"Rose seems to be bearing up well," Alison's mother then said.

"I know Graeme wasn't that close to his father," said Alison, "but it's always a terrible time when someone close to you dies."

Alison gave her mother a hug. There was a thought, at the back of Alison's mind, that her mother might not be long for this world. The pills were doing their job, but for all the good they were doing there had to be some bad mixed in there as well.

Alison knew that her mother wanted nothing more than to see her daughter happily married and producing children, before she died. Given that Alison wasn't even in a relationship, all thoughts of marriage seemed some years away.

Then again, maybe her mother didn't have those years?

Alison did have a sister. She was older and working in London. She had been away from home since she'd been twenty and apart from a letter, every six weeks or so, there had been no real attempt to maintain contact with home.

That meant her parents rather depended on Alison to provide the wedding and the kids. She also knew that her parents were concerned that, at thirty-three, Alison might never settle down.

Knowing that their daughter liked her job and was very good at it, would in no way replace the joy grandchildren would bring. Surely, she had to realise that?

Alison had never made plans, during any part of her life. She'd always wanted to be a nurse, so she'd committed to being the best nurse possible. She had had boyfriends, but none of them had instilled in her a desire to maintain a relationship and possibly, consider marriage.

In fact, it had been some time since she'd even been in a proper relationship. She, too, felt the years were passing and that the marriage ship had probably sailed.

So, why, was she grinning like a schoolgirl on her first date, simply because she'd said a few words to Graeme Ogston?

The afternoon was spent, for both Graeme and Alison, enjoying a nice lunch and chatting about anything and everything. Graeme, perhaps, spent more time talking about the funeral, but Alison had even touched on that subject in finalising arrangements with her father for Tuesday.

One subject Alison did not touch upon was that of the medical students, who were gravely ill in hospital. She also knew there were other patients, all suffering from what looked like the same disease. All very poorly and possibly, just the beginning of something that was going to get a lot worse before it ever started to get better.

She chose to say nothing to her parents. In fact, she would say nothing to anyone about what was happening at her work. The story would break in its own time and through the words of others. For just now, she would keep her conversation general and get away in good time to meet with Graeme.

*

At five o'clock, exactly, the doors of the two houses on Gordon Road opened and both Graeme and Alison exited, closing the doors behind them. They walked together down the driveway and out on to the pavement. They were both smiling, delighted to now get on with life after the dutiful family visit.

Graeme opened the doors to his car and they both climbed in. The first thing he did was light a cigarette and wind down the window. Even though his father had smoked, Graeme had never chosen to smoke in his company. He had always acted, when at his parents' house, as if he'd never smoked.

He had seen what smoking had done to his father, but it didn't make Graeme want to give up the habit. He enjoyed smoking too much and anyway, the Ogston philosophy was that cancer was meant for others; not him.

He offered Alison a cigarette, but she refused.

"Not the best habit for someone in your business, eh?" he'd then quipped.

"I've never been interested, that's all," replied Alison.

"Smoking is the only way I get through most working days," Graeme then said, with some honesty.

Alison smiled. She'd heard many of her colleagues say the same at her work. The calming influence of a cigarette seemed to outweigh any talk of them being bad for you.

Graeme started the car engine and then paused.

"I'm going for something to eat; would you care to join me?" he said.

For Alison, lunch had been nice, but quite light. The idea of having a little more to eat, before heading for home, seemed a good one and she accepted the offer without a second thought.

"I believe the Atholl Hotel does a mean high tea," Graeme then said. "My treat?"

Alison smiled again. "That sounds lovely," she said.

They drove across Anderson Drive and down King's Gate. They chatted the whole time. General stuff, nothing of any importance. They both felt it was better to keep talking. Although they knew *about* each other, they didn't really *know* each other, certainly not well enough to endure awkward silences.

Graeme parked the car at the back of the hotel and they walked round and in the front door. They were shown through to the dining room, where there was already a number of people sitting at tables; chatting across each other and awaiting the arrival of their food.

Graeme and Alison were shown to a table near the back of the room and a young girl, wearing a smartly ironed uniform, left them a menu and said she'd be back.

The meal passed all too quickly. They both enjoyed the food and the conversation, which they'd managed to keep going without much effort. Graeme had then driven Alison to her flat on Nellfield Place and stopped outside.

"I'll see you Tuesday," he then said, referring to the funeral. "I think Mum wanted to have everyone back to the house, so maybe we can talk more then?"

"That would be nice. Thank you for a lovely evening; I'll see you on Tuesday," Alison then said and got out of the car.

She walked to the front door of the property and stopped to wave in the direction of Graeme's car. He waved back. Alison let herself into the flat and Graeme drove off.

*

Davie Milne was twenty-six years old and lived in a flat on Fernhill Drive, in Mastrick. Until four weeks ago, he had lived there with his wife, Phyllis, but she had finally walked out on him.

She was now living in the same house, as an old acquaintance of Davie's, who had come to her rescue when she'd finally had enough of her husband and sought somewhere else to live.

The acquaintance was a man called Ranald Cusiter; a man Davie had spoken to on occasions, but never really liked. He should now be liking him even less, seeing as he'd stolen Phyllis. However, Davie knew exactly why Phyllis had walked out on him and, in truth, he couldn't bring himself to blame her. Anyway, she'd be a lot happier, living in Cusiter's big house on Argyll Place, than she'd ever have been remaining in the marital home.

Good riddance was, essentially, Davie's attitude. There were plenty more fish in the sea. In fact, Davie was going out with one of those 'fish' that very evening. Originally, with Phyllis in mind, he had bought tickets to see The Rolling Stones at the Capitol Theatre. Her loss would be someone else's gain.

It was Tuesday, 19th May 1964 and Davie was excited, not only to be seeing The Stones, but all the other acts on the bill. He was also excited to be seeing those acts with Sandra, the latest girl from work to catch his eye.

They both worked for William Low, who had a shop on Union Street, close to Holburn Junction. Sandra worked in the office, doing much of the manager's paperwork. She was very pretty, but quite young by Davie's usual standards. She was seven years younger, which was probably too big an age gap, but Davie was happy to give it a try.

Sandra, on the other hand, was very concerned about the age gap and had worried about going out with a man like Davie, almost to the point of calling off their date. However, she too wanted to see The Stones, so she reckoned she could put up with him for one night.

In her mid-teens, Sandra had been more a Cliff and The Shadows kind of girl, but now, as the Sixties headed towards its midpoint, she was trying to branch out with her musical tastes. She hadn't taken to The Beatles, but the rough look of The Stones had appealed and she even had a poster of Brian Jones on her wall.

Not that she'd ever have told anyone at work that, especially Davie Milne.

Sandra knew that Davie had been out with most of the girls in the shop. She also knew that Davie's wife had walked out on him; he'd made no secret of it. She worried about what Davie might have in mind, even on their first date.

She wasn't the type of girl who liked boys touching her, much as they all wanted to. She didn't even think much of kissing but, then, maybe she'd yet to meet someone who was actually good at it. She knew she wasn't. It had always turned out to be a bit of sloppy mess; not fun at all.

They left work at the same time that night. Davie walked Sandra to the Junction, where he caught his bus and she continued along Albyn Place. Davie took the bus to Summerhill Secondary School and walked up Fernhill Drive to his flat.

Once he got home, he wasted no time in washing and changing. He even managed a quick shave, splashing himself with a liberal dose of after shave. It smelled horrendous, but he hoped it would be good enough to meet Sandra's approval.

Once he'd changed, into an outfit of which he felt sure The Rolling Stones would have approved, he heated some beans and poured them over a couple of slices of toast. That was the limit if Davie's culinary skills. Firstly, his mother had cooked for him, then Phyllis. There had never been any need for Davie to cook for himself.

Until now. And the sad fact was, he couldn't.

So, beans on toast it had to be.

He sat at the kitchen table, eating the food and drinking a cup of milky tea. He was being especially careful so as not to leave any stains on his clothing. He couldn't imagine what Sandra would think of him, if he'd met her with a huge tomato stain down the front of his shirt.

His thoughts returned to Phyllis. Before she'd walked out on him, she had constantly warned him that his philandering would be the end of their relationship. Davie had had no idea what she'd meant. His only vice was liking other women and what could possibly be wrong with that?

In Davie's mind, the simple fact was that he should never have got married in the first place. Phyllis had turned his head for a little while, that was all. He should have left it as a relationship and never even considered the prospect of getting married. The only problem with that had been the fact he'd wanted sex and she'd wanted a ring.

Davie had eventually succumbed to pressure and proposed. Phyllis had accepted at once, though sex still wasn't on the agenda until after the wedding ceremony. Davie had waited for Phyllis by meeting other women, who were less fussy about what they did with their bodies.

Once he'd finished eating, he combed his hair in front of the mirror, then pulled on his jacket and viewed how he looked. He looked good; he knew he did. He only hoped Sandra would agree.

He left the house in good time and walked up to the church, where he caught a bus into the city centre. He was in high spirits; looking forward to the music, a few kisses and maybe the possibility of further dates. He certainly hoped he'd see more of Sandra. She was the kind of girl who would look good on his arm.

He didn't know much about Sandra. He knew she lived alone with her mother. That was about it.

Anyway, Davie would see Sandra home that night and at least get a better idea of how she lived. He hoped it wouldn't take him too far away from his bus route.

He got off the bus beside the statue of Rabbie Burns on Union Terrace and casually strolled up Union Street, to the Bank of Scotland which was on the corner of Holburn Street.

Five minutes later, Sandra arrived. She was looking even more beautiful, with a touch of make-up and her dark hair washed and brushed out. She was smiling as she arrived at where Davie was standing and he took her hand as they set off down Union Street.

There was already a queue waiting to get in, at the Capitol. It was mainly, as Davie would have expected, young girls. Some were chattering excitedly and others were standing, almost in reverence, as they clutched photographs of their idols to their chests.

Once inside, Davie and Sandra found their seats and settled down for the night's entertainment. Around them the chattering still went on. They had to hope that a silence would finally descend when the acts arrived on stage.

Mark Peters and the Silhouettes had the misfortune of having to open the night's proceedings. The crowd were there to see more famous faces. A band who had released but one single, which had basically gone nowhere, was of little interest to anyone.

Peter and Gordon were certainly better known, but their style was laid back and slightly pedantic. As they had simply stood at the microphone and sang, there had been little for the audience to get excited about. As a result, they received a lukewarm response at best.

Millie was far more exciting, bringing her teenage enthusiasm to the stage and getting the audience jumping about. Her session was short but still managed to inject an energy that had brought the crowd to life.

Dave Berry almost managed to kill that energy again, with his quirky style and downbeat ballads. However, the crowd hung in there long enough to welcome Freddie and The Dreamers to the stage. No one could ever accuse Freddie Garrity of not being energetic. The band's act usually involved them all jumping around the stage and generally acting the goat.

However, that night was to be different. Freddie was much more subdued, having sprained his ankle the night before. He moved around the stage with much more care than usual. The music still had energy, just not the band.

And then it was time for The Rolling Stones.

To Davie's mind, The Stones had arrived on stage that night looking bored, as if they had never wanted to drive to the north-east of Scotland in the first place. They were known for looking mean and moody at the best of times, but on that night the mood was definitely one of disinterest.

Not that the crowd seemed to mind the mood of the band. Girls leapt to their feet and screamed as loud as they could. Davie felt sure that some of the girls were actually wetting themselves with excitement, such was the hysteria that was being created.

Due to the general carnage around them, Davie and Sandra saw The Stones that night, but they could never have claimed to have *heard* them. The screaming continued until the band left the stage, thus bringing the first half of the show to an end.

An interval followed and Davie and Sandra made their way to the bar; somewhere where they knew more than half the audience wouldn't be going, due to the fact they'd have school the next day. A bottle of beer and a snowball later and they were back in their seats for the second half.

Not all the acts played the second half and again, everything was fine until The Stones returned. Once more all hell broke loose with only a few sporadic notes or words, managing to break through the general noise the young girls were making. They seemed oblivious to a band trying to play their music. Instead, they only saw five men who triggered all manner of fantasies in their young minds.

The concert ended and the theatre emptied. Davie and Sandra went for a coffee, rather than have any more alcohol when they had work next day. They chatted; becoming more comfortable in each other's company. Sandra even managed to say how sorry she was to hear that Davie's marriage had broken up. In truth she wasn't, but felt she ought to say it anyway.

Davie then saw Sandra to her front door. He was impressed by the house in which she lived. It was a terraced property on Albert Terrace, very posh in Davie's eyes. Sandra thanked him for the evening, allowed him one kiss and then turned to let herself into the house.

Davie walked the short distance to where he was able to catch a bus that would take him to Summerhill.

It was just before half past ten when Davie got home. He let himself in and made himself a cup of tea. He was just sitting down to drink it, when he heard a knock at the door. He went to the door and opened it.

"Oh, what are you doing here?" enquired Davie, looking slightly puzzled.

*

The evening had been a whole lot quieter for Sandy Burnett. Although he was Doctor Sandy Burnett, he was not, at present, working anywhere directly requiring the knowledge he had gained from years of medical study.

He was currently deputy to Doctor Ian MacQueen, the Chief Medical Officer of Health for Aberdeen, and most of his work these days was carried out behind a desk.

That evening, Sandy had got home at a little after six and enjoyed some time with his daughters, who were eight and ten in age. His wife, Mabel, was at her Civil Defence training, which was held in Queen's Gardens every Tuesday. Mabel had felt she wanted to be able to do her bit, should the Cold War escalate into something even more sinister.

Mabel also got paid for her Civil Defence duties. That payment had recently gone up thanks to Mabel becoming a qualified trainer. It was worth her giving up a few hours each week and the money gave her an element of financial independence.

Sandy had had his usual fun evening with the girls. He had cooked the evening meal, though 'cooking' might have been a bit grand as he had really only boiled some potatoes to go with a re-heated stew, which Mabel had left on the stove.

After they'd eaten, he'd played a few games of cards with the girls, before they'd eventually got ready for bed. Two stories later and both girls were settled down in bed, leaving Sandy free to go downstairs and enjoy a little time to himself.

As was customary for his Tuesday night, he poured himself a small, malt whisky, then settled down to watch the television. He'd checked the channels earlier and knew there was little on that would be of interest to him.

He watched *Highway Patrol*, at eight o'clock on Grampian and then changed to the BBC at half past eight to watch an episode in the series called *Saints and Sinners*.

Neither of them was particularly worth watching, but it filled an hour and a quarter of his evening and kept his mind off work-related matters.

He switched the television off at quarter past nine and sat back in his chair, finally letting those thoughts from work, invade his mind.

There was definitely a serious, medical issue, brewing in Aberdeen. He knew that Doctor MacQueen was a worried man which, in turn, made Sandy a worried man. He didn't usually get tense over work matters but, in this case, he couldn't help but feel that his stress levels were definitely on the up.

There were a number of seriously ill patients in Foresterhill. However, Foresterhill was not the place for keeping patients suffering from a contagious disease, and Sandy felt sure that was what they were now dealing with.

Arrangements had already been made to move those patients to the City Hospital, where staff were better equipped to deal with a major outbreak of any disease in Aberdeen. Sandy feared that they may be on the brink of just such a major outbreak.

Those seriously ill patients had all reported symptoms, similar to severe food-poisoning. However, medical opinion was that they could be dealing with something far more serious. Those patients, already in hospital, were showing no sign of recovery.

Food poisoning, no matter how severe, tends to pass relatively quickly once the patient has suffered the inevitable vomiting and diarrhoea.

However, these patients were showing other symptoms. They all had very high temperatures and some were suffering more from constipation, rather than diarrhoea. Stomach pains were prevalent as well.

Tests had been taken and the results of those tests would be known the following morning. Sandy was pretty sure what those results would be, but preferred not to ponder too much, on the consequences, until he had had them confirmed.

When Mabel got home, at a little after twenty past ten, she found her husband trying to do the crossword from that morning's paper. It was all proving too much for him, so he'd decided to make a cup of tea for them both. They'd chatted for the time it took to drink the tea and then gone to bed.

Sleep did not come easy that night. The outcome of those tests was still weighing heavily on Sandy's mind.

2   2

Sandy Burnett had made a point of getting into work early on the morning of Wednesday, 20th May. He was keen to know the outcome of the tests and still praying that what he and many others feared most, would not come to fruition.

He entered his office and took off his coat. He hung up his hat and sat down at his desk. There was the usual pile of papers demanding his attention, but Sandy could not concentrate on anything until he knew the outcome of the tests.

Ten minutes after he sat down, the intercom on his desk buzzed. His secretary informed him that Doctor MacQueen wished to see him in his office. Sandy thanked his secretary for the information and stood up. Suddenly, he felt like a pupil being called to the headmaster's office to be informed of his exam results.

Although Sandy needed to know the results that morning, there was a piece of him that wished to remain in the dark. In his heart he knew what the news would be, but until he actually heard it from Doctor MacQueen there was always that small hope that he was wrong.

Sandy walked the short distance to the office occupied by Doctor Ian MacQueen, where he knocked on the door and was invited in.

Ian MacQueen sat at his desk, with a solemn expression on his face. He was a heavy-set man, with a good head of hair and thick rimmed spectacles. He was a man who exuded an air of authority; he even *looked* like someone who knew what he was doing.

MacQueen was studying some papers, lying on the desk in front of him. He ushered Sandy to sit down. Sandy Burnett was younger, leaner and probably more enthused about his work, but MacQueen was the man in charge. There was no doubt in Sandy's mind that if there were any particular medical issues, about to arise in Aberdeen, then it would be to Doctor MacQueen that everyone would turn.

The buck, most certainly, would stop with him.

MacQueen eventually looked up and fixed a stare on Sandy. "It is what we thought," he said, his eyes tending to look over his spectacles, rather than through them.

"Typhoid?" said Burnett. MacQueen nodded, his expression one of deepening concern.

"Exactly," he said. "The news couldn't be any worse, but we have no time to feel sorry for ourselves, there's work to be done. A lot of work."

MacQueen said he'd been in his office for over an hour. He had spent that time deciding on who he would now turn to, as his first line of defence against the spread of the disease. He had decided on a small team of experts. He'd also chosen the man to lead the group: Sandy Burnett.

"Your main priority, Sandy, is to prevent panic," MacQueen now said. "Your team can be together, by lunchtime today and you need to hit the ground running. Firstly, I want all the current patients interviewed. I know some of them may be next to useless at the moment, in terms of providing useful information, but they need to be spoken to while memories might still be sharp."

Sandy was nodding.

"We'll need to know what they've eaten, in the last couple of weeks," he said.

"And perhaps, more importantly, where they bought the food they've eaten," added MacQueen. "We need to identify the source as quickly as possible, so that we can prevent further sales of contaminated food."

"You feel certain that food will be the source?" asked Sandy.

"Oh, yes," said MacQueen. "If the source had been water, or even milk, then I feel certain we'd already have far more cases than we have."

Sandy could see the sense in MacQueen's thinking. "With the high temperatures of the disease bring about hallucinations, we may end up with the wild ramblings of a seriously ill individual?"

"Indeed, we might," agreed MacQueen," but they won't all be like that. We have no option, Sandy, the quicker we find the source of the contamination, the quicker we put an end to phase one of the disease."

"Who's going to be in the team?" Sandy then enquired.

MacQueen slid a sheet of paper across his desk and Sandy picked it up. He read through the short list of names, four men and one woman; all at the top of their field of experience.

"Do we have office space yet?" was Sandy's next question.

"Being set up, as we speak," replied MacQueen. "I'm locating you down at the City Hospital, because I believe that is where most of the essential work will be done. You'll have office space and the help of a couple of administrative employees, who have still to be selected. Perhaps, you can deal with that yourself?"

"Of course," said Sandy. "I'd better get organised, in that case."

And with that he hurried from the room. Doctor MacQueen placed his pipe in his mouth and reached for the phone.

*

Detective Chief Inspector Ogston arrived at the Princess Café just as the Town House clock was striking nine. He was delighted to find Alison already there.

The previous day, at the funeral, they had spent some time in each other's company. A few people had gone back to the house for a cup of tea and a section of one of his mother's cakes. Graeme had spent most of his time in Alison's company. They had agreed that their jobs were likely to get in the way of them seeing each other, which was something they'd decided they'd like to do.

After further discussion, they agreed to meet for coffee during the day, if and when they found the time. Alison was to be working that night, but suggested they meet for a coffee as she made her way home the following morning. Graeme had thought that a good idea. The Princess Café was chosen as their first meeting place and a time agreed.

Both of them knew that it would make a pleasant change to have the opportunity to get away from work, even for a little while and be able to relax a little.

Alison knew, by the time they met that morning, that her own working life was about to get very, very busy. She had not needed word from on high, she had seen the patients who were now in quarantine. Alison knew the symptoms those patients were exhibiting.

She knew the city was experiencing its first cases of typhoid. She also knew they wouldn't be the last.

Not that she was going to say anything to Graeme, that morning. Conversation was kept light and even though they had only seen each other the day before, they found it easy to fill their time together.

A pot of tea was ordered, along with a bacon roll for Graeme and a cake for Alison. Alison was on her way home, eager to get some sleep, while Graeme's day had only started an hour or so ago.

They were together for forty-five minutes. They laughed a lot and Alison felt better for her time with Graeme. It had been the perfect foil for the pressure building at work. The timing of their meeting really couldn't have been better.

They exchanged phone numbers. They were work related, as neither of them had a phone in their flat. They hoped to see each other again, though neither felt sure as to when that might be.

Graeme paid and they made their way back on to Union Street. Graeme said he'd phone Alison, at her work, a little later in the week and maybe she'd have a clearer idea as to when they could meet again, even if it was just for another coffee.

Alison was smiling as she made her way to the bus stop. As she waited for the bus, she watched Graeme make his way down Union Street, following his back until he disappeared in to George Street. Alison felt a tremendous feeling of well-being, when she was with Graeme. It was a feeling she had never really experience before, when a man had been in her life.

Why, then, should it be different this time?

*

By one o'clock, Sandy Burnett had met with his new team and discussed how they would play those first few hours. He also found the time to arrange for a couple of admin girls to help out with the inevitable mound of paper that would arise from their enquiries.

The eight staff were housed in two rooms, neither being of any great size. In one room there were three tables, which they had pushed together to form one large workspace, around which they could all sit. The admin girls were in the other room, along with two further desks which Sandy's team could use, if they felt the need to spread out a little.

Four fourteen-drawer cabinets had been provided, along with two two-drawer cabinets. There was also a phone in each room and the switchboard had been brought up to speed on who could be found at the two extensions. The women on the switchboard had also been briefed as to the urgency of putting calls through to those extensions. They were to take priority at all times.

All this had to be done until Doctor MacQueen, himself, said otherwise.

Sandy and his colleagues drew up a brief questionnaire. Although the team now consisted of eight people, only four of them were doctors. It was agreed that only the doctors would deal with the questionnaires, so the patient number was quartered and they set about their business.

With the patients being held in quarantine, no one was being allowed near them, other than the medical staff. Most of them were too ill to receive visitors anyway.

Questions were asked, wherever possible and answers written down. The team were looking for specific information. They were seeking something, which the patients might have in common. Some of the patients were better able to answer the questions than others. However, whatever was said, it was written down. Sandy's team did not want to miss anything in those first hours of their investigation.

The questions were simple: had they eaten the same foods or visited the same shops? If they could find the common denominator, then they'd be a long way towards identifying the source of the disease.

The main problem was the two-week incubation period, that the disease carried. Even without the effects of an illness, who remembers what they ate last night, let alone over the last fourteen days and more?

Sandy decided he would start with the two medical students. They had been first to show symptoms of the disease and were now responding to the treatment they were being given. It would be a long, slow recovery, but at least they had now begun that journey.

That being the case, they were both in a slightly better condition to deal with Sandy's questions. Also, being medical students, they had a better understanding of what they were going through and why it was vitally important to answer Sandy's questions in as much detail as possible.

The two students proved to be excellent subjects. Their diet had been limited. They had tended to eat what passed as cheap and cheerful food. They could tell Sandy exactly what they'd eaten and the main shops they'd bought their food from. It had proved an excellent starting point.

Sandy noted down everything that had been said and thanked them for their help. Both students had a resigned look upon their face. They knew they were going to be in hospital for a long time, but they also knew they *would* fully recover.

By the time he returned to his new shared office, the others were already collating the information they had gathered. With the full team trying to work from the two rooms, there wasn't a great deal of space, but it was something they were just going to have to get accustomed to. For them now, it was about getting quick results, rather than showing concern for their work environment.

As the information was looked at in more detail, it already seemed as if a pattern was developing. One shop appeared on all but one's list of places they'd bought their food at.

One woman steadfastly remained adamant that she had never bought anything at that shop so it was quite impossible for her to have been infected by food from that source.

With that one patient not fitting the pattern, Sandy worried that there might be more than one source. Though the evidence might have been pointing that way, Sandy didn't want to believe that there could be more than one outlet selling contaminated food in Aberdeen.

There was also the matter of which, specific, meat had become infected. The answer to that question was to become all too obvious when information was recovered from an entire family, who were now quarantined in the City Hospital.

There were six people in the family and only five of them had taken ill. It became clear that the five infected patients had all eaten corned beef at a time when the sixth member had not.

Their youngest boy had not liked corned beef; he'd had something else.

So, Sandy was pretty sure he'd found his source. Somehow, an infected tin of corned beef had found its way into a shop on

Union Street and from there, it had been sold to the general public.

However, when Sandy presented his thoughts to Ian MacQueen, much later that afternoon, he did not find his boss instantly agreeable to his theory.

MacQueen took the view that a carrier was more likely to be the problem. In his mind, a member of staff had to be a typhoid carrier and in touching the meat, they had passed on the disease to others.

MacQueen's opinion caused Sandy even more concern, which he put into words.

"But if you are correct then we may have multiple carriers and multiple sources for the disease starting?"

"Let us hope there was just the one carrier for just now," said MacQueen. "Your initial findings seem to point to one shop, so let's concentrate our efforts there, for the moment.

He then instructed Sandy to take a team to the shop in question and to have all the staff tested for the disease. If he was right then one of them had to be a carrier of the disease and once that individual had been identified, then it would be easier to trace those unfortunate to have come into contact with him, or her. MacQueen still hoped to contain the disease, thus preventing great numbers from becoming infected.

Sandy reminded his boss that there was still one woman adamant that she'd never shopped at William Low. If she were correct, then there had to be at least one other source. Doctor MacQueen again said that, as the other patients all had William Low in common, they would concentrate on that shop until other information came to hand.

"Visit the shop," he then said, "and test all the staff. While you are there, make sure they are reminded to keep their slicing machines clean, at all times, to prevent cross contamination with other meats."

"I'm guessing most of them will only get properly cleaned at the end of the working day," said Sandy.

"And little more than wiped down at busy times," added MacQueen. "Traces of the disease will, most certainly, have been on those blades, so goodness knows how many have been infected over the last few days."

The more MacQueen thought about the problem, the more he decided that his chances of keeping the figures of infected patients low, was slim at best.

"Our first aim is to stop any more infected meat being sold," he then said. "That means William Low cleaning everywhere around their butchery department and keeping everything clean thereafter. It also means that anyone, identified as a carrier, will have to be removed from their place of work for the foreseeable future."

The problem with disease carriers is that their own host immunity system is able to tackle the infection and prevent the disease from fully attacking them. They do, however, retain the bacterium, which causes the disease and can therefore, continue to infect others without being aware of what they are doing.

The fact that a carrier could be infecting others for up to two weeks, before any symptoms would begin to show, meant that any number of people in Aberdeen might already have the disease.

This early in the life of the disease, MacQueen and his team could only guess at the number who might end up contracting the disease. Even introducing policies immediately would have no effect on those already infected.

Sandy left MacQueen's office, intent on making arrangements for the visit to William Low's, which would take place the following morning.

While he was doing that, however, matters became a little more complicated.

There was a ship, docked in Aberdeen harbour, that had recently travelled from a typhoid zone in South America. It was now possible that a carrier, or carriers, could be aboard the ship and that they had, in some way, introduced the disease to the city.

It was certainly a possibility, but in Sandy's mind, only a slight possibility. He felt the weight of evidence still pointed more towards William Low being the source but, just to be sure, he dispatched two of his team to test the crew of the ship.

Until those results came back, he would continue to keep an open mind on the subject of how the disease had arrived in the city.

While two were testing the crew of the ship in the harbour, the others had started compiling a list of all the people who could already have come into contact with the infected patients. Those in quarantine were re-interviewed for that purpose.

There was around nineteen people already in hospital. It should come as no surprise to anyone that nineteen people can come into contact with an awful lot of people, over a two-week period.

Sandy fully expected their final list to run to hundreds of names. He also knew that as those people became infected then, they in turn, would need to compile a list of contacts. It would be never-ending until they managed to break the back of the numbers being infected.

Meanwhile, Ian MacQueen had made a decision regarding how he would keep the media informed of proceedings. He recognised the need for newspapers to carry as much information as possible, but that information had to be accurate. There was no place for anything going to print that wasn't true.

To that end, he set up a twice-daily meeting with the Press. It would only be a few invited journalists and the meetings would be held in his office. There was limited space, but he felt it was the right place to hold such meetings. His desk, after all, was the centre of the investigation; journalists would expect him to have all the answers at hand.

Later that day, Sandy had returned to MacQueen's office to clarify what was expected from the visit to William Low's the following day.

"Should we be closing the shop?" Sandy had asked after sitting down and crossing his legs.

MacQueen had considered the matter for a moment and then shook his head.

"I'd rather not go public on which shop might be the source of this disease, just yet. If we did that then everyone would stop shopping there for everything. I don't want to destroy their business completely, especially as they've done nothing out of malice; they've just been unlucky."

"Surely, the public ought to know though?" Sandy had insisted.

"Perhaps, but not at the moment," insisted MacQueen. "Firstly, we need to confirm that William Low's was definitely the sole source then we can consider the best course of action to take after that. In the meantime, if we remove potential carriers and get the place cleaned, we should put an end to the first wave of the disease at least."

"Very well," Sandy said, but with little conviction.

He wasn't totally convinced by MacQueen's line of thinking, but chose to bow to his superior's opinion anyway. He left MacQueen's office and headed for home. He wanted to have a nice relaxing evening and then get a good night's sleep. He felt sure there might not be too many more, until the disease had been brought under control.

3 _____ 3

The following day, Samuel Reynolds opened William Low's shop on Union Street and let himself in. There were one or two staff already waiting at the door, so they followed him in. Overhead the sky was grey and a threat of rain hung in the air.

The front of the shop was mainly glass, affording the potential customer a clear view of what lay inside. Just inside the front window was a line of containers, each filled with a special offer for that week. Other offers were advertised on sheets of paper stuck to the window. It was all about luring customers into the shop; all about making William Low look like it would be the best shopping experience ever.

It was Thursday morning; the working week was wearing on. Reynolds had been manager of the shop since it had opened, but he had never considered it necessary to put down roots in Aberdeen. He was a career man, never seeking to marry, always concentrating on the job and where it might lead him.

Reynolds had been born in Edinburgh and hoped, one day, to return to the city of his birth. He had never considered Aberdeen as a proper city. It was too small for a start, everyone seemed to be on top of each other. There was no breathing space.

William Low's was one of those shops beginning to embrace the relatively new idea of self-service. Reynolds wasn't a fan. He saw it as the first step to massive staff cuts; the first move towards having as few people working for you as possible. He even feared a little for his own future. Maybe they wouldn't need shop managers for just a handful of staff?

The shop was long and narrow. The self-service shelves were in the middle and against the walls were the departments where it was still felt the personal touch was needed. There was no way that a customer could be expected to help themselves to their meat, bread or cheese for example. Reynolds could never see a day coming when that would ever be the case.

The butchery department was at the far end of the shop. To the right of the butchery counter was a doorway, leading through to three rooms as the very back of the building. The rooms were of varying sizes.

The manager occupied the smallest space. His office was little more than a glorified cupboard. It might have been small, but it at least gave him some space to call his own. He guarded that space as if his very life depended on it, even to the extent of not allowing the cleaner in to tidy up. He told everyone that he'd deal with that himself, but he never did.

His office, therefore, was little more than a tip. Paper lay everywhere and the surface of his desk hadn't seen the light of day in some time. The bottom, right-hand corner of his desk was the only area devoid of paper. Instead, clearly visible to the casual visitor, were ring marks left by coffee mugs being laid down.

Old Mrs Grant had often sought permission to clean the office, but had been knocked back emphatically. She was not to enter the office and she was never to touch anything belonging to the manager. There was more than enough to keep her busy elsewhere in the shop.

Reynolds went in to his office and took off his coat. Along with his desk, the room contained two chairs and a four-drawer cabinet. On the desk was a phone, a blotting pad and an ornate desk organiser, which contained two pens, a ruler and a cup for paper clips.

The desk organiser was the only sign of order.

Reynolds sat down behind his desk and moved some of the papers to the side. That was pretty much his idea of tidying up. Nothing got put away, only moved. The four-drawer cabinet was all but empty, due to the fact everything was left lying around, rather than getting filed away.

Next door to the manager's office, was the middle- sized room. This was where all the administrative work was carried out. Two staff worked there, Sandra Riddell dealt with the general staffing issues and an older woman worked on matters relating to finance.

Reynolds would openly have admitted that he'd employed Sandra purely for her looks, but she had proved herself to be a competent and very effective employee. There was an old head on young shoulders, which he now claimed he'd spotted from the start.

The largest of the three rooms was across a narrow corridor. Here the staff could hang up their coats, eat their lunch and keep a few personal items in their designated drawer, which was housed in one of two fourteen-drawer cabinets.

Everything else about the shop was visible to the customer out front. As the morning got underway, staff were out front organising themselves when Sandy and his team walked in through the front door.

Everyone could tell, immediately, that the small group entering their shop were not customers. They had arrived in a very business-like manner. Whatever they were there for, it was something important.

While the others waited at the door, Sandy sought out a member of staff and asked to speak to the manager. The young girl had then asked Sandy to follow her. She led the way through to the back and knocked on one of the doors.

A male voice beckoned her to enter. Mr Reynolds looked up as she entered the room, though his eyes were more on the man behind her, rather than the girl herself. Head Office hadn't mentioned anything about reviews being carried out, so Reynolds was instantly a worried man.

Before the girl could tell Reynolds who the man was, Sandy had brushed past her and was handing Reynolds his card.

"Doctor Burnett, Public Health," said Sandy, pausing to look at Miss Simms. His expression told her to get lost, so she did. Once the door was closed, Reynolds spoke.

"What can I do for you, Doctor Burnett?"

"We have reason to believe that your shop might be the source of a contagious disease that has been let loose on the city."

Reynolds looked as if he were about to question that statement, but Sandy held up his hand, as if demanding silence. Reynolds, therefore, said nothing and Sandy continued.

"I haven't time to debate the subject, my team are here to take blood from all your staff, including yourself. Maybe we could set up in one of the offices?"

Reynolds stood up. "We don't really have offices," he said.

"There must be somewhere, we can set up," said Sandy. "Obviously, the quicker we get those blood samples, the quicker we'll be out of your hair."

Sandy instantly saw the humour in what he had just said. Reynolds didn't really have much hair, apart from some manfully clinging around his ears and just above the back of his neck.

"Which disease are we being accused of spreading?" Reynolds then asked.

Sandy was reluctant to answer the question. People usually reacted to the word 'typhoid' as they did to the word 'plague'. In some people's eyes it was one and the same thing which, of course, it wasn't. People saw both as being caused by dirt and squalor, so no modern-day city would ever want to be associated with such thinking.

For that reason, Sandy decided not to answer the question. Instead, he asked one of his own.

"Where would be best for my team to set up?"

Reynolds again looked as if he wanted to debate the subject, but he quickly realised by the set of Sandy's jaw, that his visitor meant business. His point had already been well made; the quicker the tests were complete, the quicker they'd be on their way.

Reynolds took Sandy through to the staff room, where the furniture was rearranged to provide working space for the testing team. Sandy suggested that Reynolds should organise a rota for the staff, so they'd know when to go through to give blood. Reynolds seemed outraged at being asked to do such a menial chore.

"I'll get Miss Riddell to deal with that," he'd replied.

"Oh, and I'll need the names and addresses of any staff who aren't at work today," added Sandy.

"Miss Riddell can provide you with that as well," answered Reynolds, as he hurried from the room, obviously concerned that he might be asked to do something else.

Sandy went back out front and waved the team towards the back of the shop. He then led the way through to the staffroom and left them to organise themselves, ready for the work ahead. He explained that the staff would come through, in an orderly fashion and that all the tests were to be taken as quickly as possible.

While some of the team were dealing with taking blood, others were in the butchery department organising the cleaning of slicing machines and all other, relevant, surfaces. The machines were taken apart and every part cleaned thoroughly.

Until the work had been completed the public were being kept away. A sign had been placed in the door, claiming staff training was taking place and that they'd be opening at lunchtime.

The staff who weren't working in the butchery department, stood around waiting for further instructions. Reynolds was, by then, hiding in his office and Sandra Riddell was busy drawing up a last of staff before going through to tell them what would be happening.

Half an hour after Sandy and his team had walked into the shop, the first member of staff was having blood taken from him. Others had wanted to ask questions, but soon realised that answers were not going to be forthcoming.

They were told about the possibility of contaminated meat having been sold there and that one of them could be a carrier of a contagious disease. Again, no name was given to that disease which, in many respects, made the staff feel even more anxious.

"Could we die?" one young girl had enquired, as she had blood taken from her.

"No one is going to die," came the reply but, of course, no one could be sure of that answer being accurate.

Sandra brought the last piece of information to Sandy. These were the staff who were not at work that day. Sandy was relieved to find only four names on his list.

"I forgot to ask if anyone had been paid off, or left for any other reason, within the last two to three weeks?" he then asked.

"No one," came the reply.

Another reason for Sandy to feel relieved. He thanked Sandra for the work she'd done, then went through to the staffroom to let the others know he was going out for a little while. He had decided to visit the four names on his list personally, leaving everyone else to get on with their own jobs.

Just before he left the shop, Sandy checked his list again. Sandra had noted, beside each name, why the person was off work. Two were sick. They'd both phoned the shop two days ago to say they were unwell, but they'd be back as soon as possible. The third name on the list was on holiday and was known to be staying at home.

The fourth name was the only unknown element. He hadn't been at work since leaving on Tuesday, but there had been no phone call to explain his absence.

Sandy left the shop and walked to where he had parked his car earlier. Once seated behind the steering wheel, he looked at his list, paying particular attention to the addresses. He, mentally, planned the best route to take, which would allow him to cover all the addresses in the shortest space of time.

Once satisfied with exactly where he was going, he started the engine and set off in the direction of Garthdee.

The staff member, who was officially on holiday, was found at home. He was rejoicing in being able to stay in bed for as long as he liked. He had provided a blood sample, seen Sandy out of the house and then returned to bed.

The first of the two staff known to be sick, turned out to be suffering from a migraine headache, which had spilled into a second day. She said she'd felt a lot better, but not up to going to work. Sandy had taken blood from her and then gone on his way.

The third visit was not so straightforward. Zena Morrice lived on her own. When she had phoned in sick, she had played down the severity of her symptoms. She was in fact, very ill and Sandy knew immediately what was wrong with her. She had barely found the strength to open the door, but she knew it had been her only way of attracting help. She had no phone in the house and the nearest box was at the end of the road.

Sandy suggested she go back to bed and told her he'd be back. He'd hurried to the phone box and dialled a number, which he knew would take him straight through to the ambulance service. He gave his name and the reason for the call. He then gave them Zena's address and asked that they get there as soon as possible. He then went back to the house where he waited until the ambulance arrived.

He told them to take Zena straight to the City Hospital and then made his way back to the car. He checked his list and noted that his last call would be Fernhill Drive, in Mastrick.

Surely there would be no more excitement that day?

It was late morning when he pulled up outside the relevant tenement block. He checked the name on his list. *David Milne. Butcher. Last worked on Tuesday. No contact since.*

Sandy knew the area quite well. When he'd gone to Aberdeen Grammar School, for his secondary education, Sandy had been friends with a lad who'd lived around the corner, on Arnage Drive. They had often wandered around the area, passing time and generally larking about.

Sandy entered the building and was immediately struck by how clean everything was. Clearly, there was at least one resident who had a pride in the surroundings. Sandy checked the number he was seeking again and then started to climb the stone steps.

On the first floor, he found the address he wanted. He knocked on the door and noted it wasn't properly closed. He pushed a bit harder and the door opened a little further.

"Hello, is anyone at home!" Sandy called out. There was no reply, so he opened the door wider.

"Mister Milne! My name is Sandy Burnett, I'm from the Public Health Department. May I come in?" he then added.

Again, there was no reply. In fact, there was no sound whatsoever to indicate someone might be at home. Sandy called again and as he did so, he opened the door fully and stepped into a long and narrow hallway.

From what he could now see, the flat seemed to be in decent order, though the choice of wallpaper in the hallway would not have met with Sandy's approval. He shouted out Milne's name again and started to walk along the stretch of carpet. There were four open doors, either side of the hallway, and one closed door at the very end.

Sandy noted a bedroom and bathroom to his left and a kitchen and bedroom to his right. Eventually he reached the closed door and at that point, he paused.

He once more shouted Milne's name and again there was no response. It was now just a matter of opening the door and entering what he assumed must be living room. Something, however, was stopping him. It was as if his muscles had frozen and the simple act of stretching out a hand was now beyond him.

He stood there a few seconds more. For one last time he shouted Milne's name, as if hoping the man had been in a deep sleep and would now wake up and rush to open the door.

Nothing happened.

Sandy finally overcame his momentary muscle loss and pushed down on the door handle. It swung open.

He entered a darkened room. There were two windows, one larger than the other and the curtains were still drawn on them both. There was some sunlight filtering through, but not enough to allow Sandy to get a look at the contents of the room. He crossed the floor and pulled open the curtains on the larger window. Light flooded into the room.

He turned to have a better look around the room. His eyes fell on a sight that caused his stomach to churn. For a brief moment he thought he might vomit, but the sensation past. He moved a little closer to what turned out to be the body of a young man.

He was lying face down on the carpet. The back of his head was a mass of blood, skull fragments and brain tissue. Someone had used a particularly heavy weight, probably killing the man with one blow.

Blood had stained the carpet around the man's head and Sandy bent down to check for signs of life, even though he already knew he wouldn't find any. The body was cold and rigor mortis was evident. Sandy's medical training told him the man had been dead for less than three days, probably a lot less.

He hurried back out of the flat, closing the door behind him but ensuring it hadn't locked in the process. He went downstairs and outside, taking in gulps of fresh air to help fight the nausea that still threatened to overwhelm him.

He walked up the street, knowing there was a police building on the other side of Greenfern Road. It was positioned between Mastrick Church and the Community Centre. It was a small office, but Sandy knew there would be at least one police officer there, who would know what to do in the circumstances.

It turned out to be little more than an enquiry point, with two uniformed officers positioned behind a short counter. Sandy had noted a police car parked outside. There was also a door to the right of the counter, which Sandy thought might indicate more working space.

A fresh-faced, young man, wearing a uniform that looked as if it had just come out of the wrapping, stood up and came to the counter.

"Yes, sir, can I help you?" he enquired, with a welcoming smile.

'I am a doctor," Sandy began, "and I've just found the body of a young man, whom I believe has been murdered."

As soon as the words were out of his mouth, the second police officer sprang to his feet and came to the counter. He looked to be a lot older and, presumably, more experienced in matters pertaining to the police.

He immediately took over, asking a series of questions and mentally retaining the answers. It did not take long for him to decide that a visit would be needed to the premises in question.

Before leaving the office, the senior officer then told his junior to phone Lodge Walk and to notify CID, so that they could send someone out to take control of the investigation.

"Best let the Police Doctor know as well," the senior man added, as he reached the front door. "They'll need confirmation of death before the body can be moved."

The young officer glanced in the direction of Sandy. The older officer seemed to read the unspoken question on his colleague's face.

"We need a formal medical opinion, his won't count," said the older man, nodding towards Sandy.

The young Constable picked up the phone as the others made their way from the building. Once at the front door, of the flat on Fernhill Drive, the police officer suggested that Sandy step back. He then opened the door and entered.

Sandy was asked to wait in the kitchen.

The police officer then proceeded through to the living room, to see for himself what Sandy had found. He, also, hoped to pick up on obvious clues; CID were usually quite happy to receive assistance in the early stages of an inquiry.

Sandy sat down at the kitchen table and wondered how long he might be there. He had blood samples to get back to the lab and he also still had to get blood from Davie Milne. After all, it was still possible that the murder victim could also have been the typhoid carrier.

The first member of CID was on the scene within half an hour. He noted the man sitting in the kitchen, but thought it best to visit the crime scene first. He nodded towards the uniformed officer, as he entered the living room. He then knelt down and studied the body for a moment, though he wasn't exactly sure what he was looking for.

He then stood up and walked around the room. The uniformed officer watched, but said nothing. He hadn't found anything that seemed of much use and was now happy for his CID colleague to come to that same conclusion himself.

"Nae murder weapon?" the CID man then said.

"Not that I can see," came the reply.

The CID man then nodded, as if happy with the reply. Detective Constable Gordy Jamieson was still relatively new to his role in CID. He still had much to learn. He was twenty-six years old and wore his hair a little longer than would normally be acceptable for a police officer. As a result, nearly every working day, he expected to be told to get it cut.

Gordy really wanted to be a Beatle. He played guitar and had just started to dabble in song-writing. It was early days, but if he could find a few mates and form a band, then maybe he could leave the police and seek fame and fortune outside of Aberdeen. His life was really about music, not solving crime.

Gordy also dressed well. The downside of CID was not having a uniform, but the upside meant he could wear nice suits and show-up his colleagues in the process. He always felt he dressed better than anyone he came into contact with and that included senior officers.

Gordy turned once more to the uniformed officer.

"His the doctor been telt?"

"Aye," came the reply.

"Fine. Ma boss 'ill be here soon," added the CID man, as if that was going to make everything better, in some way.

"Do you want me to stay?" enquired the other officer.

"Aye." Gordy paused, as if suddenly remembering something. "Fa's 'at in the kitchen?" he then asked.

"Says his name is Sandy Burnett; he found the body. Oh, an' he's a doctor apparently."

Gordy nodded. "Ah'd best hae a word, then," he said and went off to the kitchen.

Gordy sat down at the kitchen table and took note of Sandy's name, address and age. He then asked why Sandy was there.

"I really do have a lot to do," Sandy had said first. He briefly explained why he was there and why it was imperative that he got away, as soon as possible.

"I appreciate yer busy, sir, but ma boss wid hae ma guts for garters, if ah let ye go afore he's seen ye."

Sandy had no other alternative, but to remain exactly where he was. Jamieson made his way to the door, but paused.

"Wid ye like a cup o' tea?"

Sandy looked around the kitchen. He got get the impression that the occupant of the flat hadn't been in there much. There was no sign of dirty dishes, no sign of cooking; in fact, no sign of anyone having done much for some time.

"If I can find tea somewhere, I'll make a pot," Sandy then said.

"Might be an idea," added Gordy, "fin I mak tea it usually kills fowk."

Sandy smiled, stood up from the table and started his search for tea, sugar and milk.

*

Detective Chief Inspector Ogston arrived twenty minutes later. He was accompanied by Detective Inspector Forrest, a tall, gangly man with a prominent Adam's apple showing from a long neck. Neither man carried the same clean-cut image as their Detective Constable.

They went through to the living room, where Jamieson was on his knees, crawling around behind the settee. Only his head became visible as the two, senior officers entered the room.

"What do we have?" asked Ogston, taking a pack of cigarettes from his pocket.

Ogston smoked Embassy Filter, which was rapidly becoming the most popular cigarette in the shops. It wasn't so much for the cigarette that he bought Embassy; it was more for the coupons inside. Many an item lying around the Ogston household had been bought from the Embassy catalogue.

Gordy came out from behind the settee. "One Davie Milne, sir. Heid bashed in, probably wi' this," he added, holding up a trophy, the base of which looked to have blood and hairs on the end of it. Jamieson held the other end with a handkerchief, so as to protect any fingerprints that might be on the item.

"Was that behind the settee?" asked Ogston.

"Aye, sir. The killer must 'a chucked it there afore scarperin'," replied Gordy, looking very pleased with himself.

"Do we know anything about Mister Milne?" enquired Ogston, finally lighting his cigarette and blowing smoke across the room.

"Naethin' so far. Ah only got the name fae Doctor Burnett, the mannie in the kitchen. Seems he's here tae tak blood fae the victim, at's if there's ony left," Gordy said, glancing down at the mess on the carpet, around the man's head.

"So, we don't know, for certain, that this is Mister Milne?" Ogston then said, also glancing down at the body.

"No, it's him a' right. There's a weddin' photay on the sideboard," Gordy replied, nodding his head in the general direction of that item of furniture.

Ogston went over to study the photo. The bride looked stunning, her face radiating happiness. The groom did not look quite so happy. They made a handsome couple all the same. He laid the photo down again and returned to the body.

He knelt down and studied it a little closer. The head wound was certainly serious and, almost definitely, the cause of death. Someone had hit him on the back of the head, with some force. It had definitely been a blow struck in anger and with intent to kill, rather than simply to maim.

Ogston was still having a look around the room, when the door opened and a thick-set man, with a mane of bushy, white hair and a round, slightly rosy face, came into the room. This was the Police Doctor, Angus McAllister.

Angus was a proud Highlander, who enjoyed a dram or two when not on duty. He was a jovial character, rarely seen with a glum face and, clearly, a man who enjoyed his work, no matter how horrific it may have been at times.

He went straight to the body and knelt down.

"I'll speak later," Ogston then said and made his way through to the kitchen.

However, Sandy Burnett wasn't in the kitchen. He had grown tired of sitting at the table and decided to take his second cup of tea out on to the balcony, which could be reached through a door off of the kitchen.

Ogston picked up the pot, in the passing and having confirmed there was still tea in it, poured himself a cup and continued out on to the balcony.

Sandy turned as the Chief Inspector came up behind him.

"I hope you don't mind, but I felt I needed some air."

"Not at all," said Ogston, "it must have been a tremendous shock. Do you want one of these?" he then enquired, holding up his cigarette.

Sandy declined. A piece of him had always wanted to be like his boss and smoke a pipe, but he had never had the inclination to smoke cigarettes. As it was, he'd never even got around to acquiring that pipe.

Ogston formally introduced himself and immediately got to the point

"DC Jamieson tells me you're in a hurry."

Sandy looked at his watch. "Well, I was," he said, sounding as irritated as he felt.

"DC Jamieson also said you were here on medical business; are you Mister Milne's GP?"

"No."

"I believe you were here to collect blood; may I ask why?"

Sandy thought for a moment. He wasn't sure how much to tell the Chief Inspector. However, as this was a murder inquiry, it would have been unlawful for him to hold back on anything that might have been of assistance to the police.

"The news of what I am about to tell you will break soon anyway, but I would ask, at least until that story does break, that you keep to yourself what I am about to tell you."

Ogston looked suitably intrigued. "I'm a police officer, Doctor Burnett, I'm good at keeping secrets."

Sandy smiled.

"Of course. We have confirmed a number of cases of typhoid in the city, Chief Inspector and are in the process of trying to identify the source of the disease. We have reason to believe that the source could well be the place where Mister Milne worked and we're taking blood samples from all the staff, in case one of them is a typhoid carrier. It is imperative, therefore, that I get the samples, I've already taken, back to the lab so they can be tested. I'll also still need a sample from Mister Milne."

"You'll need to take that up with the Police Doctor," said Ogston.

"I know Angus well enough; I'll speak with him later," added Sandy.

"So, where did Mister Milne work?" Ogston then enquired.

"Now, this is the bit I must ask you to keep to yourself," Sandy then replied. "We don't want to go public, for the moment, with the name of any particular shop as our investigation is still in its early days and we don't want to be pointing fingers unnecessarily."

"I understand," said Ogston.

"Mister Milne worked in the William Low shop on Union Street," Sandy eventually said.

Ogston juggled cigarette, tea and notebook, so that he could make a note of that last piece of information.

"So, you reckon the typhoid started in William Low's?" Ogston then asked.

"As I said, Chief Inspector, it is early days and I'm not prepared to say anything more, on that particular subject."

Ogston smiled. "You should have been a police officer, Doctor Burnett, you know when to stop answering awkward questions."

Sandy smiled as well. Ogston continued.

"Did you know what Mister Milne did for an occupation?"

"Yes, he was a butcher."

"Ah, I see why it is so important that you check if he was a carrier, or not," added Ogston.

"Exactly," agreed Sandy.

"Talk me through what happened after you arrived at the front door," Ogston then said.

Sandy described, exactly, what he had done, including the fact he had called out Milne's name, on numerous occasions.

"So, the front door was open?" Ogston now asked.

"Yes, it was just off the latch. I suppose to a passer-by, it might have looked closed, but it needed only a little pressure before it opened."

Ogston gave that some thought. The killer would have left in a hurry and presumably, in a state of panic. They hadn't stopped to think about closing doors and yet the door to the living room had been closed. Why take the time for one and not the other?

Davie Milne hadn't been about to run after them.

Ogston clarified one or two other points with Sandy, but soon decided it would be in order for Sandy to get his samples back to the laboratory.

"Very well, Doctor Burnett, I'll not keep you here any longer. I'll leave you to speak to Doctor McAllister, about the blood sample and I'd also like you to come down to Lodge Walk later, and give us a formal statement. Could I also ask, at the same time, that you let us take a set of your fingerprints? You may not have touched anything while you were here but, if you did, it would allow us to eliminate you from our inquiries."

"I'll do that on my way home tonight," said Sandy.

"Thank you," added Ogston, returning to the living room as Sandy Burnett left the flat.

*

While Doctor McAllister arranged for Davie Milne's body to be moved to the mortuary and DI Forrest and DC Jamieson were interviewing the neighbours, Ogston took another look around the flat.

Firstly, he stood over the body again. The wound was on the back of the victim's head, so he had to have turned his back on his killer. He obviously hadn't felt under threat at that moment.

There was also the little matter of the front door. It had to have been the killer who had left it open. That meant the killer had to have been allowed into the house by Milne, seeing as there was no sign of forced entry.

It also meant that Davie Milne had known his killer and had not felt threatened by inviting that person into his home. Why, then, had the meeting turned to murder?

Ogston began to wander around the room.

There wasn't much to see in the living room. He searched the sideboard, assuming that any personal, or financial, papers would be in there. He found a bankbook, in which was noted a balance of thirty-three pounds, five shillings and sixpence.

There was also a small book, which detailed the payments that were being made on a television set. Ogston assumed it was the small set that sat in the corner. He also found another book. This time it was payments being made to the Northern Co-Operative Society, by way of lessening the financial blow of Christmas.

The second book indicated an element of forward planning, which Ogston would not have associated with many men. It would, therefore, have been Mrs Milne who was probably making those payments, all be it from her husband's income.

Which brough Ogston's thoughts to *Mrs* Milne. Where was she? Clearly, she was not living there at that moment, or she would have been in the house when her husband had been killed. Or, did that suggest that she might be the killer?

Ogston thought about the damage to the back of Davie Milne's head. It was damage caused by a violent blow. Could a woman had delivered such a blow?

Ogston looked at the wedding photograph again. He got the impression the photograph hadn't been taken that long ago, which meant, if Mrs Milne was now elsewhere, then the marriage hadn't lasted.

Why would that be?

He moved on to the rest of the flat.

There were two bedrooms, but only one of them looked like it had ever been used. Although there were beds in them both, one seemed cold and uninviting, not to mention slightly lacking in other furniture.

In, what Ogston assumed was the main bedroom he found two wardrobes, placed side by side at the end of the bed. There wasn't much space, between wardrobes and bed, to get the doors open and search inside. Only one of the wardrobes had anything hanging in it and it was all men's clothing.

It seemed clear to Ogston that Mrs Milne had left the marital home for good. Something had happened to the marriage and now something had happened to the ex-husband. Could there be a connection?

Ogston went through to the kitchen. The larder was all but empty and there was only what was left of a pint of milk and a small piece of cheese in the small refrigerator. Ogston was quite impressed that a young couple could afford to have a refrigerator; it certainly wasn't something many people had in their home.

Ogston heard voices in the hallway. He left the kitchen to investigate. It was Doctor McAllister and two men. The men were there to collect the body and McAllister was back to collect his bag.

"Initial thoughts, Doctor?" Ogston asked.

"Single blow, delivered with force. The blow was definitely meant to kill. I'd say the victim has been dead for around forty hours, putting the time of death sometime late Tuesday night, early Wednesday morning. I'll get a report to you, as soon as possible."

"Well, thanks for giving me something to work with, doctor," Ogston had then said. Moments later McAllister and the two men were heading out the door. No doubt, what was being carried would cause some debate amongst the neighbours.

Ogston had no sooner been left on his own, when DC Jamieson came back in to the flat.

"Did the neighbours have much to say?" Ogston enquired.

"Aye, that Davie boy couldnae keep it in his troosers, if ye ken fit ah mean?" replied Jamieson, rather bluntly.

Ogston knew exactly what he meant.

"Any mention of Mrs Milne?" added Ogston.

"She left aboot a month ago. Went aff wi' some flash mannie, wi' an expensive car, according tae the wifie across the landin'."

"I don't suppose the 'wifie across the landin' had any idea where Mrs Milne is now?" Ogston then enquired, more in hope than expectation.

Jamieson grinned. He held up a piece of paper. "Phyllis Milne left 'is wi' the neighbour, jist in case there might a been ony need tae contact her."

Ogston took the paper from his DC. Written on it was an address on Argyll Place.

"Wonder why she left this with a neighbour?"

"Still thinkin' aboot her man, ah suppose," added Jamieson.

Ogston could only presume that that had been the case. None the less, he found it hard to understand why any woman would walk out on her husband, but still care about him enough as to leave a contact address with the neighbours. Surely, any feelings she may have had would have walked out the door with her?

Whatever her reasons, however, Ogston was grateful for her thoughtfulness, At least it gave him a direct contact to her and a whole lot quicker than might have been the case. Ogston put the paper in his pocket, then turned back to face Jamieson.

"Arrange for the fingerprint boys to go over every square inch of the flat. It looks surprisingly clean, but you never know."

"Aye, sir," said Jamieson.

"Once the fingerprints have been checked, have a Council joiner secure the property, then head back to Lodge Walk."

"On it, sir."

At that moment DI Forrest came back. He'd got tied up with one of the neighbours, who was hard of hearing and long-winded when talking. The interview had taken forever and very little, of any use, had come of it.

It was then agreed that Jamieson would work with the fingerprint team, while Forrest gave Ogston a lift to the address given by Mrs Milne. Forrest would then continue back to Lodge Walk. Jamieson would also return to Lodge Walk, but he'd have to take the bus.

Jamieson went up to the police office to make the call that would bring the fingerprint team to him. At the same time, he arranged for one of the officers to give him a lift back to Lodge Walk once he'd finished at the flat. A bus journey was not for Gordy Jamieson when a lift could be cadged from somewhere.

Finally, he phoned the Council offices and arranged for a joiner to call, a little later that afternoon. Gordy Jamieson then went to the shops and bought himself something for lunch, along with a few snacks for the afternoon.

It was likely to be a long day.

*

Ogston was dropped off at the traffic lights at the top of Argyll Place. He made his way down the street, which was made up of a number of large, terraced properties. Most of the properties were on the left-hand side of the road. The opposite side was mainly taken up by the Victoria Park.

He walked down to the number he'd been given by DC Jamieson. His first impression, as he viewed the properties he passed, was that Phyllis Milne had certainly gone up in the world.

Outside the house in question, there was a man washing a car. It was a Series 3, jet black, Humber Hawk. The man was tall, handsome and up to his elbows in suds. His shirt sleeves were rolled up and his, slightly scruffy trousers, were held up by blue braces, with thin white stripes.

He had the look of a man intent on some hard labour.

The door to the property Ogston was seeking, was open and he assumed the man washing the car might live there.

"This where Phyllis Milne is now living?" Ogston asked, nodding in the direction of the property.

The man stopped washing the car and dropped the sponge, he'd been using, back into his bucket of soapy water.

"Who wants to know?" he asked. It wasn't a hostile question, but certainly one that was coming from a man intent on giving little away.

Ogston showed his identification card. "The police want to know," he said.

The man relaxed a little. "In that case, you'd better come in," he said and led the way into the house.

"Phyllis?!" he called out, as he passed through the front door," the police are here to see you."

An attractive woman appeared from a room at the end of the entrance hallway. Ogston recognised her, immediately, from the wedding photograph he'd seen earlier that day. She was drying her hands and there was a look of concern on her face.

Ogston introduced himself and was then shown into the living room, where he was invited to sit down. Phyllis sat across from him and the man began to leave the room.

"It might be an idea if you stayed, Mister.....eh?" Ogston said.

The man paused at the door, then came back into the room.

"Cusiter," he replied, "Ranald Cusiter."

Ogston thought it might be a good idea for Phyllis to have someone with her, when he broke the news about her husband's death. Cusiter sat down beside her and instantly took her hand.

"I'm here about your husband, Mrs Milne," Ogston then said.

"I'd prefer if you used my maiden name, Chief Inspector," Phyllis quickly said.

"Which is?"

"Duncan. I'd like to be Phyllis Duncan again. The less I have to do with that husband of mine, the better."

Ogston noted her name in his notebook, along with Ranald Cusiter.

"Had there been problems in your marriage, for a while?" he then asked.

"Look, Chief Inspector, would you mind telling me why you are here?" Phyllis then said.

"Well, it's actually about your husband."

"What's he done now?" came the instant retort.

"It's more about what someone else has done to him, I'm afraid," said Ogston. "I'm sorry to tell you this, but your husband was found dead this morning."

It took a second for the words to sink in and then Phyllis Duncan's expression changed to one of shock and horror.

"Dead? Davie can't be dead."

Cusiter took a tighter grip of Phyllis's hand and turned to Ogston.

"What happened to him?"

"It looks like he was murdered. Of course, I'm saying the victim was Mister Milne, but until we have a formal identification, I can't say that with certainty. Would you be able to carry out that formal identification for me, Miss Duncan?"

It took another moment before there was any response. As if by magic, Phyllis suddenly produced a handkerchief from the left sleeve of the light cardigan she wore. She started dabbing at her eyes.

"Would Ranald be able to come with me?" she then asked.

"That won't be a problem."

"In that case I'll do the identification."

"Thank you," added Ogston.

"Would you like a drink of some kind?" Cusiter then asked Phyllis. "It might help with the shock."

"A cup of tea would be better," Phyllis replied.

Cusiter stood up. "Would you like tea as well, Chief Inspector?"

"A coffee would be lovely, Mister Cusiter, if it's not too much trouble. Milk and one sugar, please."

Cusiter glanced down at Phyllis once more, as if checking she'd be okay while he was out of the room. She managed to smile back and he continued on his way.

Nothing much was said until Cusiter returned with the tea, coffee and a few biscuits on a plate. Once he was seated again, Ogston returned to the questions he felt needed to be asked.

"What brought an end to your marriage?"

"Davie and his liking for the ladies," replied Phyllis. "I knew what I was getting, before I married him but, I suppose I thought I'd be the one to change him. I was stupid enough to think that I would be the *only* woman for Davie when, in truth, I always knew he'd never change. It was who he was."

"Can you think of anyone who would want him dead?"

Phyllis laughed bitterly. "I expect there were a few husbands who wouldn't have been too pleased with him, but whether any of them would see that as motive for murder, I wouldn't know."

"Did your husband have any other family?"

"Just his mother, she lives in Cummings Park."

"What happened to his father?"

"Died young. Heart attack, I think. Davie was pretty much brought up by his mother, on her own."

Ogston considered that for a moment. "Were they close?"

"Not really. Davie effectively left home when he reached sixteen. He hadn't seen that much of his mother in the last few years. In fact, our wedding was probably the last time they spent any time together."

Ogston asked for and received an address for Davie's mother. He then moved on.

"How about male friends? Did Davie have many of them?"

Phyllis shook her head. "No one ever came to the flat, so I'm guessing no one was that close to him. His best man was Craig Talbot, but he moved to Australia just after the wedding and hasn't been heard of since."

"But your husband must have had *some* male friends?" insisted Ogston.

"None that I ever knew about," replied Phyllis. "Davie spent all his spare time with the ladies, though precious little of it with me."

"And that didn't bother you?" asked Ogston, failing to believe that any wife could, willingly, let her husband live that way.

"Well, of course, it bothered me, but there didn't seem to be much I could do about it. I tried being the loving wife, hoping that alone might change him; but it didn't. In hindsight, I should never have married him."

"Was Davie ever violent towards you?" Ogston enquired.

"Good heavens, no," came the rather outraged reply. "In his own way, Davie loved me; he'd never have harmed me. In fact, I doubt if he would ever have harmed any woman."

"He must have interests though?" added Ogston, quickly adding, "other than women?"

"He used to go to Pittodrie, but even that stopped when we got married. He went out every Monday, said he was playing darts, but I never knew whether to believe that or not."

"Where did he play his darts?"

"That's just it, he never said and to be honest, I never saw Davie with a set of darts in all the time I knew him."

"Was Monday the only night your husband went out?"

"No. He went dancing on a Wednesday and sometimes on a Saturday, though there was more chance of me being invited along at the weekend. It was as if he did actually see that as being our time together, brief though it may have been."

"How did you come to meet Davie?"

"We met at a party. Actually, you were at that party as well, weren't you, darling?" Phyllis then said, directing the last few words towards Cusiter.

Ogston felt sure the words weren't that well received. Cusiter looked like a man being put on the spot. It took a few seconds for him to respond.

"Now that you mention it, I believe I was."

Ogston noted that, much as Cusiter tried to straighten his speech, there was still a strong hint of the *Aiberdeen loon* shining through.

"Do you remember whose party that was?" Ogston then asked, glancing both at Phyllis and Cusiter. It was Cusiter who answered first.

"I'm afraid I don't, Chief Inspector. I went to so many parties back in the day, that it's difficult to isolate one from the other."

"Miss Duncan?" added Ogston, now looking straight at Phyllis.

"I remember meeting Davie, but I have no recollection as to whose party it might have been."

"Someone must have invited you?" Ogston then said.

Phyllis gave the question some thought, though Ogston couldn't help but think that Cusiter was now being less than helpful. Had the man something to hide? Eventually, Phyllis spoke.

"I'm pretty sure it was one of those parties, which I attended with my friend Caroline. She would go on to be my bridesmaid, but she used to get invited to all manner of events and would often ask me to go with her. Caroline could be quite harum- scarum at times, so she liked me along to bring an air of sanity to proceedings. She always saw me as having my feet on the ground."

"Caroline?" prompted Ogston.

"Caroline O'Hara, but you'll not be able to speak with her either, Chief Inspector," replied Phyllis.

"Don't tell me," said Ogston, "she went to Australia with the Best Man?"

Phyllis smiled. "Not quite; but she did go to London over a year ago and I've lost contact with her."

Ogston then looked at Cusiter. "And you, Mister Cusiter, what did *you* think about Davie Milne?"

Cusiter glanced at Phyllis before speaking.

"Oh, I didn't really know him. As I said, I remember meeting him briefly at the party where he met Phyllis but, to be honest, my eyes were more on Phyllis. I was somewhat upset that she chose Davie that night."

Ogston noticed the smile that passed between them.

"So, you remember Phyllis and Davie, but you don't remember who threw the party?" he then said, directing the question at Cusiter.

"Pretty much, yes," came the reply.

Ogston couldn't bring himself to believe Cusiter, but he was going to have to set that to one side, at least for the moment.

Ogston paused for a few seconds. He was making a few notes, while they were fresh in his mind. He then looked up.

"When did the two of you get together?"

Phyllis looked at Cusiter again. It was as if she were seeking permission to answer.

"My marriage started to really fall apart around eight months ago. About six months ago, I was walking down Union Street and literally bumped into Ranald. We went for lunch and I rather unburdened my problems on to him. He was lovely. Took it all on the chin and still came out smiling."

"Pleased to offer a shoulder, eh, Mister Cusiter?" Ogston then said.

"I have never concealed the fact that I find Phyllis extremely attractive and wish, one day, to marry her. Obviously, I did not like to see her so upset and was keen to offer my help, in whatever way was possible."

"Which brought Miss Duncan here," Ogston then said.

"Yes, but there's nothing untoward, Chief Inspector. There are enough rooms in this house for Phyllis to have her own space. In no way am I forcing myself upon her. She is free to live here, for as long as she might choose whether, or not, that leads to us having a lasting relationship."

"You have to understand, Chief Inspector," Phyllis then added, "Ranald has acted the perfect gentleman towards me, at all times. I contacted him and told him I had to get away from Davie. The womanising had finally got to me. Ranald suggested I came here and, as he says, I have my own room and everything."

"Had you spoken to your husband about getting a divorce?" Ogston enquired.

"We had, as a matter of fact. Davie had told me that he would not contest such a request. He was quite happy for me to cite his adultery as the reason for the divorce and he even said he'd get me the photographic evidence, should I ever require it."

"Did he really?" said Ogston, while all the time thinking *why ever would he do that?*

"Considering you had thoughts of marrying Miss Duncan yourself, Mister Cusiter, you must be delighted to hear that Davie Milne is dead?"

It was a blunt question. It was, frankly, quite rude but Ogston wanted to goad Cusiter a little, just to see how he reacted. Anger immediately rushed to the surface.

"Look, Chief Inspector, are you accusing me of something?"

"I'm merely suggesting that you no longer need to wait for a divorce, the road is clear for you both to be together whenever you want."

"But the divorce would have been a formality," insisted Phyllis. "There was no reason for either of us needing Davie out of the way."

"Much as you tell me there would not have been any problems with a divorce, Miss Duncan, some might still view your situation as being the perfect motive for murder," suggested Ogston.

Phyllis almost shouted her next sentence.

"I didn't kill Davie!"

"How dare you suggest such a thing, Chief Inspector," added Cusiter, jumping to his feet.

"You both have a motive for wanting Davie Milne dead," insisted Ogston, "whether you like to hear that, or not. Now, Miss Duncan, what else can you tell me about your husband?"

Phyllis calmed down. "Nothing, that I can think of."

Ogston let a few seconds of silence pass between them, before speaking again.

"Very well, that will be all, for just now." Ogston stood up. "However, I must ask that when you visit Lodge Walk later, to identify the body, you also provide us with a set of your fingerprints. That goes for both of you."

"But why......?" Cusiter started to say.

"We'll have collected various sets of fingerprints from the flat and we need to know who owns them all. You've both been there so, presumably, you'll both have left fingerprints as you moved around the property. Eliminating you from our enquiries will help the investigation a lot."

Both Cusiter and Phyllis seemed to see the sense in that, even though Cusiter maintained he'd only really been there the day he'd gone to collect Phyllis and take her to his own home.

"Never the less, Mister Cusiter, you'll still have left fingerprints," was all that Ogston would say. He thanked them for their time and then made his way to the front door.

Cusiter went with him and as he held the front door open, he beckoned Ogston a little closer. In soft tones, he said:

"Neither Phyllis, nor I, had anything to do with Davie's death. I admit I never liked the man and the way he treated women was atrocious, but I had no need to harm him. He proved no threat to me, Chief Inspector, none whatsoever."

"Perhaps," concluded Ogston, as he passed Cusiter and exited the house.

Once outside, Ogston paused on the pavement and lit a cigarette. He gave some thought to the route he would take going back to Lodge Walk. He had already decided to walk, so he crossed the road and made his way through the Victoria Park. He was almost alone, with only a couple of young mums out pushing prams. He then cut down through Rosemount and onwards to Lodge Walk.

As he walked, he allowed a number of random thoughts to form a connection in his mind. They were mainly about Ranald Cusiter. There was something about the man that just didn't ring true. Ogston was sure he was hiding something, yet could hazard no guess as to what that might be.

What he had decided, by the time he reached his office, however, was that he'd have someone do a lot more digging into the life and times of Ranald Cusiter.

4   4

Later that Thursday, when Sandy's medical team had met again, it came to light that the patient who had claimed to have had no contact with William Low, now remembered she had been there. It hadn't been normal for her to shop there, which was why it had slipped her mind.

With what appeared to be the last piece of the jigsaw in place, the team now felt one hundred per cent certain that they had not only confirmed the source of the disease, but also the shop from where that source material had been contaminated.

The span of information the team had gathered, was quite impressive. There would be hundreds of people to contact, although many of them would be informed through reading the local newspapers. The first, leading article would be in the Friday editions, after Ian MacQueen had held the first of his press conferences that afternoon.

He had chosen to be as honest as possible. There seemed little point in hiding pertinent facts from either the Press, or the public. However, he still had to be careful in exactly what was said and therefore, written.

The Press were notorious for putting their own spin on any article they wrote. Many a true word had been knocked out of shape by the manner in which it had been reported. An angle was usually sought, prior to a word being written.

Seeking an angle might have sold papers, but it distorted facts along the way.

MacQueen did not want to be the instigator of panic and chaos throughout the city. He did not want to give the journalists any latitude to start writing what appeared to be facts, but facts that simply weren't true.

He thought, that in giving the journalists as much information as he could he would, in some way, maintain their confidence in him throughout the crisis.

He did not mention the specific meat that was suspected and he, certainly, was not going to tell them which shop may have been responsible for selling the infected meat. He did, however, reveal that they were fairly sure that it *had* been meat, of some kind, which had caused the outbreak.

He further said that a lot more work would have to be carried out, before anything, by way of specific information, could be provided.

He went on to say that everyone, believed to have come into contact with the infected meat, had now been tested to ensure that no one among them, was a carrier of the disease. He asked for time to complete the tests and to assess the findings.

At that stage of the investigation, Ian MacQueen was still firmly of the opinion that he was looking for a carrier of the disease, rather than the meat itself having arrived in the shop already infected. MacQueen found it hard to imagine that contaminated tins of meat would be arriving in the country. It made more sense for the contamination to be introduced *after* the tin had been opened.

He explained that the incubation period, for typhoid, could be twelve to twenty days and that it created the problem of people failing to remember exactly what they had eaten, or even what they had bought, over the relevant period. At the time of the press conference, MacQueen had not known that the patient, who had appeared to be out of line with the others, had now remembered shopping at Low's.

MacQueen had continued along the lines of poor, personal hygiene being the likely reason for the disease spreading. He stressed the need for people to wash their hands after each visit to the toilet and also stated that local butchers ought to be particularly mindful of cross contamination.

"If cutting machines are not cleaned after every cut of meat, then the chances of cross contamination rise markedly," he had said.

Sandy was still at his desk as seven o'clock came and went. They were still awaiting the results from some of the blood tests, taken from the staff at William Low. In all the excitement of the afternoon, he had completely forgotten about Davie Mine. He'd picked up the phone, acquired an outside line and then phoned the number for the police mortuary.

As luck would have it, Doctor McAllister was still there. In fact, he was working on Davie Milne's body. He would be happy to see Sandy, were he to call immediately. Sandy was secretly delighted; it gave him a legitimate excuse for leaving the office.

*

The City Hospital staff were also in for longer hours than usual. The patients, who had already been confirmed as having typhoid, would take a little time to respond to the medication they were being given.

For the nursing staff, it would be about keeping the patients and the wards, spotlessly clean. It would be about clearing away any possible areas of contamination and keeping infected patients well away from anyone else.

Numbers were still quite low, but everyone knew that those numbers would start to rise. It was just a matter of how quickly and to what level.

More and more people would be calling their General Practitioners, seeking their help for individuals and whole families who were now falling sick. As those people were identified, they would be referred to the hospital for tests. If confirmed, then they would join those already in isolation.

Alison Young had come in earlier that day. She wanted to be as useful as possible, but she also wanted to hear if there had been any further spread of the disease. Her day-shift colleagues had little news.

Matron was bustling around with her usual air of efficiency. She had stopped Alison in the corridor, just after Alison's shift had started.

"Your hat's not straight, Nurse Young. We can't let standards slip, no matter how busy we may get."

"Sorry Matron," Alison had responded and then hurried to find a mirror. Matron liked everything in the wards to be just so; but she was fair in her assessments and thoughtful towards those staff beneath her. Having said that, no one would have wanted to cross her; her temper was legendary.

Matron had informed Doctor MacQueen that her staff were up to the task of helping those patients admitted with typhoid. She knew she had a conscientious group of well-trained nurses, who would do whatever was necessary to maintain the high standards of the hospital.

However, she remained less certain that there would be enough of those nurses. If patient numbers started to get out of hand, then the need for additional nurses would become essential.

For the moment, Matron was content to believe that they *could* cope. Time would tell if she was right.

*

By the time Alison finished her shift on the Friday morning, there had been no new patients admitted and there was a sense, among the nurses at least, that all might not be as bad as everyone had first thought.

She'd been delayed at work, so it was nearer ten before she got away. On speck, she had telephoned Graeme, on the off-chance he'd be able to meet her again at the Princess Café.

Even on a busy day, Detective Chief Inspector Ogston liked to have a break and when the opportunity of enjoying that break, in the company of an attractive woman, presented itself he was not going to say no.

Yet again, Alison was already seated by the time he got to the café. Graeme sat down and ordered a coffee, accompanied, once more, by a bacon roll. Alison was just having a coffee. Graeme would have also have liked a cigarette, but he decided against such an idea whilst in Alison's company.

"I guess you're busier than ever?" he then said.

Alison was looking even more tired than the last time they'd met. Even though it had only been forty-eight hours ago, so much had happened to both of them in their working lives that it would have been no surprise to read tiredness in both their faces.

They enjoyed their time together. It was an oasis of calm in the midst of turmoil. Alison felt more relaxed as a result of seeing Graeme. She'd been quite wound up when she'd arrived. They'd agreed having coffee together seemed good for them both and that they should meet as often as possible.

"That won't discount a night out, though?" Graeme had then asked.

"If we can find the time, we'll have that night out," answered Alison. "It's just, with the likelihood of the typhoid getting worse, I don't think I'll be seeing much time off, just at the moment."

"And I'm in the middle of a big case," Graeme then said, "so my time will be tied as well."

"Then the odd coffee break it may have to be," said Alison, smiling.

"Looking forward to the next one already," added Graeme.

Alison rose on to her tiptoes and pecked him on the cheek.

"Me too," she said and turned to make her way to the bus stop.

Graeme once more became Detective Chief Inspector Ogston and made his way back to Lodge Walk.

Alison caught the bus almost at once and was soon back at the flat she shared with two other nurses. They worked the day shift, so Alison returned to an empty flat.

She was still thinking about Graeme. It really did make a pleasant change to have a man in her life again, even if the chance of a proper relationship forming was still pretty remote, at least as long as work kept getting in the way.

It had been a long time since she'd had a boyfriend in her life. Fifteen months, to be exact. He had, not surprisingly, been a doctor.

It had been doomed from the start; two people with little to talk about, other than what had happened in the hospital that particular day. Basically, it had gone nowhere fast and they had both finally agreed that it would be tantamount to flogging a dead horse, were they to go on seeing each other.

Alison had returned to enjoying her own company, content in the thought that she had her work and that that would take up enough of her life to keep all thoughts of boyfriends at bay.

But now she had Graeme Ogston sounding keen to see her, in a social capacity. After all these years, they had finally spent some time together and she'd enjoyed it immensely. For the first time, in a long time, she was annoyed with the impact her job had on her life. She longed for a weekend off, a chance for her and Graeme to spend some quality time together.

She laughed out loud. Of course, if she got a weekend off, he'd probably be up to his neck in a murder, or something. Maybe they were destined to be nothing more than good friends? Would she be happy with that?

Probably not.

At thirty-three, even Alison knew that time was running out if she wanted to settle down with someone. She wasn't that bothered about having kids, but didn't fancy being single the rest of her days.

Alison made herself a cup of tea and sat at the kitchen table to drink it. The morning paper was lying on the table, which she found a bit of a surprise. Her flatmates were rarely out that early to bring a paper back; they'd usually just set off for work and had no reason for bringing anything back to the flat.

Alison opened the paper and studied the front page. It announced to the world that Aberdeen had confirmed typhoid was in the city.

Alison knew that it wasn't just the medical implications of having typhoid in the city. The effect, in general, that it would have on the city would be immense. Summer was approaching and the whole city would normally benefit from visiting tourists. Surely, no one would come to a city in the grip of a typhoid epidemic?

Dark days lay ahead for Aberdeen and Alison knew that she would be at the sharp end, as events unfolded. That meant getting a good sleep every time she was given the chance.

She finished her tea and went to bed. She fell asleep, that morning, thinking of Graeme Ogston and wondering if love might finally be coming into her life.

*

When Detective Chief Inspector Ogston had got back to Lodge Walk, he had found a report lying on his desk. He had sent one of the Detective Constables out to interview Davie Milne's mother. The report of that interview was short but very much to the point. The relationship, between mother and son, had not been good for some time. In fact, there was only really one quote from Davie's mother, which read:

"Davie wis as big a womaniser and waster as his Da, he wis nae son o' mine."

Harsh words indeed.

Ogston cleared up some more paperwork and then made his way up Union Street to the premises of William Low. He knew the shop had already been visited by the medical profession and that all the staff would be on their guard against saying anything to anyone.

However, he still needed to find out what he could about Davie Milne.

It seemed, from what he'd been told already, that Davie Milne had lived a very strange life. He had had few real friends, mainly passing his time in short relationships with women. Was he incapable of forming proper relationships or had Davie Milne been chasing something; something he was never likely to find?

Ogston found the shop quite busy but, of course, no one knew that they were doing their shopping a matter of feet from where the typhoid outbreak had effectively began. A part of him wanted to let people know, but the other part knew he'd be starting an unnecessary panic in the process.

Ogston entered the shop and asked a girl, who was stacking shelves, if she could direct him to the manager. She assumed it was another medical visit and asked Ogston to follow her. She then asked him to wait, as she disappeared through a door to the right of the butchery department.

When the girl reappeared, she was being followed by a rather anxious looking man, who announced himself as being the manager, before enquiring as to what more the medical profession could want from his premises.

"I'm not from the medical profession," Ogston had said, holding out his identification.

Samuel Reynolds looked at the card in disbelief. What could the police want with him, or his staff? Surely it couldn't be linked to the typhoid. Was he to be charged with something?

Ogston asked if they might go somewhere, a little quieter, to conduct their business. Reynolds seemed a little shell-shocked and took a few seconds to pull himself together. Eventually he spoke.

"Yes, we can go to my office."

The office was its usual mess. Reynolds noticed the look of almost disgust on the police officer's face, as he surveyed the small room. There were papers everywhere, including on top of the only chairs Ogston had any hope of sitting on. Reynolds reacted to Ogston's quizzical expression.

Paper was lifted from chairs and dropped in the corner behind where Reynolds would be sitting. Other papers were moved off his desk to create an illusion of tidiness. Both men then sat down.

Reynolds was still fighting the tension rising inside him, as he spoke.

"What can I do for you, Chief Inspector?"

"I'm here about Davie Milne."

"What's he done?" Reynolds asked.

"Why would you think he'd done something, Mister Reynolds?"

"He's a waster that one. I should have given him his cards a long time ago."

"You won't have to worry yourself about that now, Mister Reynolds. Mister Milne's dead body was found, in his flat, yesterday morning."

Samuel Reynolds sat back in his chair.

"Well, I must say, I didn't expect that."

"What can you tell me about Mister Milne?" Ogston then asked.

When Reynolds replied, it did not amount to much. He said that he was not in the habit of knowing his staff on a personal level. Standards had to be maintained and he found it easier to 'crack the whip,' as he said, more easily if he were not on personal terms with anyone.

"So, you knew nothing about Mister Milne, nothing at all?" pressed Ogston.

Reynolds thought for a moment. "I did hear that his marriage had broken up after a mere two years. Hardly worth buying a wedding gift for a two-year marriage, was it?"

Ogston would have assumed most people would have been joking, in making that comment, but with Samuel Reynolds it was patently clear that he was being perfectly serious. He was a strange man, well dressed and yet working in what looked like a constant mess.

Ogston wondered if this man ever tidied up around him. In fact, Ogston wondered if the man's general lack of motivation, might have permeated to his staff. Was it no more than collective laziness that had led to the typhoid breaking out from Reynolds' premises?

"Can you tell me anything else about Mister Milne?" Ogston then said.

Reynolds seemed to think for a moment. Finally, he spoke.

"You might want to talk to Sandra Riddell, she works in the office."

"Did she know Mister Milne?"

"I heard that she was Davie's latest conquest from amongst my female staff."

For someone who claimed not to know his staff on a personal level, he certainly seemed to *hear* an awful lot. Ogston was obviously keen to speak to anyone who might have known Davie Milne particularly well.

"Did many of the female staff go out with Mister Milne?"

"Quite a few, I believe. Davie never spent much of his time here actually doing any work. He was always far too busy chatting up some poor, unsuspecting victim. He was like a spider luring them in to his web."

There was disgust in Reynolds' tone. Ogston didn't have to guess that the manager had clearly had no liking for Davie Milne. However, how much of that was down to jealousy, more than anything else? Davie had had a way with the ladies yet it seemed beyond Ogston's comprehension that Mr Reynolds had ever had much success with the opposite sex.

"Is there somewhere I can talk with Sandra?" Ogston then asked.

It was obvious from the manager's expression that he felt there wasn't. Ogston had no intention of interviewing anyone in the pigsty that Reynolds called an office. If there wasn't a spare room, then he'd just have to take Sandra somewhere else; not that he wanted that to be Lodge Walk.

"There's nowhere that would guarantee you peace and quiet," Reynolds eventually said.

"Very well, Mister Reynolds," Ogston then said, "if you would introduce me to Sandra, then I'll take her away from here for a little while."

"Of course," said Reynolds, feeling a sense of relief that the police officer would be leaving. The last thing he wanted was for his staff to lose any more time away from their workplace. After all, they were only talking about Davie Milne; it wasn't as if it was important.

Reynolds left the office, but was only gone a matter of a moment or two. When he returned, he was in the company of a rather nervous looking, young woman. She relaxed a little once she had been introduced to the Chief Inspector. She had assumed Reynolds had wanted to see her on a work matter.

Ogston explained that he wanted to talk to her about a personal matter and that it might be better if they went elsewhere. He suggested that Sandra put on her coat and he'd buy her a coffee.

Sandra had wanted to ask more, but felt that everything would be explained in good time. She went through to the staffroom, to put on her coat and Ogston went with her.

Ogston noted the line of pegs on the wall and the fourteen-drawer cabinets placed against one wall. There was also a table, with six chairs round it. In the corner a kettle sat beside a small sink. To the right of the kettle was a jar of coffee, packet of sugar and a half-empty bottle of milk.

"What are they for?" asked Ogston, nodding towards the fourteen-drawer cabinets. He would not have expected to find them in a staffroom.

"Each member of staff has their own drawer. You can't keep much in them, but I suppose it's better than nothing."

"Do they lock?"

"Good grief, no."

"I wanted to talk to you about Davie Milne. Which drawer would be his?"

"His name should be on the front. I didn't really know Davie; I only went out with him the once."

"Which was last Tuesday?" prompted Ogston.

Sandra seemed surprised that the Chief Inspector already knew that.

"Yes, that's right," she replied.

Ogston, by that time, had found the drawer with Davie's name on it. He pulled it open and checked the contents. It didn't amount to much. There was a jersey and a scarf, presumably for colder days. There were a number of pens and some scrunched up pieces of paper; none of which had anything of interest written on them.

"Has something happened to Davie?" Sandra asked, as she finished buttoning up her coat.

"He's dead, I'm afraid."

"Oh, my God," said Sandra. "How?"

"Let's go somewhere else and I'll tell you what I can," Ogston then said and led the way out of the shop.

A few of the staff watched their departure with interest, most of them wondering what Sandra could possibly have done wrong.

They went around the corner, into Holburn Street and stopped off at the Kit Kat Café. It was quite a small establishment, but Ogston knew they made good coffee and also offered a variety of cakes, all baked especially for the café and changed on a daily basis.

It was almost lunchtime and the café was already showing signs of getting busier. There was a young waitress serving three women, by the window. She nodded in the direction of a table and said she'd be across as soon as possible.

Ogston and Sandra went to the table, indicated, and sat down. As they did so, a dark-haired woman emerged through a door at the back.

Ogston knew this to be Mrs Signorini, the owner of the premises. Most of the cafes in Aberdeen were owned by Italians, or people of Italian descent. Ogston had noted, on previous visits, that Mrs Signorini did not appear to serve in her own café, though she did make the coffee more often than not.

Ogston kept the chat very general as he waited for the waitress to take their order. Sandra was obviously keen to learn more about Davie, but Ogston wanted to be sure that no one would be within listening distance, before he said anything more on that subject.

The waitress eventually came to their table and two coffees, with two cakes were ordered. A note was made on the page of a small notebook and a smile offered, before the waitress made her way back to the counter.

Ogston took the chance to ask some questions.

"Could you just confirm where you went with Davie Milne, last Tuesday evening?"

"Yes. We went to the concert at the Capitol."

"Did you do anything else?"

"We had a coffee and then he walked me home."

"What time would that have been?"

"He would have left me around half past ten. He didn't want to miss his last bus."

"If you don't mind me asking, Miss Riddell, why did you go out with Davie in the first place; isn't he a bit old for you?"

"There was just something about Davie that attracted women to him. I was no different, in that respect."

"Did you know he was married?" Ogston enquired.

"He told me he was in the process of getting a divorce," Sandra replied. "Wasn't that true?"

"No, that appears to have been the truth. Do you know if any other girls, at work, went out with him?"

"There were a few. Most of them were for one night only, though."

"How about you, Miss Riddell, would you have seen Davie again?"

"I wouldn't have thought so. As you said, he was a lot older than me and I'm not sure if I'd have been comfortable with that. I know, for a fact, my Mum wouldn't have been happy."

"How old are you, Miss Riddell?"

"Nineteen."

And Davie Milne was twenty-six. Was seven years really a big age gap? There were ten years between himself and Alison.

At that moment, the waitress returned to the table with a trolley, on which were a selection of cakes lying underneath glass domes. Cakes were chosen and lifted on to plates, which were then placed in front of Ogston and Sandra. The waitress then returned to the counter, where Mrs Signorini had managed to prepare two white coffees. These were then brought to the table and Ogston and Sandra left alone to enjoy their snack.

"Where do you live, Miss Riddell?"

She gave him her address on Albert Terrace. She also explained how her father was now dead and that she was alone with her Mum.

"Oh, I'm sorry to hear about your father," said Ogston.

"There's no need, Chief Inspector, I never knew him. I was only one when he was killed."

"At least that was something you would have had in common with Davie," Ogston then said.

Sandra's expression was blank.

"You *did* know that Davie's Dad died young and that he was brought up by his mother?"

Sandra looked surprised. "That wasn't the way Davie told it. He said his father was in the Merchant Navy and rarely at home. He didn't say much about his mother, other than she lived in a big house beside Seafield Playing Fields."

Not quite Cummings Park, thought Ogston. *So, Davie had re-invented himself. Had his entire life been a lie?*

Ogston decided not to shatter the illusion which Davie had created. The full story might, one day, come out in the papers but at least for the moment, he was happy to leave the staff of William Low believing what they wanted about their colleague.

"Maybe I got it wrong," he added. "Did Davie tell you anything else about himself?"

Sandra cut her cake in two and sipped some of the coffee, which was still quite hot. Her attention was drawn to the door, as two women entered. They were talking. One of them laughed out loud, obviously reacting to a joke of some kind. They took off their coats and sat down, a suitable distance from Ogston and Sandra.

Sandra began speaking again. "Davie talked about little else, but himself. He liked the ladies and was always trying to impress us. I suppose I knew that I was always going to be little more than another name in his little black book. It would have been a long list, that's for sure."

Ogston smiled. "Do you happen to know if he had a little black book?"

"I was just joking, though it wouldn't have surprised me."

Ogston pondered, for a moment, on the possibility that Davie Milne *had* written about his love-life somewhere. There certainly had been nothing left lying around the flat. Had that been something the killer took away with him, or had it never existed?

"You said he talked about himself; in what way?"

"Just stories half the time. To be honest, I never believed the half of what he said. There's a word for someone who makes things up about themselves?"

"A fantasist."

"Well, Davie would have been one of them," added Sandra, biting into her cake and finding her coffee a little cooler to drink.

Ogston lit a cigarette and drank some of his coffee. He had ordered a cake, but he wasn't really in the mood for eating it.

"Did you know anything about Davie playing darts on a Monday?" he then asked.

"He never mentioned that in my company. However, I do know when he met another girl from work it was always on a Monday evening. They used to talk about how it put a smile on their face at the start of the working week."

So, the darts was just an excuse to get out of the house, thought Ogston. *What a lovely man.*

"Were you ever aware of Davie being in any trouble?" Ogston then asked.

"What kind of trouble?"

"I don't know, financial problems, for example," said Ogston.

"As I said, I really didn't know him that well, but he always came across as a happy-go-lucky kind of character, who rarely seemed bothered by anything. He was immensely self-confident and cared little for what others thought of him."

"Was he well-liked at work?"

"Oh, definitely not. The men hated him for constantly chatting up the girls and some of the girls hated him for never attracting his attention. Mister Reynolds didn't like him because of his poor work record. I know that Davie had received more than one warning about his attendance. In fact, I saw them arguing at the end of last week."

"Davie and Mister Reynolds?"

"Yes. They weren't exactly shouting at each other, but their voices were definitely raised."

"What were they arguing about?"

"Oh, I couldn't make out what they were saying, but it was probably to do with Davie's time-keeping. Davie never saw the point of getting to work for opening time; it seemed to be beyond him."

"Why didn't Mister Reynolds just sack him, then?"

"I don't know," replied Sandra, eating some more cake. "Davie did bring custom to the shop. His ladies would queue up for their pound of steak, or whatever and he'd fire off the one-liners and make them all laugh. Maybe Reynolds would have missed their business had he got rid of Davie."

In light of what he now knew about the typhoid, Ogston wondered how many women might now be ill because their infatuation with Davie Milne had caused them to shop with William Low.

"Did Davie ever mention a man by the name of Ranald Cusiter?"

Sandra thought for a moment. "No, I don't think so."

Ogston felt there was little more to be gained from questioning Sandra Riddell, even though it had been a very pleasurable experience. They finished their coffee and Sandra asked if she could have Ogston's cake. He readily agreed and wrapped it in a napkin for her.

"It'll do for lunch," she said. "I'll not get out again after this."

Ogston walked Sandra back to the shop. He wanted a quick word with Reynolds anyway.

"Might I ask that you say nothing about Davie's death, for the moment. It'll be in the papers soon, so you'll be able to talk about it then," he said.

"My lips are sealed, Chief Inspector," replied Sandra with a smile. "Thank you for the coffee and cakes."

"My pleasure," replied Ogston, opening the door and letting Sandra enter the shop first.

Ogston went through the back and straight to Reynolds' office. The manager did not look overjoyed to have the police back to see him. Ogston sat down.

"I believe you were arguing with Davie Milne at the end of last week, Mister Reynolds. What was that about?"

"The usual," Reynolds replied. "I questioned Davie's attitude towards getting here in the morning. I suggested it would be nice if he got here *before* the doors opened and he had his usual alternative view."

"Why not sack him then?" suggested Ogston.

"I really don't know."

"Did he, perhaps, bring in some extra custom?" suggested Ogston.

"I don't deny our lady customers were very taken with our Davie and yes, it probably did help the figures over a year."

Ogston thanked Reynolds for his time and stood up. "I'll send a couple of men along to interview the rest of your staff, Mister Reynolds but, for just now, I'll leave you alone."

Reynolds was not sorry to see the Chief Inspector leave his office. It had not been a good week at work and all he wanted now, was for a bit of peace and quiet.

Oh, yes, and a good week of sales.

*

Back at the office, Ogston tasked someone with finding Caroline O'Hara, wherever, in London she might be. He found it hard to believe that neither Phyllis, nor Cusiter, could remember whose party they'd met at. They seemed rather besotted with each other and it would be normal, in circumstances such as that, for every detail of their relationship to be locked into their memories.

Hopefully, Caroline's memory would be better.

Ogston still wanted to find out all that he could about Ranald Cusiter. He gave that task to another officer. He wanted to know *everything* about Cusiter, absolutely everything.

Ogston felt sure there was a stone, somewhere, waiting to be turned. He pondered, for a moment, on what might crawl out.

5   5

By Saturday, 23rd May, there were 23 patients in hospital, 20 of them now confirmed to have typhoid.

Ian MacQueen had been talking to the media, warning that numbers could rise quite dramatically, as doctors erred on the side of caution and admitted to hospital anyone experiencing symptoms, even remotely attributable to typhoid.

The names and addresses of those already confirmed, were in the local papers that day, along with a message from Mr MacQueen suggesting that anyone, who may have received food from any of those named, might like 'to have a word' with their GP.

The weekend turned out to be almost perfect in terms of the weather. A temperature of 72 degrees was recorded at Strathdon, though Aberdeen, itself, never quite reached such dizzy heights.

Much as the residents of Aberdeen wanted to enjoy the fine weather, there was an air of uncertainty hanging over the city. Most people were generally ignorant, with regard to typhoid and rumour and counter-rumour was flying around the city, without question. As a result of not knowing what to believe, many residents had stopped doing much of what had previously been described as normal living.

The fear of death was prevalent everywhere. Typhoid, to the average man and woman in the street, was in the same category as the Plague. Catch the disease and death would quickly follow.

The newspapers tried to educate Aberdonians, by printing various articles on the subject of typhoid. The message from Doctor MacQueen and his team remained the same; clean hands thoroughly at all times and do not share food with others, under any circumstances.

Ron Smith was, by that time, lead reporter with the *Evening Express*, on the subject of typhoid, He had fallen into the role, due to the fact three other journalists were now off sick, one of them already in hospital, believed to have the disease himself.

Ron had been called into the editor's office and told to read up on everything related to typhoid. The local papers would become the main source of information, for the people of Aberdeen and the editor wanted much of what they wrote to be educational as well as informative.

Ron had gone to the Central Library that morning and taken out every medical book he could get his hands on. He would take his role seriously.

He had also started attending Doctor MacQueen's twice-daily conferences. Ron had taken to MacQueen almost immediately, finding the man keen to pass on as much information as possible. Ron sensed that MacQueen almost relished being thrust in to the spotlight.

With the meetings taking place in MacQueen's office, space was limited and journalists would perch on desks and windowsills, as well as the lucky ones finding the odd chair that might be free. MacQueen, himself, would sit behind his desk, pipe in hand and answering questions with a relaxed ease.

Those who met the man came away thinking that if Ian MacQueen was anything to go by, then there was really no need for panic in the city. If the Chief Medical Officer could be *that* relaxed, then no one else should fear anything.

It was rare, indeed, for a journalist to interview someone in the public eye, who actually *wanted* to tell the Press as much as he could. MacQueen had recognised, very early in the process, that the media would be of tremendous help to him to both spread the word and also issue the occasional warning. It was, therefore, to his advantage to have the Press on his side.

Ron's mini, and temporary, promotion had led to him being given a new desk. The fact that the previous occupant was now off work, with suspected typhoid, had not filled Ron with much joy as he had first sat down. He now knew that he could not catch the disease by simply touching items left by his colleague, but the half-eaten sandwich, which was found in the top, right-hand drawer, was swiftly dispatched into the nearest bucket.

*

By the time Sandy Burnett got back to his desk, on the Monday morning, the number of typhoid cases had risen to 59 and the medical profession now had two major concerns. The first was for the numbers that might catch the disease before they got the spread under control. The second was for the staff who were expected to deal with the ever-increasing number of patients.

There weren't enough nurses, experienced in such diseases, to man the wards.

Doctor MacQueen instigated a press release, asking for retired nurses to return to service for the duration of the epidemic. It was obvious to the likes of Alison Young that the service provided to the patients would suffer and standards be compromised, if the nursing numbers remained as they were.

Alison knew what she was doing, but others didn't. Some of the younger nurses were constantly concerned that they too might contract the disease. Ignorance was one of the biggest enemies.

While Sandy was at his desk studying the information that had come in over the weekend, Alison was finishing her shift, or at least trying to. With the number of patients rising at some pace, it was putting a strain on the staff already working at the City Hospital. She knew that arrangements were being made for other hospitals to be used, should the numbers continue to rise at their current rate.

Alison also knew that the staff, in those other hospitals, would be less able to cope with a contagious disease. There would need to be an increase in on-the-job training, to try and bring other nurses up to speed on what would be expected of them.

While Alison mopped up, after another accident in the ward, Sandy was now making his way through to Doctor MacQueen's office for their daily meeting. This had been another idea of Doctor MacQueen's.

Doctor MacQueen could only keep the Press up to date if he, himself, was kept up to date. That meant regular contact with Sandy in particular, but also through contact with others.

To that end, he had set up a small team, who would meet each day and exchange ideas. MacQueen and Sandy would cover the medical issues, the other two attending the meeting would represent the interests of others.

Gary Quinn represented the City Council and was responsible for feeding back, any relevant information, directly to the Lord Provost and other Councillors. Obviously, the Councillors were constantly being contacted by their worried constituents and the more the Councillors knew, the better prepared they were for dealing with those queries.

The other person was Peter Shepherd, Head of the Retail Section of the Chamber of Commerce. Peter represented the interests of all retail outlets in Aberdeen where, it was feared, trade could be greatly affected by the fear and rumour that was already spreading throughout the city.

The four men met in MacQueen's office, each sworn to silence on matters which would not be made public until Doctor MacQueen decided to do so.

That morning there was growing concern regarding the numbers of patients now in hospital. Peter, in particular, was pushing for MacQueen to name the shop from where they believed the bad meat had been sold.

Peter Shepherd was thirty-eight years old and took his position, in the Chamber of Commerce, very seriously. He did not want anyone, in the retail trade, to suffer a loss of income through anything he might have done wrong.

Although he took his duties seriously, Peter did not look the type to be particularly bothered by anything. He dressed casually at all times and often appeared to lose interest at meetings, as if his mind had drifted to other matters.

It was an illusion, however. Peter Shepherd was a sharp individual, who missed nothing. At meetings, even when appearing to be distracted, he would be listening intently to what others might be saying. He had little need for notes as his memory was exceptional.

"I really think we should be naming the shop in question," Peter was saying, for more than the first time, at their meeting that morning.

Ian MacQueen looked irritated, which was not an uncommon sight, away from public viewing. He did not suffer fools gladly and he did not like his authority being questioned, especially by someone outside of the medical profession.

"At the moment, there is no need to name the shop," MacQueen replied, trying to keep his rising anger under control.

"But there are stories sweeping the city, Doctor MacQueen, which point the finger of suspicion at a number of outlets. Customers will stop going to those shops if they think, even for a few days, that the typhoid started there. We need to give them all the facts, so that they'll know it is perfectly safe to go on shopping at their usual haunts."

"We need more time, Peter," insisted MacQueen," so as to be absolutely certain that the source was only in the one place. We are confident that corned beef was the source and we also now know, that the strain of typhoid is that found in Spain and South America. "

"Exactly," said Peter, "and the corned beef used by William Low came from Argentina. Do we really need to know any more?"

"In terms of the disease and its spread, it is still early days," MacQueen insisted. "In getting to William Low as quickly as we did, I think we can safely say that there will be no possibility of contaminated meat being sold from there anymore. It might also be safe to say that their hygiene record, from now on, will be second to none. Why then, affect future business by attributing the source of the disease to them just at the moment? There will be a better time for that, I can assure you."

"But they *were* the source of the disease and I think people need to know that," insisted Peter.

MacQueen shook his head. "No, it is too early. We need to understand the spread of the disease better, just in case there are other sources, which we haven't yet identified."

"But surely we *know* the source now," said Peter, almost pleading with McQueen to change his mind.

"We might *think* we know everything, Peter, but, as I keep stressing, we have much still to do. As for the rumours, well we'll never stop them, no matter how much information we give out. People will continue to believe what they want, it's human nature."

Peter Shepherd was not sold on MacQueen's argument, but knew that he could not say anything, publicly, without breaking the trust of the others sitting in the room. For the moment, all he could do was to try and counter any of the rumours, which reached his own ears.

"Where do you think we are with this disease?" Gary then asked. "Councillors are concerned as to what the final numbers might be."

MacQueen smiled. "The Councillors are concerned about the numbers, is that really all that concerns them? Me, I'm more concerned for the people who catch this disease. While it may no longer be fatal, if caught and treated early enough, it is still an extremely violent illness, which will be long remembered by those who contract it. Councillors should give some thought to the people they represent and give less thought to the numbers."

"I didn't mean to sound quite so callous," confessed Gary. "Obviously, they are mindful of the effects the disease has but, equally, it *will* be the numbers that everyone else will focus on. People, outside of Aberdeen, will look at the paper each day and they'll see that number rising. Whether we like it, or not, it will be the *only* talking point until the number starts to fall again."

Although the idea annoyed him, even Doctor MacQueen had to admit that Gary had a point. The numbers *would* keep rising and the headlines would not make good reading, for some time to come. It would just be the number at the top of the page that people would concentrate on.

"Gary," MacQueen then said, "you asked where you thought we were with the disease. I shall be telling the Press later that I believe the first wave should be over in a day, or so."

"First wave?" said Gary, looking deeply concerned and casting an eye at both Peter and Sandy, before looking back at MacQueen.

"Yes, the first wave are those cases who were directly infected by the contaminated meat. However, those people will have been carrying the disease for anything up to two weeks and would have come into contact with many others in that time. It is those 'others' who will constitute the second wave of the disease. They will have become infected by the first wave and those numbers could be considerable."

"My God," said Gary.

"Not even He can help us now," added MacQueen.

There was a stunned silence in the room for a moment. Sandy understood the gravity of the situation but for the other two, ignorant of all medical matters, it was a giant learning curve, one which neither was particularly enjoying.

"So, this could go on for long enough," Peter eventually said.

MacQueen nodded. "As I say, it is still early days."

*

Detective Chief Inspector Ogston was in his office. He had just received the post-mortem report on Davie Milne. There were no real surprises in the report and but for the fact the time of death had been recorded with a little more certainty, there might not have been any need for the report at all.

The base of the trophy had been confirmed as the murder weapon. It had only taken the one blow, delivered with force and clearly intended to kill. Time of death was set at some time between ten o'clock on the Tuesday and two o'clock on the Wednesday morning.

Ogston already knew, from speaking to Sandra, that Davie probably hadn't been home any earlier than around a quarter to eleven. That meant he may have died almost as soon as he had got home, which suggested someone must have been waiting for him.

The report went on to deduce that the blow to the back of Davie Milne's head had been delivered by someone of at least the same height, possibly slightly taller. That mean the killer had to be around five feet nine upwards.

Which definitely took Phyllis out of the equation, though not Cusiter.

If someone had been waiting for Davie to return, then maybe one of the neighbours might have noticed something? No one had said anything during the question sessions with Forrest and DC Jamieson. Had they really not noticed anything, or simply chosen not to mention it?

Ogston decided to send some uniformed officers around the Fernhill Drive area, to ask residents if they'd seen anyone hanging around outside that night. They were also to check for any cars that might have sat outside the property for a while. A car registration would have been of particular help.

Ogston put the report down and lit a cigarette. He sat back in his chair and gave some thought to what he already knew. It didn't take long.

As it stood, there was next to nothing to go on. They had no obvious motive for anyone wanting Davie Milne dead, short of an irate husband. However, without knowing the names of the wives, no one was ever going to identify the husbands.

No one had really offered any opinion as to who Davie Milne really was. Not even his wife seemed to know him. All anyone talked about, was his liking for the ladies. There had to be more than that.

Ogston was now convinced that there had never been any darts played on a Monday night. It had been no more than an excuse to get Davie out of the house. Maybe there had been one, special woman and maybe if had been her husband who had done the deed.

Maybe? That was really all he had, a list of maybes. Certainly nothing to keep an investigation going.

Along with the post-mortem report was the outcome of the fingerprints taken from Davie Milne's flat. That, too, proved to be of little help to the investigation other than add the fact that Ranald Cusiter's fingerprints had been found in the bedroom.

Maybe the friendship with Phyllis had already moved to another level before she finally decided to leave her husband?

Ogston still retained a nagging suspicion about Ranald Cusiter. No matter what else he did, he simply couldn't shake that suspicion.

He was still deep in thought when there was a knock at the door and Andy Forrest stuck his head round the door.

"Bad news, boss," he said. "Gordy's phoned in sick. Doesn't sound good. He's waiting for the doctor to call and then he'll let us know the outcome."

"Okay," Ogston replied, "thanks for letting me know."

"You're looking a little concerned, sir?" Forrest then said.

"It's this bloody murder," Ogston said, sounding slightly exasperated. "I can't, for the life of me, see a motive other than some irate husband, which I just don't buy."

"Irate husbands have turned to murder many times in the past," Forrest added.

"Agreed. But in this case, how would an irate husband know where to find Davie Milne? As far as we know all his romantic dalliances were well away from his own home. On the night of his murder he let someone in to his flat who, he felt, posed no threat to him. Some unknown husband would never had fallen into that category. As soon as Davie reached the front path the husband would have been on him."

Forrest could see the sense in that statement. Ogston continued.

"Plus, that someone waiting, clearly knew that Davie was coming home otherwise he'd not have hung about. Who would have known what Davie was doing that night?"

Forrest thought for a moment. "Someone from his work, maybe?"

"Perhaps," agreed Ogston, "though we have no reason to believe that anyone from his work would want to harm him, let alone kill him. That blow was delivered with a great deal of anger."

Forrest thought some more. Eventually, he spoke again.

"Maybe it's time to release the story to the papers; see what happens?"

Ogston nodded. He knew his Inspector was correct; it was time to make the story public and, in the process, ask for anyone with information to come forward. Ogston had held off, hoping something of value would come to light from their own efforts.

That had proved not to be the case. Every lead had fizzled out, and Ogston now conceded that the investigation was unlikely to go anywhere unless new information came to light. The problem with passing a story to the papers was that it invited every nutcase, in the north-east of Scotland, to pick up a phone and tell the police any old rubbish. Their idea of helping the police was to thrust themselves into the limelight. It was their own needs they were meeting, no one else's.

There had already been a suggestion, from one of the female staff members at William Low, that it might have been her husband who had attacked Davie. Forrest had looked in to the suggestion himself and found that the husband had made some threats towards Davie Milne but they'd been made under the influence of drink and that he'd never had any intention of actually going through with those threats.

Forrest had believed him.

Ogston had even had the trophy checked out, just in case the murderer had brought it with him. After all, no one had ever spoken about Davie being sporty, unless sex could be classified as a sport.

It turned out that the trophy had been awarded to Davie when he'd been sixteen. He had been part of a squad of football players, who had taken part in a local competition. They had finished winners and every member of the squad had been given a trophy. Davie hadn't even played, but he'd got one anyway.

Ironically, it meant a trophy he'd never really earned, was to be the very thing that killed him.

That appeared to have been the only time that Davie had taken any part in a team game. After that it had all been about doing things on his own. At least until he met Phyllis.

He'd, literally, lived for the ladies.

Ogston suggested that he and Forrest return to the Fernhill Drive property that afternoon and have one final look around. He knew he was suggesting it out of a sense of grasping at straws; there was no real plan to what they'd be doing, other than a vague hope that something may have been missed the first time.

A time was arranged for later and Ogston then picked up the phone as Forrest set off to deal with other business. Ogston got his outside line and dialled a number from memory.

The call was answered almost at once and a meeting arranged for lunchtime that day. Ogston then put on his coat and left the office.

*

Ogston arrived at the Roosevelt Café, on Belmont Street, twenty minutes after walking away from his desk. It was the usual meeting place, when he had a story for the Press. When he arrived, his contact was already sitting at one of the tables.

Ron Smith had been Ogston's contact for the last three years, having taken over from an old hack, called Alec Collier, who had retired two months before a lifetime of drinking, finally saw him off.

Ron had explained he was up to his ears in typhoid stories, but Ogston had insisted on talking to no one else. On the back of a long and trusting relationship, Ron had agreed to meet and then he'd decide how best to pass on whatever information he received.

The café was filling up, which didn't take long, such was the size of the place. They both ordered pie and chips along with a pot of tea. The food did not take long to prepare and both men were soon tucking in to a meal that they hoped would fill a gap.

They were both busy, both working longer hours than might normally be the case and both unclear as to when the next meal might come along. They ate in relative silence and it was not until both plates had been cleared that they settled down to the business in hand.

Had it not been for the typhoid, Ron would probably have dealt with the Davie Milne murder. It would, therefore, not come as a surprise to anyone, in the Journals, to know that the police wanted Ron to get the details of the case. Some younger, and certainly more eager, journalist would get the privilege of writing the story for the evening paper.

Ron took some notes. There wasn't that much to write, particularly as the police appeared to have gathered little in the way of useful information, so far. The story was being released more to attract information than impart any.

"Put in the usual bit about us seeking information from anyone who knew Davie Milne," added Ogston. "To be honest, it would be nice to speak to a man who saw Davie as a friend. So far, he's been painted as public enemy number one and only the women ever wanted to be seen with him. Because of that, we really do know absolutely nothing about our victim."

"Has the typhoid affected you directly?" Ron then asked, choosing to change the subject.

Ogston was taken slightly aback by the swift change of direction but, given that Ron's working world was rather full of that one story, it perhaps shouldn't have come as such a surprise.

"We have a few more off sick than might be normal," answered Ogston, "but, as far as I am aware, we don't have any confirmed cases amongst police officers. How about you?"

"The chap I'm covering for has typhoid," said Ron, "but, so far, he seems to be the only confirmed case. Word from Ian MacQueen is that a lot of people could be affected by this disease so I think we can expect to lose a few more colleagues as time goes by."

"I've been following your work in the papers," said Ogston. "I think we're all aware of the fact that numbers will rise. Have they given any indication as to where it all started?"

Ogston wondered when they would finally come clean with that particular piece of information. For the moment, he was just checking how much Ron knew.

"They're certain 'how' it started and I'm pretty sure, they know the 'where' as well; however, no one seems in any hurry to tell the likes of me that."

"Meanwhile, people will be making up their own stories," added Ogston.

"Far better than anything I could ever write," said Ron, laughing. "Some of the tales I've heard already are truly unbelievable."

They finished their tea over more general conversation. Ogston got to the point where he was happy that Ron had all he'd need to run the Davie Milne story. Just before they parted, however, he had one last question to ask the journalist.

"Ever crossed paths with Ranald Cusiter?"

Ron laughed again. "You mean *Ronnie* Cusiter. The *Ranald* only came along when he started getting a bit more successful in business. I imagine he though Ranald sounded better when moving in higher circles."

"Tell me about him," prompted Ogston.

"He's a man desperate to bury his past. If he could, I'm sure Ronnie would erase his past completely."

"Why?"

"Because he's ashamed of his upbringing. Ronnie was born in Aberdeen and brought up in Torry. He lived in a tenement flat, occupied by himself, his parents and his five brothers and sisters. He grew up with nothing, other than a giant chip on his shoulder and a burning desire to move up in the world."

"And now he's doing alright for himself," said Ogston.

"Indeed, he is. Three shops have his name above the door and he occupies a house on Argyll Place. I even hear he now has a rather attractive woman living there with him."

"So, how does some impoverished lad from Torry get enough cash together to start a business?" Ogston then asked.

"Ah," Ron replied, "the sixty-four million-dollar question and one which you may struggle in getting the correct answer."

"What would Ronnie's answer be?" said Ogston.

"That he received a loan from an anonymous backer. He's never named that backer, but insists that was where the money came from."

"When was this?"

"First half of Sixty-One, if I remember correctly. He opened the first shop around then and filled it with clothes he'd bought in London and brought back to Aberdeen. He advertised his clothing as being unavailable anywhere else in Scotland and began to attract customers from all over the place. In fairness to him, it was a roaring success almost from day one."

"And the other shops followed?" asked Ogston.

"The second in Sixty-Two and the last at the beginning of this year."

"Does he still depend on London clothing for his stock?"

"I believe he now employs someone to design a line of his own. It's not my scene, Graeme, but I believe there's a lot of money to be made in fashion. Young people, nowadays, have more money to spend on themselves and clothing is one area where they seem happy to splash the cash. Even the blokes want to look good; I expect we can blame all these pop stars for that."

Ogston instantly thought about Gordy Jamieson. He seemed to spend every penny he earned on making himself look good.

Ogston laughed. "I guess neither you, nor I, will ever be what's termed as fashionable."

"My idea of fashion was to dress like my father," said Ron, "so I'm not likely to be seen donning Beatle gear now."

Ogston laughed again. He had a mental picture of Ron, with his Beatle haircut and smart suit. It was a comical thought.

"Going back to Cusiter," he then said, "have you ever heard any whisper of him being crooked?"

Ron thought for a moment. "No. Why, you're not investigating him, are you?"

Ogston shook his head. "No, nothing like that. His name cropped up and I was just curious."

"About what?" pressed Ron, his journalist's nose starting to twitch.

"I suppose it goes back to the money he received for starting his business. I just wondered if it might have been money earned illegally."

Ron Smith did not look convinced. "Surely, if Ronnie Cusiter had been up to no good then he'd have crossed your radar long by now?"

It seemed a valid point. Maybe Ogston was allowing his dislike of Cusiter to cloud his judgement. It would just make life so much simpler if Ronnie could turn out to not only be crooked, but to also be Davie Milne's murderer.

Ogston could even come up with a strong motive. Cusiter, keen to have Phyllis for himself, went to see Davie and they'd argued. One thing had led to another and Cusiter had delivered the fatal blow.

If that could just be the case then everything would be tied up. Neat and tidy, just as Ogston liked everything in his life. There was only one problem, one major problem. There was no evidence to tie Cusiter to Davie Milne, other than the fact they both knew Phyllis.

"If you, or any of your colleagues, come across anything which might blacken Ronnie Cusiter's name I'd be delighted to hear about it," Ogston then said.

Ron laughed. "My God, you've really got it in for poor Ronnie, haven't you?"

"There's something about the man, I just don't like," was all that Ogston was prepared to say.

The two men put on their coats and Ogston paid their bill. They parted company outside the café and Ogston made his way back to Lodge Walk, where he found Forrest waiting at the front door.

"I have a car round the back, sir," he said and led the way out the back door.

They were soon on their way back to Fernhill Drive.

Both officers felt a chill in the flat, even though the outside temperature was still very pleasant. Ogston wondered if the new occupants would be put off by the fact a murder had taken place in their living room.

He led the way along the hallway to the kitchen. He suggested that Forrest take the bedrooms and Ogston would deal with the living room and kitchen himself.

It had all been searched before, more than once, but in the absence of anything else of value, there seemed nothing wrong with returning to the scene of the crime and hoping someone had missed something first time around.

Ogston entered the living room and looked around. The dark stain, on the carpet, was a little distracting, but Ogston managed to put it to the back of his mind and concentrate on what else might be in the room.

A jacket still lay over the back of the settee. He knew Gordy would have been through it, but he still found himself picking it up and once more going through the pockets. The tickets for the concert were there, along with his wallet. There was nothing of interest in the wallet. A few pounds and some receipts for purchases made.

Ogston put the jacket down again and moved over to the sideboard. He knew he'd been through it before, but he still searched all the drawers once more and yet again, came up with nothing.

Satisfied that the living room had no secrets to reveal, Ogston then made his way through to the kitchen. He now felt as if he were truly scraping the barrel for ideas. He didn't expect to find anything of interest in a kitchen, after all that was usually the domain of the woman of the house.

Ogston couldn't picture someone like Davie Milne doing much in a kitchen. He certainly wouldn't be likely to hide anything directly under his wife's nose. Would he?

Ogston checked the cupboards, the larder and the refrigerator. Not surprisingly, nothing had changed since the last time he'd looked, apart from the fact the milk had gone off. Ogston poured the milk down the sink and left the empty bottle on the kitchen table.

He assumed Phyllis would have to clear the house of all its contents before it could be offered to someone else. She'd definitely need to remove the carpet in the living room; new tenants could hardly be expected to stare at a bloodstain every day. He expected Phyllis would leave it all up to Ronnie Cusiter. He'd probably pay for someone to go in and clean the property thoroughly, before keys needed to be handed over.

Ogston found a few bills on the kitchen table. Bills that, probably, would not be paid now.

If asked later, the Chief Inspector would have been hard pushed to explain why he went back into the larder. He already knew there was nothing but a few tins in there but, something, made him go back.

Was it that old police officer's intuition, or something else, that simply can't be explained? Whatever made him do it, he was to meet with some success as a result.

With the kitchen having a balcony attached to it, the larder was situated with its back to the outside wall. The larder was built to remain colder than the rest of the property, so the walls and floor were bare brick. Towards the top of the larder was a small ventilation grill, which allowed some air to circulate and prevent damp from forming.

This time, when Ogston opened the larder door, he did not look at the shelves but down at the floor. About four inches above the floor were some wooden slats, designed to allow tins and other products to be placed upon them. Ogston got down on his knees and studied the slats a little closer.

He fiddled with them and realised they weren't as solid as they probably should have been. In fact, some of them could be moved easily.

A wave of excitement passed through Ogston. Maybe he was finally getting somewhere? Or maybe, he'd just found some loose slats.

One slat came away altogether and another could be raised at one end, though not detached altogether. There appeared to be enough space for someone to hide something, were they of a mind to do so.

Ogston put a hand into the space and started fishing around. It appeared to be empty and his excitement began to drain away.

His mind, however, was in overdrive. Had this been a hiding place for Davie, or Phyllis? What would they have kept in there and why was it now empty? Had the contents of this space been the reason for Davie Milne's murder?

Had the killer taken away the contents?

So many questions and so few answers.

Ogston continued moving his hand around inside the space and was just about to give up, when his finger touched something. It was stuck in the corner and, no matter how he tried, he simply couldn't get enough grip to pull it out.

At that moment, Forrest came into the kitchen. Ogston instructed him to phone for a joiner and to get him there as soon as possible. Forrest did not waste time asking why, but hurried down to the car to make the call back to Lodge Walk.

Within half an hour there was a knock at the door. Forrest opened it and was greeted by a small, almost pot-bellied man wearing a flat cap, dungarees and a checked shirt with the sleeves rolled up. He carried a tool box and had a pencil behind his ear. There was also a half-smoked cigarette, dangling from the corner of his mouth.

"Someone want a joiner?" he enquired, rather more cheerfully than Forrest might have expected. Surely no one could enjoy their work that much?

Twenty minutes later and the slats were all removed. The little man had also got through a cup of coffee and half a pack of, slightly soft, biscuits. On top of that, two more cigarettes had been smoked and a few tunes whistled in between puffs.

Having been told to invoice Lodge Walk, the little man then went on his way, content that his services had been of vital importance to a police inquiry.

Ogston, by then, was back on his knees. He was now able to see exactly what his fingers had been touching. It looked to be a photograph and, once more, his excitement rose.

He carefully tugged at the item until, eventually, he released it from whatever had been gripping it. He stood up and both officers now studied the picture.

It was of a man and a woman. They were sitting on a bench in a park. Ogston felt sure it was the Victoria Park. The man and woman were sitting, facing each other. The man was holding one of the woman's hands between his own. They were looking into each other's eyes and seemed to be deep in conversation.

At first, Ogston wondered how anyone had managed to get close enough to take such a picture until Forrest had enlightened him to the effect of a zoom lens.

Whoever had taken the picture had to have been good at what he, or she, did for the clarity was second to none. In being so clear, both Ogston and Forrest were able to identify the man in the photograph.

It was Councillor MacLean. They didn't know who the woman was, but they did know it *wasn't* Mrs MacLean.

"Now, what would that be doing here?" said Forrest.

"Maybe Davie had a wee side-line on the go," Ogston then said.

"A spot of blackmail, do you mean?" added Forrest.

"Could well be. I can't see any other reason for having photographs like this in your possession. The question now is had Davie taken the photographs himself, or was he working with someone else?"

"A falling out between crooks?" suggested Forrest.

"Perhaps. If it were, at least we'd have a motive for the murder, which would be a massive step in the right direction."

Forrest nodded. "So, what do we do now?"

"For starters, let's have another look around for any sign of photographic material. If Davie did take the pictures, then there must be at least a camera somewhere."

Another circuit of the flat proved fruitless. No sign of anything, even remotely, connected to photography. Ogston had also taken the time to check, once more, for evidence of another bank account. If Davie Milne had been in to blackmail, then he had to have hidden money somewhere.

The bankbook, with thirty-three pounds, five shillings and sixpence in it, was found and Ogston noted the branch as being the Bank of Scotland at 501, Union Street. Ogston also noted the balance, though he doubted that could have been inaccurate in any way.

Ogston and Forrest stood by one of the windows in the living room. The Detective Chief Inspector was looking puzzled.

"So, we appear to have evidence of what we believe was blackmail and yet we have nothing to confirm that. Milne would surely have been extorting money from probably more than one source, which means he had to have stored that money somewhere. But where?"

"Maybe the money was in the hiding place with the photographs?" suggested Forrest.

"Maybe?" added Ogston, but with little conviction.

"It was maybe the money that they murderer came for," Forrest then said, "which was why there was always the intent to kill Davie Milne and not just hurt him."

It was a strong theory and one that provided the strongest motive yet. Ogston mulled things over for a moment before saying anything further.

"It would all add up, I agree, but it just doesn't seem right to me."

"In what way, sir?"

"It's the fact we found the hiding place in the kitchen," Ogston explained. "I just think that brought risk. I mean Davie Milne was hardly likely to have been in the kitchen that much, whereas his wife would have been in there all the time. There would always have been a high risk of her finding that hiding place, if only by accident. Now, Davie might have been able to explain why he had photographs hidden there, but he'd never have been able to explain a bundle of money."

Forrest nodded. That made sense to him, Ogston continued.

"No, I feel certain that the money is elsewhere. In fact, I'd go as far to say that there's every chance Davie Milne has a second bank account, especially if his extortion racket had been profitable."

"And do we still think there's an accomplice?" said Forrest.

"Without a shadow of doubt," Ogston replied. "Davie didn't take that photograph, someone else did."

"But why would a man like Davie Milne have anything on Councillor MacLean in the first place?" Forrest next enquired.

"A very good question, Inspector," said Ogston, "and one that might lead to yet another player in this game."

"Not a second accomplice?" added Forrest with horror. "We haven't even identified the first one yet."

Ogston smiled. "It would be nice to know we were at least looking for one."

Forrest looked around the room. "Could it be possible that those involved in the blackmail scam fell out and one of them killed Milne?"

"It's possible, but I don't think so. They all needed each other; nothing worked without the input of all involved. With Davie dead, I'm guessing their wee income died with him."

"Which still leaves us with the fact that Davie Milne willingly let his murderer into his home on the night he was killed," said Forrest. "He had to have known his killer well enough as to trust them not to get violent with him."

Ogston nodded. "Only no one reported seeing anyone hanging around the property that night. No reports of mystery cars or lurking strangers. Yet, someone had to be waiting for him."

"Another mystery we need to solve, sir," said Forrest.

"At the moment, Inspector, we have too many mysteries and a sad lack of facts," said Ogston, making his way to the door. He put the photograph in his pocket, opened the living room door and started walking along the hallway.

They secured the property with the key to the replacement lock and went downstairs. Outside, the clouds were gathering and a threat of rain hung in the air.

They drove back to Lodge Walk and while Forrest parked the car, Ogston made his way back to his office. He sat down at his desk and lit a cigarette. He glanced at his watch. Hopefully, he'd get away soon. He could feel a headache forming and looked forward to getting home and putting his feet up.

He tried clearing some of the paperwork that had been left on his desk in his absence. However, the sheer effort of concentrating seemed to make the headache all the worse. There was now a tell-tale sign of spots starting to drift across his vision; a clear indication that a migraine was developing.

Ogston no longer got migraines that often, but when he did there was no other solution than to head for a darkened room and get some sleep. There was no point in fighting it; no one ever beat a migraine simply by willing it to go away.

He packed up, put on his coat and left the office. Yet again he rejoiced at home being so close. There was no need for a troublesome drive home, or having to take a seat on a busy bus. He could walk and be home in five minutes.

Ogston wasn't in the mood for eating, but did make himself a cup of tea, before going to bed. He'd drawn the curtains, got into bed and then pulled the blankets over his head, to darken the room even further.

Just as he was dropping off, an image of Alison appeared in his mind's eye.

Even in a time of pain, it was enough to put a smile on his face.

6 6

6

Ian MacQueen's meeting on the morning of Tuesday, 26th May was a fraught one. Morale amongst the medical staff was dropping rather dramatically, with many of them working fourteen or fifteen hours per day. MacQueen had received a letter from the Lord Provost, which he had decided to circulate amongst the staff in the hope that it might stabilise, if not raise, morale.

At least Doctor MacQueen was able to report that the signs were good that the first wave of the disease was passing. He had no indication at that moment if, or when, the second wave might begin to have an impact

As of that morning, there were 94 confirmed cases of typhoid, with another 14 suspected.

Peter Shepherd was still hounding MacQueen to go public with the name of the store. However, MacQueen continued to stand his ground, claiming to have plenty time in which to make such an announcement.

"I shall be telling the Press later," he said, "that we suspect corned beef to be the source, but that the contamination of that meat took place many miles away and had nothing to do with the shop which had the misfortune to sell it. As I have said before, the disease could have originated anywhere."

"But it didn't, did it?" Shepherd snapped back.

MacQueen gave Shepherd a withering look, but chose to say nothing. Sensing a major clash growing between the two men, Gary Quinn tried changing the subject.

"What do we know about the source of the corned beef?"

"As already stated, we know the typhoid strain was that found in Spain and South America. We now, also, know for certain that the infected corned beef did arrive from Argentina, though we still haven't pinpointed the supplier. We have inspectors working with the shipping and beef companies, so I'd hope to have that information any day now."

"And then you'll name the shop in question," insisted Peter.

Quinn's attempt at changing the subject hadn't lasted very long.

MacQueen sighed deeply. He turned his gaze on Quinn and stared at him for a few seconds.

"Perhaps, not even then, Peter," he eventually said. "William Low do not deserve to be punished for what has happened, they did not do any of this on purpose."

"Whether it was done on purpose, or not, Doctor MacQueen has no relevance on us announcing that they *were* the source of the infection. It's the news the public are waiting for with the greatest interest," Shepherd said,

"Then, they shall just have to wait a bit longer," was MacQueen's final comment on the matter.

Neither Gary Quinn, nor Peter Shepherd, seemed entirely happy with the way in which Doctor MacQueen was handling things but, from Sandy Burnett's viewpoint, there wasn't much else he could do. MacQueen cut the meeting short at that point, his irritation obvious to everyone else in the room.

*

Ron Smith was in his usual seat for the press conference. He had his typhoid hat on again, after spending much of the day before ensuring Detective Chief Inspector Ogston's murder found its way on to the pages of the *Evening Express*.

Smith had also prepared a full-page article on typhoid, which would be in the following day's *Evening Express.* He had covered everything, from the cause of the disease through to how best to prevent its spread. He was both proud and pleased with the piece and hoped it might springboard him towards a permanent, better job.

Everyone sat up as Doctor MacQueen entered the room. Some put out cigarettes, while others lit them. Notebooks were perched on thighs and pens and pencils held at the ready. Nothing was said as MacQueen sat behind his desk, his trusty pipe in hand, though rarely lit.

For the first time, MacQueen said a little more about the actual source of the disease.

"I now firmly believe that the source of this disease was one tin of corned beef. The infected corned beef was sold by a large shop in the city, but I must stress that the shop in question has not been negligent and its hygiene had been acceptable, prior to the first patient becoming infected."

"Which shop was that, Doctor MacQueen?" someone shouted out.

"I'm not prepared to answer that question at the moment," was all that MacQueen would say.

No one, in the room, pressed the point. Another question was fired at MacQueen.

"Having found the source of the infection, does that mean the end of the disease in the city?"

"It isn't quite that simple," replied Doctor MacQueen. "I said that the corned beef was the source of the contamination. However, it was not just the corned beef that ultimately became infected. When meat is cut, either by hand or machine, then any bacterium that may be left upon the knife, or slicing machine, will be passed to the next piece of meat, if that knife or slicing blade is not cleaned immediately. That means customers buying other meats, from the same butchery department, stood the risk of catching the disease."

"Which means?" asked one of the journalists.

"Which means people who don't like corned beef should not, necessarily feel safe," said MacQueen and although it had not been meant as a joke, it did raise laughter in the room.

MacQueen continued. "We should also not lose sight of the possibility of disease carriers still being out there. As they touch and contaminate food, they spread the disease without realising it. It means that, although we've stopped sales of the contaminated meat, we haven't stopped the spread of the disease."

Ron Smith had not exactly been filled with joy as he wrote down what MacQueen was saying. Everyone was looking for good news and there didn't seem to be any forthcoming. Much as Doctor MacQueen was trying to keep spirits up, the constant undercurrent was one of doom and gloom.

Another area of doom and gloom was the effect the disease was having on the local medical services. Medical staff were stretched and patient numbers continued to rise. Would the day come when breaking point would be reached and the local hospitals simply would no longer be able to deal with the number of patients in their care?

*

The same question was passing through Alison Young's mind as she made her way through the ward. She had been on duty since seven o'clock the previous evening and it was now lunchtime. She was desperately tired and in need of a break, even if that break didn't actually lead to sleep.

The doctors were all in the same condition. It was questionable if they were in any fit state to make accurate decisions. Meetings were held and collective decisions taken, mainly to prevent any one person being blamed were anything major to go wrong.

The call for retired nurses to come forward had been partially successful, but some of those who volunteered had been away from the profession for a few years and needed brought up to speed on almost everything, which stole time from a nurse who could have been doing something more useful.

Alison had been taken off her main duties and asked to become an unofficial trainer. Whilst it kept her away from the front line against the disease, it now tied her down to watching over others rather than doing things herself. She now had a responsibility to those nurses, under her training and it meant the idea of going home no longer entered her head.

Eventually, however, Alison was cornered by Matron and ordered to get some sleep. She was given the details of a free room in the nurses' home and told to stay away for at least five hours.

Alison found the room easily enough, only to find that another nurse had also been told of the room being free. They were both too tired to debate the rights and wrongs of the situation. They stripped to their underwear and climbed into bed.

They were asleep almost before their heads hit the pillow.

*

Ogston and Forrest had an appointment to see Councillor MacLean. At two o'clock they made their way to an office in the Council buildings, where they had been told Councillor MacLean would be waiting. The contact had asked what the meeting would be about, but Ogston had taken the precaution of saying it was a police matter in which they hoped the Councillor might be of some assistance.

Percy MacLean was a white-haired man of fifty-seven. His face was deeply lined and he looked a good five to ten years older than he was. He was overweight, having enjoyed too many dinners on council expenses over the years. He also looked very worried as Ogston and Forrest entered the room and accepted the seats they were offered.

"Now, what can I do for you, Chief Inspector?" MacLean eventually said, sounding as if he'd rather not do *anything* for the police.

"Do you know a man by the name of Davie Milne?" Ogston began.

MacLean gave the question some thought, before announcing that he didn't.

"So, you've never heard of Davie Milne?" Ogston asked again.

"Not unless he's one of my constituents," said MacLean. "I see a lot of them and don't always remember their names."

Ogston took the photograph from his pocket and slid it across the table. MacLean looked down and the blood drained from his face.

"Where did you get that?"

"Effectively, from Davie Milne," replied Ogston. "Still say you don't know the name?"

MacLean stared at the photograph for what seemed like forever. Ogston was happy to give him time, now knowing that the photograph was in the hands of the police, had come as a tremendous shock to him. MacLean eventually looked up.

"The only name I know connected to that photograph, is Mitchell."

Ogston looked at Forrest, who was looking back. *Who the hell was Mitchell?*

"Mitchell?" Ogston repeated.

"Yes."

"As in a surname?" Ogston then said.

"No idea, it was just Mitchell."

Ogston thought for a moment. Had Davie Milne used the name Mitchell, or were they looking for yet another accomplice? It, perhaps, explained the missing money. It was probably in one of the banks in an account for Mitchell. But whose account?

Ogston moved on. "I take it you were being blackmailed?"

MacLean nodded. He looked down again. "This photograph makes it look a lot more sinister. It really was all very innocent."

"Tell me about it, anyway," said Ogston.

MacLean sat back in his chair. He took a packet of cigarettes from his pocket and removed one. He placed it between his lips and lit the end, using a silver lighter. Through the whole process, his hand had been shaking.

He inhaled deeply, then let the smoke trickle out through his nose. He flicked the end of the cigarette over an ashtray, which was already lying on the table. Only then did he seem ready to speak.

"There were six photographs altogether. As you probably guessed, they were taken while Violet and I were talking in the Victoria Park. Violet had recently lost her husband and I was consoling her; nothing more. We are good friends, not lovers."

"Then why not simply say so and be done with the threat of blackmail?" asked Ogston.

"I am married to a very jealous woman, Chief Inspector. I doubt if she would have believed me, had I tried to say how innocent it all was. I have previous, if you get my meaning."

Ogston got the meaning. No smoke without fire and all that.

"When were you first contacted?"

"About three months ago. That photograph would have been taken around November of last year. Contact was made at the beginning of February."

"How was that contact made?"

"By letter. It was sent to my office and contained copies of the photographs and instructions as to how I was to make monthly payments."

"And how were you to make those payments?"

"I was told to put the money in an envelope and write the name *Mitchell* on the front. I then went to Tam's Bookshop, on George Street, where I handed the envelope to the reprobate behind the counter. He handed me a brown paper bag in which would be a copy of some disgusting magazine. I'd leave the shop, dump the bag in the nearest bin and go back to whatever I was doing that day."

Ogston knew Tam's Bookshop very well. It was situated on the corner of Gerrard Street and George Street and was well known to the Aberdeen City Police for stocking items that contravened every pornography law that had ever been placed on the statute books.

It was no longer Tam who ran the shop. He had died a couple of years back from an excess of alcohol and nicotine. His body had been buried, rather than cremated, for fear of causing an explosion.

The shop was now run by Tam's son, Shuggie, who was a small, thin Glaswegian with long straggly hair and a general unwashed appearance. Shuggie, like his father before him, was never seen without a cigarette in his hand. He was certainly in the right trade as he looked every bit as questionable as most of his stock and many of his customers.

"And you did that every month?"

"I did."

"Did you get any reaction from the shop owner, when you handed over the envelopes?"

"None whatsoever, just a look of complete indifference as he handed the paper bag to me."

"If you were only going to dump it somewhere, why accept the paper bag in the first place?" Ogston enquired.

"I thought it would look more natural to leave the shop carrying something."

That made some sense to Ogston, although personally he would not have liked to have been seen coming out of an establishment like Tam's Bookshop carrying a plain brown paper bag.

"How much were you paying?"

"Twenty pounds a month."

"That's a lot of money," added Ogston.

"It certainly is."

"Then why, if your meetings with Violet were so innocent, did you agree to pay the money in the first place?"

"As I've already said, Chief Inspector," MacLean replied. "the time I've spent with women in the past hasn't been quite so innocent. My wife knows about many of those affairs and would be unlikely to believe me, on this occasion, when I claimed it was nothing other than a close friendship. Anyway, I assume you are only here because the blackmailer has now been apprehended?"

"Not exactly," said Ogston.

"But you do know it must be this Davie Milne?" pressed MacLean.

"Davie Milne certainly appears to have played a part, yes."

"And you have him in custody?" MacLean then asked.

"Not in custody, Councillor, in the mortuary."

MacLean's expression was one of shock, though Ogston felt he noticed some relief in there as well. Getting rid of a blackmailer was definitely a motive for murder, though Ogston could not see Councillor MacLean as that murderer.

Of course, he might have arranged for someone else to commit the crime. There was no way he'd have got his hands dirty himself.

However, had that been the case then the Councillor would have known that Milne was dead; yet his reaction to the news had seemed genuine enough. Either he was hearing the news for the first time, or his acting talents were worthy of an Oscar nomination.

"Did you ever have direct contact with your blackmailer?" Ogston now asked.

"No. There was just that one letter. I suppose after I started paying the money, there was no reason for anyone to contact me again."

"We'll need to speak to Violet," Ogston said. "Would you be good enough to give us her contact details?"

"Does she have to be involved, Chief Inspector," pleaded MacLean, "she really has nothing to do with any of this?"

"Councillor MacLean, she's in the photograph. That means she had *everything* to do with this."

MacLean finished his cigarette and squashed the last of it into the ashtray. He seemed to be giving the matter some thought. Eventually he reached a decision.

"In that case, you might as well speak to her now. She works along the corridor."

MacLean went to fetch Violet and while he was away, Forrest sought an answer from his superior officer.

"Do you want me to arrange for Shuggie Gemmell to be taken to Lodge Walk?"

"Not at the moment. What you can do, however, is arrange for a car to be parked across the road from Tam's Bookshop. Then set up a surveillance team. Eyes have to be kept on that shop as long as it's open. I want a note of any known face who goes into the shop. We have to assume that Councillor MacLean was not the only person paying money to Davie Milne and his accomplice."

"I'll deal with that the moment we get back to the office," said Forrest, as the door opened and MacLean came back into the room. He was in the company of a very prim and proper woman, who was probably in her early to mid-forties. Her hair was in a perm and she wore a grey jumper and skirt. She looked quite calm, so Ogston assumed that MacLean had taken the opportunity to quickly explain why she was about to be interviewed by the police.

Both Ogston and Forrest recognised her as being the woman in the photograph, so at least they were speaking to the right woman and not just anybody the Councillor had brought along.

She sat down and MacLean was asked to leave. He did so reluctantly. Once left on her own, Violet looked a little more nervous.

She gave her name as Violet Yates and her address as being on Thomson Street. That explained their meeting being in the Victoria Park; it was at the bottom of Thomson Street.

Ogston showed Violet the photograph and shock registered on her face.

"Did that get Percy in some kind of trouble?" she asked.

"He was being blackmailed," answered Ogston.

"Blackmailed?" repeated Violet. "Why ever would he pay blackmail money for something so innocent?"

"Mainly because it doesn't look that innocent, Mrs Yates?" said Ogston. "You're holding hands and looking at each other in a manner that suggests more than just being good friends."

"But that *is* all that we are," said Violet. "Percy was just giving me some much-needed support after the death of my husband. I haven't dealt with it very well, I'm afraid. However, it would have been a lot worse had it not been for Percy being so thoughtful. It's terrible to think he found himself in trouble simply for showing me some kindness."

Actually, it was his previous indiscretions that, effectively, got him into trouble, thought Ogston, though he chose to keep that to himself. Instead he asked:

"When did your husband die?"

"Last August. He was only fifty; died of a heart attack while digging the garden. I was in bits for weeks and it was only thanks to Percy that I was able to get through those dark days and start to build by life again."

"Did you see Councillor MacLean socially at all?" Ogston then asked.

"We might have had lunch a couple of times, but we were never out together at any other time. I know the Councillor is married, so I would never have done anything to jeopardise that marriage."

"Well, someone must have thought there was more to your relationship before photographs were taken and money elicited from the Councillor," said Ogston.

Violet thought for a moment. "I suppose someone in the office might have got the wrong impression, even though we did nothing to justify that."

"Did you meet in the park a lot?"

"A few times, just to talk of course. Percy thought if we spoke out in the open it would prevent the very thing that seems to have happened."

"So, you are prepared to swear that there was nothing romantic going on between yourself and the Councillor?"

Violet looked offended. "Of course I am. How many more times do I need to tell you?"

It seemed clear to Ogston that Violet was telling the truth. He asked her to leave and for the Councillor to come back.

MacLean sat down again and lit another cigarette. This time, Ogston joined him by lighting one of his own.

Ogston was still a little confused as to how Davie Milne could have got wind of the Councillor meeting with Violet, especially if all the meetings had been so innocent. Had Milne heard about the Councillor's previous indiscretions and just presumed he was at it again?

With no direct link between Davie Milne and the offices of the local Council, it meant there had to have been someone working in those Council offices and passing on information.

In Councillor MacLean's case, the 'source' had got it sadly wrong, However, even in getting it wrong, it hadn't actually affected anything, seeing as MacLean paid up anyway.

Then there was the matter of the photograph. There was no way that Milne, himself, could be the photographer. Was the Council source also the photographer, or were there three of them involved in the blackmail?

The only other name in the frame that was in any way connected to the blackmail, was that of Shuggie Gemmell. Surely, he couldn't be the accomplice? Although his mucky books were full of photographs, there had never been any evidence of him actually taking pictures himself. It was also unlikely that a man like Shuggie Gemmell, would know anything about the personal lives of Councillors, other than which books they might prefer from the world of pornography.

Ogston found himself leaning towards the idea that there had been three people involved in the blackmail. One, working with the Council, gathered the information; a second took any photographs that might be needed for applying pressure and then Davie would come along and apply that pressure.

Ogston was convinced that Davie Milne had been the puppet master. The fact he had hidden the photographs told Ogston that he had been the one in control. Davie had also probably dealt with the finances. The accomplices had received their cut but had never been directly involved in collecting the money in the first place.

Ogston expected Davie and Shuggie to have come to some arrangement over the collecting of the money. It kept their illegal income away from the banks. Did that mean the money hadn't found its way into a bank account? Did Shuggie still have it?

Ogston looked across at Councillor MacLean and asked his next question.

"Did you ever talk to anyone else about your friendship with Violet?"

"Not to my knowledge. Look, it was a passing close friendship, I simply was there for her after her husband died."

"But you did see rather a lot of her?" pressed Ogston.

"Not socially, no," replied MacLean. "We had lunch here at work and we met in the park, because it was close to her home."

"Were you in the habit of having lunch with women, other than Violet, when you were at work?"

MacLean thought for a moment. "My personal assistant, if we were discussing a particular issue, but no one else."

"So, having lunch with Violet might have been misinterpreted by others?" suggested Ogston.

"I suppose," conceded MacLean.

"You also hadn't been in the habit of having lunch together whilst Violet's husband had been alive, had you?"

"No, but she didn't need my support then."

"You do see what I'm suggesting, Councillor?" Ogston then said. The Councillor' expression remained blank. "Violet's husband dies and you are suddenly seen in her company. You are seen to be holding her hand, looking at her as if she means something to you. It would be easy for someone to get the wrong idea, wouldn't it?"

"I suppose," the Councillor said again.

And that someone had to be close to both the Councillor and Violet, thought Ogston, which confirmed his belief that they had to have worked in the Council offices. *They also had to have known Davie Milne. So, if the Council contact knew Davie Milne, there was every chance they had to be looking for a woman.*

Ogston drew the interview to a conclusion and then he and Forrest, returned to Lodge Walk. Forrest went away to organise the surveillance on Tam's Bookshop. The officers involved, would have to be briefed and a rota drawn up.

It would take a little time.

Ogston went to his office and found a short report had been typed out and left lying on his desk.

One of the young Detective Constables had discovered all that he could about Ranald 'Ronnie' Cusiter. It hadn't amounted to very much, most of which Ogston had already got from Ron Smith.

Ogston lit a cigarette and sat back in his chair to read the report.

As already mentioned by Ron Smith, Cusiter had been brought up in Torry. The family had lived in a tenement flat on Menzies Road. Cusiter had gone to Victoria Road Primary School and then the secondary school in Torry. He had left with little in the way of exams and got a job as an Aberdeen Corporation bus conductor.

Throughout his twenties, Cusiter had changed jobs on a regular basis but, at the age of twenty-eight, all that changed. Almost out of nowhere he acquired money, from a source as yet unknown, and opened the first of his shops.

Cusiter had never married, though his attraction for Phyllis might have filled his thoughts these last couple of years. There was little doubt, in Ogston's mind, that they'd be getting married at the first opportunity.

Much as he had taken a dislike to Cusiter, he did wish Phyllis some happiness in her life.

Cusiter had lived in a flat, off George Street, until the money started to pour in from his budding empire. By the time the third shop had opened, he was moved into Argyll Place and living the life he had always promised himself.

Cusiter's bank accounts were all healthy and his parents now lived in a semi-detached house in Torry; apparently unwilling to move from the area they'd known best.

Ogston put the report sheet on his desk and puffed on his cigarette. He gave some more thought to Ronnie Cusiter.

There was nothing, in the brief report, to indicate that there was anything unlawful about Cusiter and yet Ogston continued to have a grumble in his stomach, which usually meant he was on to something.

Now, whether his stomach grumbling was an indication that he'd found his murderer, was another matter. Cusiter could still be a crook, but not a murderer.

Ogston put the report with the other paperwork already gathered in the name of Davie Milne. There still wasn't a great deal, still no obvious picture of Davie Milne and the man he'd been. They knew he'd been a womaniser and a blackmailer, but beyond that, not much else.

He was just getting ready to leave the office, when there was a knock at his door. The door opened and Sergeant Alan Sangster, one of the uniformed Sergeants, came into the room. Ogston invited him to sit down.

"What can I do for you, Alan?" enquired Ogston.

Alan Sangster was based in the Sergeants' room, which was located across the corridor from the front office. Being uniform, Alan dealt with what amounted to petty crime. Only the CID got to deal with the serious stuff, so no murders for Alan.

Sangster had been a cop for twenty years, and had reached that point in his career, where he was quite happy with his lot. He did not seek the extra hassle of being an Inspector, much as the extra salary would have come in handy. Alan was happy to see out the rest of his years and take his pension.

Beyond that, he had no plans for the future, other than, perhaps, growing old disgracefully.

"Do you still have that contact at the Journals?" Sangster asked, holding out a pack of cigarettes. Ogston accepted one and both men lit their cigarettes, before anything further was said.

"Yes."

"Could I ask that you contact him, there's something he needs to know."

Ogston was intrigued.

"Go on," he said.

"As part of this typhoid business the papers have been in the habit of printing the names and addresses of the patients."

Ogston nodded. "Yes, I know. Doctor MacQueen wanted the general public to know who was already in hospital, so that they could seek medical advice, if they felt they'd come into contact with any of those listed."

"An admirable intention," said Sangster, "only, in printing all those names and addresses, they've also tipped off every petty thief in the city that there were certain houses likely to be lying empty. Some of those houses have now received a visit and items have been stolen."

"How many burglaries have you dealt with?" Ogston asked.

"Four in the last two days."

"And they were all properties occupied by current typhoid patients?" said Ogston, by way of clarification.

"They were. That being the case, you're going to have to ask them to stop printing the names of any more patients."

Ogston nodded; of course, the habit of printing names and addresses would have to stop. However, it had been Doctor MacQueen's idea in the first place, so it made more sense to have a word with someone at Doctor MacQueen's office rather than go to the Journals.

Ogston told Sangster he'd deal with it. Once the Sergeant had left the room, Ogston phoned the number for Doctor MacQueen's office and by the time his call was over, he had arranged an appointment to see Sandy Burnett, the following morning.

*

Sandy broke away from Doctor MacQueen's daily meeting to go and speak with Detective Chief Inspector Ogston.

"I would never have considered the possibility of someone stooping that low," Sandy said, after Ogston had explained why he was there.

"Oh, there are many criminals who would stoop even lower, if they felt it would line their pockets in the process. I appreciate you asked for those names to be listed, in good faith," Ogston added, "but I really am going to have to ask you to stop."

"Of course, Chief Inspector. I'll explain to Doctor MacQueen and notify the Press immediately. There will be no more names in papers from now on."

"My thanks, Doctor Burnett."

"May I ask how your investigation is coming along, with regard to Mister Milne's murder?"

"Not moving as fast as I would like, Doctor Burnett. Sometimes, the pieces just refuse to fall into place."

"It can be the same in the medical world," Sandy said. "deciding what is wrong with a patient often needs the same skills as when you set about solving a crime."

Ogston understood at once. It was all about gathering relevant information and then coming to an educated conclusion. It wasn't always the right conclusion and sometimes nothing more than a best guess scenario.

"Anyway, I'm sure you'll get there eventually, Chief Inspector," Sandy then said with a smile.

"I wish I shared your confidence," added Ogston.

The two men shook hands and Ogston went on his way. Sandy sat at his desk a little longer. It really was difficult to comprehend how some human beings constantly sought to benefit from the suffering of others.

It was a cruel world indeed.

7   7

By the morning of Friday, 29th, there were 113 confirmed cases of typhoid, with another 23 suspected. The numbers continued to rise and Doctor MacQueen's initial optimism, that the disease might be on the wane, now seemed a trifle misplaced.

In fact, Ian MacQueen was looking particularly worried at the daily meeting. He had been giving some thought to the closure of places where people might meet in numbers. It made sense, if they were to prevent a mass transference of the disease, to keep people away from each other, as much as possible.

He would start by closing the schools. It would be a decision that might not go down well in some quarters, but he felt it was too high a risk to continue allowing pupils to gather and potentially spread the disease amongst each other. The young and elderly still needed the most protection.

He had also decided to either close other venues, or at least restrict in some way the numbers who might attend. The places he had in mind were dancehalls, cinemas, perhaps even the pubs.

Whatever his final decision, it would be unpopular. However, he was not doing his job to win a popularity contest; he was doing it to prevent further spread of a potentially deadly disease.

There had been a steady rise in patient numbers from day one. Much as he was trying to remain upbeat, even Ian MacQueen was beginning to wonder how bad things were going to get. In many respects it was fighting the unknown and no one can beat an enemy when they can't even see them.

Peter Shepherd stuck to his usual mantra. He wanted MacQueen to go public with the name of the shop involved and he wanted it made clear that nowhere else in Aberdeen posed a threat.

MacQueen stuck to his guns. He was almost getting fed up having the same conversation every day. Why wouldn't Shepherd just take no for an answer, why keep banging on every day about the same thing?

They hadn't realised that the mounting pressure was starting to get to them all. Answers were expected and they were the select few who should be providing those answers. The problem was, they didn't always have them.

Sandy Burnett brought the conversation back to the matter of closing public places. It had been mentioned earlier and then, rather skimmed over.

"You mentioned the need to start closing places where people meet in numbers but you didn't elaborate on, exactly, what you meant?"

MacQueen put his pipe in his mouth. Much of the time he never smoked his pipe, treating it more like a child's comfort blanket.

"Okay, gentlemen, how do you feel about us ordering the closure of the schools, for a start?"

The consensus in the room, was favourable. Sandy then spoke next.

"But we can't stop there; what about the universities?"

MacQueen shook his head. "Not just yet. I'm concentrating more on the young and the elderly at the moment."

"But isn't it just about keeping people away from each other?" pressed Sandy.

MacQueen pondered for a moment.

"You're quite right, Sandy, it is about keeping people away from each other, but I still feel we need to maintain a sense of proportion in the action we take. If we announce too much, too quickly then we'll just trigger that panic we've worked so hard to avoid. Any closures we make must be seen as a precaution and not be mistaken for us, in some way, losing the battle with the disease."

"Agreed," said Sandy," but can we at least draw up a list of the places we are *likely* to close."

"Very well," agreed MacQueen. He slid a piece of paper in front of him and took the top off his fountain pen. He started to write, speaking as he went along. "We start with the schools. Firstly, we'll reiterate our message to children not to share food with anyone else, then we'll get an agreement with the Education authorities to close the schools altogether."

"That will mean children being deprived of their school milk and meals," said Gary Quinn. "For some kids that's the only meal of the day that's worth having."

"I'm sure it is, Gary, but even if we continued to allow children to attend school, we'd have to stop giving them meals. There will be less chance of them catching the disease if they are at home and we'll just have to hope that their parents find some way of feeding them, even if that is less nutritional in the long run."

MacQueen looked down at his piece of paper again and began writing once more.

"Dancehalls. Bingo venues. Youth clubs," he said out loud.

"Cinemas?" added Sandy.

MacQueen paused. "I'd rather not close them."

"Why not?" said Sandy, rather more bluntly than he'd intended.

"For the same reason I won't close the pubs. The people of Aberdeen need something to lighten their day; we can't take everything away from them."

"But cinemas attract people into a relatively confined space," said Sandy. "Where there is contact, there is a threat of the disease spreading."

"Agreed," said MacQueen," but if life is already at an all-time low, being provided with some form of entertainment becomes all the more essential. For just now the cinemas and pubs remain open."

Sandy thought for a moment. "Okay, if we are aiming to protect the young and the old, why don't we at least stop children from going to the cinema?

Gary and Peter were nodding in agreement with the suggestion. MacQueen gave it some thought and could see the sense in adding an age restriction to those attending the cinema, for the foreseeable future.

"Very well, "MacQueen then said, "we'll say that under eighteens will only be allowed in to a cinema, if accompanied by an adult; that way the decision to take them out will rest with the parents."

"Excellent," said Sandy and the other two were still nodding. "Now, what about the football?"

"What about the football?" asked MacQueen.

"Aberdeen are due to play their first leg of the Summer Cup Final; can we honestly allow that to happen in the midst of closing so many other places? Surely we don't want people travelling from Edinburgh at a time like that?"

"Sandy's right," said Gary, "we can't possibly allow a major football match to be played under the current circumstances."

MacQueen felt as if he were being backed into a corner. He did not like that, even though he recognised his colleagues were only thinking of what might be best in everyone's interest. Before MacQueen could say anything, Sandy spoke again.

"It's highly unlikely that anyone would come up from Edinburgh anyway. We all know what the rest of the country thinks about this city at the moment. No, it's best that they either play the game somewhere else, or don't play it until we're clear of the disease."

"I don't have the authority to insist the game is postponed," MacQueen finally said, "but I will speak to those who are in a position to make such a decision."

Sandy left the meeting feeling more confident that the right decisions were being made. Action had to be taken and it had to be taken quickly.

By the time Ian MacQueen spoke to the Press, later that day, he had added both the Bon Accord and Beach baths to his list of places closing.

On making that announcement there was an audible reaction from the journalists.

"Does this mean you're losing the battle with the disease?" was the obvious question asked.

MacQueen took a deep breath. That was exactly the message he did not want splattered across the front pages of all the major newspapers.

"We are not losing a battle," he said, trying to keep his voice calm and his speech measured. "Everything we are doing is as a precaution against the spread of the disease. You can't just switch off an infection." MacQueen then continued, "To some degree, it is always a matter of time before corners are turned. Nature itself is the cure, we can only help it on its way."

Ron Smith asked about the universities and another journalist wanted to know about the football. MacQueen answered both questions in a manner which seemed to satisfy his audience.

Notes were taken, before the small group of journalists headed off to expand those notes into a complete piece, ready for the later editions of their newspapers.

*

Alison found herself working with more groups of inexperienced nurses. They all looked so young and yet every one of them was keen to learn, keen to play their part in getting the ever-increasing number of patients on the path to recovery.

All patients were quarantined. No one, except medical staff, was allowed near them. All visitors had to speak to patients through windows, which meant at visiting time there was a general tussle for space at one of those ward windows.

Many patients, of course, were too sick to receive visitors. The disease past through a stage where temperatures soared and individuals thought they were seeing all manner of things. Nurses heard the most ridiculous outbursts from patients as the hallucinations kicked in.

One girl, for example, had felt sure that the doctors gathering around her were giant seagulls. The more the doctors tried to help her, the more anxious she became.

Alison had hardly found time to go home in the last three days. Her energy levels were low and the few, short, naps she had managed to grab had done her little good.

Yet still the patients kept coming. Still there was no sign of the disease abating.

Just after lunch, that day, Matron gathered a group of nurses around her.

"The decision has been taken to create some space at Woodend, so that future patients can be taken there as well as coming here. Now, obviously, the staff at Woodend have limited experience in dealing with infectious diseases, particularly something so virulent as typhoid. To help matters we have agreed to exchange some staff so that more nurses can be trained. We appreciate that you are all very tired and as such, your ability to do your job properly is being severely compromised. You need to get rest and you need that rest to come at regular intervals, otherwise mistakes will be made and we can't have that happening, can we? To that end, you are all to report to Woodend Hospital tomorrow, at nine o'clock in the morning. Alison, you will be the senior of this group and it is to you that the others must turn, should they have any problems. You can then take those issues to Matron, or some other senior member of the team at Woodend. Until nine o'clock tomorrow, you are all to go home and get some sleep."

No one argued. No one asked any questions. No one did anything to keep them there a minute longer. They had heard the words 'go home', so nothing else mattered.

Although she was very tired, Alison took the chance to telephone Graeme, just before she left work. They hadn't had a chance to see each other for a few days and she just craved a few moments of normality, before going to bed and sleeping for as long as possible.

As luck would have it, Graeme was free to meet for a coffee. They agreed to meet at the Kit Kat Café, which was that little bit closer to Alison's flat.

*

Graeme studied Alison, as he entered the café and made his way over to where she was sitting. He thought she looked tired, though she did manage a smile for him as he approached her table. Suddenly, Alison leapt to her feet and threw her arms around Graeme's neck. Without thinking, he put his arms around her and they held each other tightly.

They stood like that for a moment, saying nothing but holding each other close. They got some strange looks from others in the café, but neither Graeme nor Alison were caring. For a few seconds they were in their own little bubble. Eventually, Alison let go.

"I'm sorry, it's just so good to see someone who isn't ill, or doesn't wear a white coat," she said, as they both sat down.

Graeme was smiling. "Feel free to do that anytime," he said, "it was most enjoyable."

Coffee was ordered, though neither of them sought any food. Alison spoke about how things were going at her work and that she was now moving to Woodend. Graeme said he, too, was busy with the murder inquiry. He was honest enough to admit that his enquiries weren't really going anywhere.

Alison reached across the table and took Graeme's hand in her own. She was smiling again, her eyes finally twinkling from within a tired and haggard face.

"You'll get this murderer; I have every confidence."

"Everyone seems to have such confidence in me," Graeme said, thinking about Ron Smith's comment as well.

They spoke of more general things as they finished their coffee. They talked about having a night out together and wondered when that might be possible.

"Not that there are many places to go, at the moment," Graeme had then said, referring to the news about closures of certain public venues.

"And it'll only get worse in the near future," said Alison.

"Much worse?" queried Graeme.

Alison explained the concept of the disease coming in waves. No one could predict how long that process might last, which was why no one was prepared to even estimate the final figure of those who would be affected.

"So, basically, there's not a lot you can do to stop it?" added Graeme.

"All that can really be done is what's been done already. Stop people sharing food with each other and improve cleanliness, throughout the city."

Graeme squeezed Alison's hand. "Maybe things will be a bit better for you at Woodend."

"I doubt it. I'll be working with less experienced staff."

"Anyway, keep in touch. I'll try to be available, if you get some free time," Graeme then said and Alison smiled again.

They left the café. Before parting, Graeme pulled Alison closer and kissed her. She responded, almost at once and the kiss lasted longer than had been intended.

As they pulled away from each other they laughed, though more out of embarrassment than anything else. Graeme was about to apologise, but the look on Alison's face told him an apology would not be necessary. The passion in the kiss had rather surprised them both.

They stood for a moment, not saying anything but looking into each other's eyes. They so wanted to spend more time together, but this really wasn't the time to be trying to develop a budding relationship. Eventually, Alison gave Graeme one last peck on the lips and then turned to leave.

Graeme watched her for a while and when she turned, he waved. She waved back; a smile evident on her face. He then made his way to Lodge Walk, his mind already turning back to Davie Milne.

*

Andy Forrest was sitting in Ogston's office. He felt sure he detected a lighter tone to the DCI's voice and perhaps a smile still lingering in his eyes. Clearly, his boss was in a better mood after he had returned to the office than he'd been before. Whoever the DCI had met had done him nothing but good. Forrest assumed it had to have been a woman.

The two officers spent some time talking about the Milne case. They agreed they were looking for a photographer and an employee of the Council. The blackmail had to have been a team affair.

"So, where does Shuggie Gemmell fit in?" Forrest had then said.

"Nothing more than a middle man, I should think," Ogston had replied.

"Do we haul him in yet?"

Ogston shook his head. "We'll let that run a little while longer, see if anything develops. I'd still bet my last penny, however, that Shuggie won't have much to tell us."

Forrest thought for a moment, as Ogston lit a cigarette and sat back in his chair. He really was a lot more relaxed than he'd been earlier. It didn't go unnoticed with Forrest, who now spoke again.

"Why is it that so many people in positions of authority seem to become targets for blackmail?"

"Anyone with a secret to keep can become a target for blackmail," added Ogston.

"We keep secrets," said Forrest with a grin.

"We don't keep *personal* secrets and that's what the blackmailer is really looking for," said Ogston.

"So, local Councillors are in to keeping personal secrets."

"Obviously some of them are. I suppose like all types of politician, Councillors are more accustomed than most to keeping secrets."

"I suppose if you get the likes of Profumo and the mess he created for himself, you must get prospective blackmailers hovering around politicians like vultures, just waiting for that one snippet of gossip that might turn in to a money-spinner for them."

"Classic case in point," said Ogston. "Powerful man, with every chance of becoming Prime Minister one day and he blows the lot on a dalliance with a young woman who may, or may not, have been a prostitute. Bring that down to local level and the photograph of Councillor MacLean and Violet suddenly takes on a new meaning, at least in the eyes of those who see what they want to see."

Forrest nodded. "Add to that the fact that there is always someone looking to knock people in authority off their perch and you begin to see why they become blackmail victims, I suppose."

"People in authority are always worried about protecting their reputation," Ogston then said. "Profumo got himself in a mess through trying to do just that. As it was, the more he said and did, the more he damaged that reputation; damaged it to the point where it could no longer be repaired."

"And he lost everything," said Forrest.

"Just as Councillor MacLean may well lose all that he has as well," added Ogston. "What may have been innocent enough has been tarnished by the actions he took once Davie Milne contacted him. No one will believe his innocence now, not after making blackmail payments. People will assume he must have had something to hide."

"Mrs MacLean will certainly assume that," said Forrest.

Ogston took one last drag on his cigarette, then leaned forward and squashed what remained of it, into the ashtray. As the last of the smoke escaped from his nose, he made one final comment on that particular subject.

"Life can be complicated enough as it is, Andy, without doing something stupid to make matters worse."

"Going back to the Davie Milne case, sir," Forrest then said. "What do you suggest we do next?"

"We interview every Councillor and try to get those who were being blackmailed, to open up about their situation. We'll make it known that anything they tell us will be in the strictest confidence as we are building a picture rather than trying to put any one of them under a spotlight. Maybe the offer of anonymity will loosen a few tongues."

"Very good, sir," Forrest then said, standing up and leaving the room.

8   8

Monday, the 1st of June had arrived. The weekend had been anything but restful for those involved in matters pertaining to typhoid and murder.

Nothing changed, however, for Doctor MacQueen. He still met twice with the Press and had his daily meeting with his own little group. There were now 197 confirmed cases of typhoid, with 30 others suspected of having the disease. Woodend Hospital was now accepting patients and Alison was already heavily involved in training those around her.

She had taken well to the role of senior nurse. The others seemed to find it easy to come to her and had quickly recognised her ability to remain calm at all times, even when those around her might have been getting a little hot under their collective collars.

Woodend Hospital was not designed, in the same way as the City Hospital, for dealing with issues like a typhoid epidemic. The City Hospital had been specifically built to deal with infectious diseases. The first hospital had been built in 1874, but major improvements were made to the design and the hospital was, effectively, reopened in 1895, with more modern facilities and a less, prison-like, demeanour.

Woodend, on the other hand, opened in 1907 and had been one of the last poorhouses to be built in Scotland. During the First World War, Woodend had been used as a hospital for the maimed and wounded. After the war, the building had rather fallen in to disrepair with no one finding an immediate use for it.

In 1927, however, it re-opened as Woodend Municipal Hospital. Although the City Hospital continued to be the main location for infectious diseases, Woodend soon became an alternative, though one that was to be used only when necessary.

The Royal Infirmary, at Foresterhill, was deemed too busy to find time to deal with one-off outbreaks of any disease and Woolmanhill was far too close to the city centre to entertain the notion of looking after patients with highly infectious diseases.

It made more sense for the Council to use The City and Woodend as they were both outside the city centre and, therefore, easier to quarantine.

While Alison was rallying the troops at Woodend, Doctor MacQueen was sitting with a group of journalists in his office. Although he had tried to be open and honest, at every meeting, he was getting more and more annoyed with some of the stories finding their way into the papers, all be it mainly outside the city.

A paper in Spain, for example, had reported that the dead were being piled up on Aberdeen beach, prior to burial somewhere safe. No one, in Aberdeen at any rate, had any idea as to how a story like that found its way in to print. Perhaps it had started as a joke and some journalist had missed the attempt at humour.

There had clearly been no attempt to check the validity of the information but there had been numerous occasions, over the years, when the Press hadn't let truth get in the way of a good story.

The facts would have told the worst of journalists that there had been no deaths and it remained everyone's hope that there never would be. An elderly woman had died after contracting typhoid, but the cause of death had been, correctly, attributed to the many other medical problems she had been suffering from.

Whether there were deaths, or not, Aberdeen was now being ostracised by the rest of the country. Anyone, however remotely connected to the city, was no longer deemed welcome in other towns and cities. Aberdeen was being treated as if the typhoid were killing hundreds and would kill hundreds more.

In one town, fresh vegetables were being sold with a handwritten note beside them, which simply stated:

Tomatoes

3/8d LB

NOT HANDLED IN ABERDEEN

Businesses were suffering and there was little sign of good news on the horizon. It was becoming clear to many that businesses in Aberdeen might never recover, were the disease to maintain its grip on the city for many more weeks to come. Even in educated times, people still chose to believe what they wanted.

MacQueen stressed, once again, that he was confident an infected batch of corned beef had been to blame for the outbreak of the disease. He went a little further that day, however, by naming two brands of corned beef one of which, he felt sure, was the source. He did not go as far as to say which one.

The journalists continued to push for the name of the shop and MacQueen continued to refuse to give out that information. It had almost got to the point where the more they asked the more determined he became not to answer.

One journalist then moved on to another story that had broken that day. It had been reported that two Ratings, members of a submarine crew at Faslane, had been taken to hospital with suspected typhoid. Another man, who had been on holiday in Aberdeen, was in hospital in Newcastle though only under observation for the moment.

A school in Manchester had found two tins of mouldy corned beef when preparing school meals one day.

The journalists asked MacQueen if there was any danger of the typhoid spreading across the rest of the country.

"By the very nature of the disease," Doctor MacQueen had said," there could always be the possibility of sporadic outbreaks, elsewhere, if people in that area came into contact with an infected person. We were not able to stop the movement of individuals and given that the incubation period for the disease is fourteen days, then it is perfectly possible that a number of infected people *may* have left the city. However, I am of the firm belief that we *have* contained the disease to the best of our abilities and that cases reported, outside the city, ought to be few and far between."

MacQueen then confirmed that three staff members, of the shop where the typhoid began, had been infected. It was perfectly possible, therefore, that at least one of them may have played a part in spreading the first wave of the disease.

Something else that had come to light and which had not gone down too well with the public at large, was the fact that the Ministry of Agriculture now admitted to being in the habit of stockpiling tins of corned beef. MacQueen, himself, had said the contaminated tin in Aberdeen could well have been imported up to thirteen years ago.

To allay fears that corned beef could become contaminated with typhoid through age alone, statements were issued explaining the disease would have had to have been present in the meat when it was sealed, or become infected through being handled after the tin was opened.

The fact that the strain of typhoid had already been connected to South America, rather implied the disease was present at the time the tin was sealed. A major investigation was already underway to ascertain exactly how the tin had come to be infected.

The public were not happy. Sales of corned beef dropped and not just in Aberdeen. Cooked meats, in general, were no longer being bought. Confidence in such products was low and it was likely to be some time before sales picked up again. If ever.

For one of the few times, since he had begun his twice-daily sessions with the Press, Doctor Ian MacQueen felt under fire from the journalists. They were no longer happy, simply receiving information. They wanted to ask questions, probing questions; questions which Doctor MacQueen might not have wanted to answer.

The journalists were now looking for a scapegoat; someone to blame for everything that had happened in Aberdeen over the last few weeks. It was another failing of the Press, they always wanted to apportion blame to someone for everything that occurred.

It was that collective baying for blood that made MacQueen dig his heels in, over naming the shop where the infection had started. In MacQueen's eyes William Low did not have to be blamed for anything.

Doctor MacQueen had therefore, stood his ground with regard to many of the questions asked and quite a few had, as yet, remained unanswered.

*

Over the weekend, police officers had visited every councillor currently working within the city of Aberdeen. They had all denied any possibility that they were being blackmailed, some more emphatically than others. However, three of them were to almost instantly change their mind, once presented with photographic evidence that they had visited Tam's Bookshop.

It seemed that admitting to being blackmailed was seen as being slightly more acceptable than owning up to shopping in Tam's.

All three had then asked to be interviewed at Lodge Walk, well away from the prying ears of family members. This was readily agreed and interview times were set up.

The first of those interviews had been planned for two o'clock that Monday afternoon and so it was, at just after that hour, Ogston and Forrest found themselves sitting in one of the interview rooms with a rather fat, balding man, in his mid-forties who was sweating profusely and trying to get a cigarette out of the packet he had taken from his jacket pocket.

Councillor Hamish MacCallum looked a worried man. He took longer than normal to get the cigarette into his mouth and Ogston quickly offered him a light, for fear that he might burn himself using his own lighter.

Ogston took the chance to light his own cigarette at the same time.

"I believe you now have something to tell us, Mister MacCallum," Ogston then said.

MacCallum looked more nervous than ever. The sweat on his brow was prominent enough to merit attention from his handkerchief and there was general concern, from both police officers, that the Councillor may be about to pass out.

"I don't want my wife to know about any of this," MacCallum then began.

"Our intention is to keep much of what you tell us out of our reports," Ogston said. "I would hope that no one else need be made aware of what is said here today."

MacCallum seemed to relax a little on hearing that. He knew he would have to tell the truth; he couldn't be sure of what the police already knew. However, the thought of his wife finding out about what he had been doing was almost too much for him to bear.

Ogston provided MacCallum with a little more thinking time, by going through the formalities of checking the Councillor's personal details. He then started asking more pertinent questions.

MacCallum quickly confirmed that he had been paying money to someone known only as Mitchell. He had never heard the name *Davie Milne*.

"Why were you being blackmailed?" Ogston eventually asked. It was the question MacCallum knew was coming, but which he was dreading all the same. He inhaled some smoke, enjoyed the nicotine hit, then let it out slowly.

He then began to speak.

"I have, for some time, been less than truthful when it came to my expenses claims. It was just a little here and there, nothing of any consequence. At first, I told myself I was doing nothing wrong, certainly nothing more than many other Councillors would have been doing. It was just a few pounds; it wouldn't hurt anyone. However, it rather became a habit I couldn't break."

"How much do you reckon you have fraudulently claimed?" asked Ogston.

"No idea. A lot, I should think."

"How long have you been a Councillor?"

"Six years; long enough to know better."

"And how long were you being blackmailed?" was Ogston's next question.

"Just over a year."

"How was contact made by the blackmailer?"

MacCallum finished one cigarette and lit another. He rarely made eye contact with anyone as he spoke.

"There was an envelope in my pigeon-hole one morning. Inside was a letter in which some of my financial indiscretions were listed. The letter went on to say that it was known that I was fiddling my expenses and that if I wanted to keep that fact a secret, I was to put five pounds, every week, into an envelope, write the name *Mitchell* on the front and take it to Tam's Bookshop, on George Street."

"How does mail normally get into your pigeon-hole?"

"Everything is sorted in the mail room and then put in each Councillor's pigeon-hole, ready for us to pick up as we pass."

"Had the blackmail envelope been posted?"

"That was the funny thing," MacCallum said, "it hadn't been."

"Because, had it been, it would have been opened in the mail room?" suggested Ogston.

"Only if it weren't marked *personal*, the mail room doesn't open anything marked *personal.*"

"But you distinctly remember it hadn't been posted?" said Ogston.

"That day is burned into my mind forever, Chief Inspector. I will remember every detail until the day I die."

"Then how did it get in to your pigeon-hole?" was the next, obvious question.

"Someone had to have put it there. I did ask if anyone knew anything about it, but I drew a blank, I'm afraid."

"Are the pigeon-holes accessible to everyone?"

"The public can't get to them, if that was what you meant."

"I'm more interested in who *can* get to them," said Ogston.

"Staff only. Whoever put the envelope in my pigeon-hole had to be working in the building. Visitors are never allowed to wander about, without someone accompanying them, so it had to be a member of staff."

"Did you ever hazard a guess as to who might be blackmailing you?" enquired Ogston.

"I had my suspicions," replied MacCallum, "but never anything concrete. I couldn't give you a name, if that was what you were hoping. However, even I could see that it had to be someone in the building, probably in the Finance Department. They would have been the only members of staff scrutinising my claims and therefore, noticing my figures didn't always add up."

"Are there many working in the Finance Department?"

"Quite a few, though I couldn't tell you the exact figure, Chief Inspector. I'm pretty sure, however, that not one of them will have the word 'blackmailer' written across their forehead."

"Is there a particular section, which deals with expenses?" Andy Forrest asked. He had been taken notes and trying to leave the questions to the Chief Inspector. But, just occasionally, curiosity would get the better of him.

"Different sections do deal with different things, but they all work in essentially the same large room, so I suspect it would not be too difficult to pick up on what colleagues might be doing."

"Is the Finance Department locked?" Ogston then asked.

"Not to my knowledge."

"So, anyone could go in and snoop around?"

"I suppose," was all the Councillor could say.

In fact, MacCallum had little else to say about anything. He was allowed to leave and Ogston and Forrest moved on to the other two Councillors, now wishing to change their story.

They both turned out to be similarly sheepish about having to attend the police office and even more reticent about having to tell the truth. Ogston was firmly of the opinion that, no matter what the level of politics, the first rule of thumb was *never* tell the truth, unless absolutely necessary.

Grudging though it may have been, they both eventually told a version of the truth.

Councillor Taylor had a sorry story to tell about needing funds for some essential house repairs. However, much as he tried to put a different spin on his actions, it still boiled down to fiddling expenses.

Councillor Wright was a different kettle of fish altogether. He was young, handsome and married. However, having a marriage licence had not detracted him from seeking the company of other women and at that precise moment in time, he was engaged in an affair with Miss Travers, from the Legal Department.

There was the usual, *please don't tell my wife*, which came from all men who thought they could have their cake and eat it. Again, Ogston made no promises. In fact, there was a piece of him eager to tell all wives of the indiscretions of their husbands. He knew that he would never treat any wife of his in that manner,

Why did an image of Alison leap into his mind when he had thoughts about wives? He hardly knew her, surely all thoughts of marriage should be well down the line.

"Do you think anyone at work was aware of your affair with Miss Travers?" Ogston enquired.

Councillor Wright thought for a moment. "I wouldn't have thought so, we were very careful in everything that we did."

"Where did you meet?"

"Always at a hotel, usually outside Aberdeen where I was less likely to be recognised."

Ogston doubted if Councillor Wright would have been recognised outside his own circle of friends, but if he wished to entertain such delusions then who was Ogston to destroy them.

"Where, exactly, did you go?" Ogston pressed.

Wright seemed unwilling, at first, to give too much away. However, even he knew that he would not get out of that room without telling the police *everything* they wanted to know.

He explained that they usually went to Ellon, though sometimes they had gone to Banchory. They always signed in as Mr and Mrs Smith (*how original,* thought Ogston) and they always only stayed one night.

"How did the blackmailer make contact?" Ogston then asked.

"I found a note on the windscreen of my car."

"Saying?"

"The note claimed that there was photographic evidence of Miss Travers and I together at the Buchan Hotel in Ellon. At first, I dismissed it all, choosing to believe that it was simply someone trying to con money out of me."

"But," added Ogston, knowing there had to be a *but.*

"An envelope came through the post," Wright then explained.

"With photographs in it?" added Ogston.

"Yes. I mean, it came to my home. What if my wife had opened that envelope?" said Wright.

Then she would finally have known what a louse she'd married, thought Ogston. What he actually said, however, was:

"What were the photographs of?"

"Oh, it was nothing scandalous; no naked bodies or anything," replied Wright.

"But they were of you and Miss Travers together?"

"Yes. Photographs of us kissing in the car. There was one of us entering the Buchan Hotel and another of us leaving. I have to say the photographs looked very professional."

"So, you'd reckon they were taken by someone who knew what they were doing with a camera?" enquired Ogston.

"Definitely."

Forrest made a note of the Councillor's opinion. Ogston paused for a moment, to better digest what he had just been told. He then continued.

"When were you asked to start paying?"

"Six months ago. There was another note on the windscreen of my car, telling me to pay five pounds every week and explaining how it would be done."

"Through Tam's Bookshop?" prompted Ogston.

"Exactly."

"Did you ever give any thought as to who your blackmailer might be?"

"You can't help but run through some options in your mind. I had no idea who it was, but I felt it had to be someone inside the Council as no one else would be interested, would they?"

"Interested in you having an affair, Mister Wright?" said Ogston. "Oh, I should think the local papers would have ran with that, had they been aware of what you were up to."

"Which shows how careful we were," added Wright," as the local papers clearly *didn't* know anything. That was why I felt it was someone inside the Council; someone close to me; someone I might have met and spoken with nearly every day there was Council business."

Ogston agreed. The more he heard, the more he was convinced that Milne's accomplice was working for the Council. Half the time they were doing their job and the other half they were watching and listening, for any titbit of information that might provide them with an opportunity for blackmail.

But who would that be?

Once the interviews were complete and the formal statements had been taken, Ogston and Forrest returned to their desks. The Chief Inspector was delighted to find that the permission, from on high, had come through that would allow his officers to formally approach the banks in their search for an account that might exist in the name of Mitchell.

Of course, the biggest problem was not knowing if Mitchell was a first, or second name. It would mean checking all accounts, with Mitchell in them, in the hope that Davie Milne had at least set it up using his own address.

The search would begin at the Bank of Scotland branch where Davie Milne's personal account was held. Ogston did not expect to find anything there, however. If he was running two accounts, under two different names, then he'd want to keep them in separate banks.

He would not want to run the risk of being recognised under one guise, while trying to pay money in under another.

Ogston did think, however, that Davie would have been unlikely to have wandered far from his work environment. He would have wanted his bank accounts close, so that probably meant his *Mitchell* account was going to be in one of the other banks at Holburn Junction.

Were that to be the case then the search might not take that long. He called Forrest through to his office and asked him to send a couple of DCs to the banks at the top of Union Street. They were looking for the *Mitchell* account and they were to turn up armed with the warrant allowing them access to such accounts, as well as all Davie Milne's personal details. There had to be a link somewhere.

Forrest went off to comply with Ogston's request. He had no sooner left the office when the door opened and the Desk Sergeant looked in.

"Someone in the waiting room is asking to see you, sir."

"Do we know who?"

"Gave his name as Archie Pearson, says he was a friend of Davie Milne."

"A rare breed, indeed," added Ogston. "Okay, give me a minute to round up Andy and we'll be right there."

As it happened, they weren't 'right there.' In fact, half an hour went by before Ogston and Forrest were finally able to go to the interview room. Forrest had taken longer than expected to find a couple of DCs who weren't already up to their armpits in work.

Archie Pearson was not a pretty sight. His hair was long and straggly. It looked like he hadn't washed it in days. He looked nervous, sitting at the table with one leg pumping up and down, as if operating separately from the rest of his body.

He was thin, badly dressed and had a slight facial deformity that tended to catch the eye of anyone talking to him. It was only a slight misalignment of the nose, but it was obvious and somewhat distracting.

Archie was puffing on a cigarette when Ogston and Forrest entered the room. He sat up, like a pupil reacting to the teacher coming into the room.

Ogston and Forrest sat down, Forrest's trusty notebook forever at the ready.

"Mister Pearson?" Ogston began.

"Aye."

"I believe you were a friend of Davie Milne's?"

"Aye, ah wis."

"Were you a close friend?"

"Naebody wis 'at close tae Davie. At least nae if ye werenae a bird."

"Why are you here, Mister Pearson?" Ogston then said, already surmising that Archie Pearson might not be the sharpest knife in the drawer.

"I kent fit Davie wis up to," Pearson then said, dragging back ever harder on his cigarette.

"What do you mean, you knew what Davie was up to?" prompted Ogston.

"Ah kent he wis getting money fae fowk."

"How did you know that?"

"Davie telt me. Davie telt me lots a things; ah'm sure he thocht ah wis nae right in the heid, half the time, an' that ah'd nivver remember fit he said."

Ogston was still wondering the same, if he were being brutally honest.

"So, what did he say?" Ogston then asked.

"Fit?" replied Archie, stubbing out his cigarette and reaching for the packet again.

"You said that Davie told you things; what kind of things?"

"This 'n that."

Ogston was beginning to get a little annoyed with Archie Pearson. He didn't think he was being deliberately obtuse, but if he didn't start saying something relevant, in the next minute or two, then Forrest would be instructed to show him the door.

"What did Mister Milne tell you, Mister Pearson?" Ogston said again, only this time his voice was raised and the anger clearly showing on his face.

Archie lit his cigarette and sat back in his chair.

"Oh, aye, sorry," he then said.

When Archie began speaking again, he seemed to forget to stop. Forrest was struggling to write everything down, reverting to a form of writing that he felt sure he'd not be able to decipher later.

Davie had been in need of money. He hadn't been making enough as a butcher, to live the kind of live he wanted. He was tired of being married and had been actively seeking a way out. He had assumed that his constant womanising would have been enough to force Phyllis into divorcing him. He'd even said he'd have supplied the necessary photographic proof, were she ever to need it.

Ogston remembered Phyllis saying something similar.

"This reference to Davie getting photographic evidence, were Phyllis to need it, interests me. Did Davie know someone who could have taken those photographs for him?"

"Nae that I ken," Archie replied.

"Then how was Davie to get the photographic proof, if it were needed?" asked Ogston.

"Dinna ken," was the immediate and somewhat honest reply.

"I thought you said Mister Milne told you things?"

"He did."

"But he didn't tell you that?"

"No."

"Okay, carry on," prompted Ogston.

Archie spoke more about Davie's masterplan to get rich. Davie had acquired information, which he felt sure others would pay good money to keep out of the public domain. Archie didn't know the specifics of the information, or who exactly was going to be blackmailed. However, he did know why Davie had set up his other account in the name of *Mitchell*.

"Mitchell is Davie's middle name."

Ogston looked at Forrest. "See if you can catch those DCs, tell them they're probably looking for an account in the name of Mitchell Milne."

"Will do," said Forrest and he hurried from the room.

Ogston then looked back at Archie. He thought about pausing the interview until Forrest returned, but decided to continue.

"We believe that Davie's little blackmail plan had involved him working with someone else. Would you have any idea who that might have been?"

"Ah canna gie ye a name, but ah bet it wis a quine. Wi' Davie it wis aye aboot the quines."

"Did Davie ever know anyone who worked for the Council?" Ogston asked next.

Archie thought for a moment, lighting another cigarette as he did so. He then spoke.

"Aboot six months ago, he went oot wi' a Cooncillor's daughter."

"Do you remember her name?"

Archie thought some more. It seemed a painful process, judging by the expression on his face. Ogston was happy to wait for an answer.

"Isla," he eventually said, "Isla Montgomery."

"Daughter of Councillor Patrick Montgomery?" asked Ogston, by way of clarification.

Patrick Montgomery had been a relatively new arrival in the City Council, on the back of a successful career in the hospitality trade. He had made money over the years and now had a part-share in three hotels around the city. He was married with two daughters, Isla being the younger one.

Was it possible that Isla Montgomery was Davie's accomplice? Surely not.

Archie didn't have much else to say. He had thought he was bringing new information to the police but he was now of the opinion that only Isla Montgomery and Davie's middle name, had been of any real interest to them.

Forrest returned just in time to show Archie to the door. Archie had asked why his information hadn't led to him receiving some kind of financial payment. Forrest hadn't even graced the question with an answer, assuming his withering look had said enough.

Archie had set off along Lodge Walk trying to come up with another plan for getting the money he'd need for that week's rent. He was staring at eviction if he didn't come up with a plan quickly. The only problem was that Archie's brain never did anything quickly.

Forrest met up with Ogston back in the DCI's office. He was keen to hear if he'd missed anything.

Before saying more about Archie, Ogston asked if Andy had managed to catch the two DCs.

"They were literally at the door, but I did manage to catch them."

"Good."

Ogston then told Forrest about the Isla Montgomery connection. Forrest's eyebrows went up. Ogston then continued.

"Andy, I want you to find out all you can about Councillor Patrick Montgomery. Perhaps he's been telling tales at home and Isla was passing them on to Davie."

"Do you want me to look into Isla while I'm at it?"

"Not for the moment. If Patrick Montgomery turns out to be the main source of information then Isla might get away with a smack on the wrists."

Forrest nodded and left the office. Ogston decided to make good his escape, just in case something else came up. He packed everything away in his drawers, put on his coat and left the building.

9   9

Ron Smith was at his desk early that Tuesday morning. He hadn't slept very well the night before and had decided he might as well be at his desk than lying in bed. As it was, he couldn't seem to stop himself from yawning as he scribbled some notes, hoping that a story would spring from the few facts he was writing down.

He suddenly became aware of someone standing behind him. Nothing was said, the person simply stood there. Ron could hear him breathing and wondered who it could be. He eventually looked round. It was Robbie Shearer.

Robbie was new to the newsroom at Aberdeen Journals. It was his first job and he was keen to impress. He was in his mid-twenties, rather scruffy but with that permanent expression of keenness that only the young possess. Life tends to wipe that look off most people's faces as the years go by.

"Yes?" Ron asked, feeling slightly annoyed at being interrupted. He had hoped that coming in as early as he had, he would have been accorded some peace and quiet to organise his thoughts.

Robbie looked a trifle awkward, as if he didn't really know what to say next.

"I was wondering..........," he began, almost cautiously.

"Yes, what were you wondering?" added Ron, trying to speed things along a little.

"I was wondering if I might take on the Davie Milne murder story?"

Ron turned in his chair. "I'm not sure there is a story."

"Only because we haven't exactly pushed for one, have we?" Robbie then said. "I mean, you've been too busy to run with it and no one else has shown the slightest interest in taking the crime stories off you."

"Are you now saying that *you* want to cover the crime stories?" Ron asked, a slight tone of disbelief in his voice.

Robbie picked up on the fact Ron did not appear to have much confidence in him.

"Someone should be keeping in touch with the police, noting any developments that might occur."

"Had there been any developments, the police would have contacted us," Ron then said. "We have to assume that their investigation isn't going anywhere fast."

"Do we actually know that?" Robbie then said. "I mean, when did you last speak to anyone from the police?"

"Just before we ran the story about Davie Milne having been murdered," admitted Ron, "but my contact with the police has always been on the basis that they tell me things, I don't ask. That being the case, if they've not made contact then it's because they have nothing to say."

"Or, they are not saying anything because they know their usual contact isn't covering crime at the moment?" suggested Robbie.

Ron had to admit that Shearer's question was a valid one. Had he still been on the crime desk he'd have been hounding Graeme Ogston for a story, any story. As it was, no one was even making contact to enquire if any progress was being made.

Maybe they were missing out on something big simply through a lack of effort on their part. Young Shearer was clearly putting himself forward for a wee step up the ladder; it was a bold move, but his thought process was sound enough.

Ron considered the matter for a moment. He wasn't particularly keen on some young whipper-snapper taking his job, even if it was only until typhoid fell off the front pages. On the other hand, Shearer was an able enough journalist and his point was well made; murder usually held the front page and at the moment it didn't have a place on any of the pages.

"I'll make some calls first," he eventually said, "and get back to you."

Shearer went away grinning. Ron couldn't help thinking that he was making a big mistake, only he couldn't work out exactly what that mistake might be.

*

Tam's Bookshop had not opened that morning. The proprietor, Shuggie Gemmell, was otherwise engaged.

At ten o'clock he was sitting in an interview room, at Lodge Walk, smoking an untipped cigarette and nursing a half-cold cup of tea. He had been sitting there for more than an hour and was beginning to get a little annoyed.

He had a fair idea as to why he was there, but the idea that he should be left to stew in his own juices, repelled him. He deserved better than that, being a pillar of the community.

Well, at least he was in his own head.

Shuggie was only a little over five feet tall and almost as wide. His shirts rarely managed to restrain his stomach, without the odd button popping along the way. In the summer, he'd wear tee shirts, all of which sat across his girth, rather than covering it.

Today was a tee shirt day, making Shuggie a less than pre-possessing sight. His face was unshaven and his hair uncombed. There was a strong smell of body odour coming off of him and the cigarette smoke was doing little to combat it.

There had be no real reason for the delay in interviewing Shuggie Gemmell. Ogston had been clearing a few other matters and receiving a report from the Detective Constables who had spent most of the previous afternoon in the banks at the top of Union Street.

They had been there a little longer because their DCI had got it wrong. There had been no account under the name of Mitchell Milne. In fact, there hadn't even been an account under the name of David Mitchell. Instead, Davie Milne had chosen to open a business account under the name of Mitchell and Co.

The business account had been opened in the British Linen Bank at 484, Union Street, just a few doors down from his work. Business accounts were dealt with in a different part of the bank from the personal accounts, which meant different staff usually worked on them. As soon as the DCs were introduced to the right staff, the pieces quickly fell into place.

Davie was recognised from the photograph they'd taken with them. He was known to the staff as the accountant for Mitchell and Co; at least that had been the story he'd spun. Every penny he had even paid in had always been in cash. He had usually attended the bank during late-night opening on a Thursday and lunchtime Fridays.

The DCs had looked through the pages in the ledger dedicated to Mitchell and Co. The details of the account were that David Mitchell was the owner and David Milne, the accountant. No one at the bank had ever twigged to the fact they were one and the same person.

The balance was noted: one thousand six hundred and forty-three pounds. Alongside the money being paid every Friday were the withdrawals that had been made on a Thursday, when the bank was open later. Needless to say, the money coming out was significantly lower than that going in.

In short, Davie Milne had been a rich man, not that anyone would now see a penny of it.

Ogston had added everything discovered at the bank, to the file he'd began on the murder. It was beginning to take some shape even if most of it was irrelevant to actually finding the murderer.

Once he'd finished with the Detective Constables, he collected Forrest and made his way to the interview room. When they entered the room, they were immediately struck by the smell of stale sweat and cigarette smoke. Rather than one dominate the other, they seemed to merge together into one incredibly offensive aroma.

Ogston almost recoiled as he entered the room. Had there been a window, he would have opened it. Only there wasn't; just a pane of glass, set just below the ceiling, where light got in but not air.

As Ogston sat down he vowed to himself to make the interview as short as possible. Before doing anything, however, he lit a cigarette of his own and watched Shuggie lit another of his own. Much as Ogston enjoyed a smoke, he had never taken to untipped cigarettes. Not only were they stronger but they had that annoying habit of depositing tobacco in your mouth as you smoked them.

He had watched colleagues forever picking strands from their mouths and knew that that was not for him.

"I've been here for ages, Mister Ogston, you can't treat me like that, you know, I have a business to run."

"So sorry, Shuggie, if I've upset your normal routine. You see, mine's been upset for a few days now thanks to Davie Milne getting himself murdered. You'll remember Davie?"

Shuggie drew back on his cigarette and then exhaled.

"I read about it somewhere," he then said.

"Is there anything you'd like to tell us about Davie?" Ogston then enquired.

"I know nothing about murder, Mister Ogston, I just sell books and magazines and keep masel to masel."

"We don't have to talk about the murder itself, Shuggie," Ogston then said. "I have a feeling, however, that you'll be able to help us with something else."

"No idea what you're talking about, Mister Ogston."

"How about the envelopes you've been collecting for Mister Mitchell," Ogston then said, studying Shuggie's reaction as he spoke.

Shit, thought Shuggie, *they know about the blackmail.*

Much as he was thinking that, he still tried to appear vague when he actually started to speak again.

"Mister Mitchell?"

Ogston gave him a withering look. "Yes, Shuggie, the ones with the money in them, don't try and tell me you don't know what I'm talking about."

Shuggie took two quick hits from his cigarette and looked down at the floor. He took a moment to respond.

"Ah, those envelopes," he eventually said.

"Tell us about them," added Ogston.

Again, Shuggie took a moment, finding his cigarette far more interesting than answering any questions. Eventually, he spoke.

"About what?"

Ogston's eyes flashed with anger. "About the bloody envelopes with *Mitchell* written on the front!"

Shuggie's chair nearly moved back with the force of Ogston's words. He now knew he had pushed the police officer far enough and it was time to tell him all he knew.

"I was just helping a mate."

"To do what?" pressed Ogston.

"I never really knew. Davie asked me to collect some envelopes and hand them over to him when he called at the shop. I never bothered to ask what was in those envelopes."

Ogston and Forrest looked at each other. Their expressions said: *Aye, that'll be right.*

"So, you got the envelopes, Davie collected them and you got nothing out of it?" Ogston then said.

"Something like that, Mister Ogston. Look, we were mates and I was just doing him a favour."

"Doing him a favour?" repeated Ogston in a tone that clearly told Shuggie he didn't believe a word. "Well, Shuggie, why don't you do yourself a favour and start telling us the truth for a change."

Shuggie finished his cigarette. He was obviously thinking things through. Eventually, he spoke again.

"Okay, I knew the envelopes contained money."

"And you never thought to ask Davie why you were being asked to collect envelopes with money in them?" said Ogston.

"Not me, Mister Ogston, I'm a trusting soul," said Shuggie, taking another cigarette from its packet. Ogston held up a hand.

"No more of them just now, Shuggie, my Inspector wants to get out of this room alive."

Shuggie gave Ogston a look of annoyance, but there was no way he was going to argue. He was enough mess as it was.

"You must have known what Davie Milne was doing was illegal," Ogston then said, making it sound more like a statement than a question.

"Never really thought about it."

"Shuggie, it was blackmail money and you were handling it, which just happens to be a crime. Now, I suggest you cut all the crap and start telling us something useful."

"I never knew nothing about blackmail," Shuggie then said, trying to sound as if he meant it.

Ogston was for none of it. "Shuggie, you've been around the block a few times and committed a few indiscretions, yourself, along the way. Don't sit there and try and tell me that you saw nothing illegal in what you were doing."

"I thought he might be collecting gambling debts," Shuggie then said.

"Was Davie Milne in the habit of gambling?"

"I don't know."

"Then why would it have been gambling debts?" Ogston asked, his anger rising again.

"Just a guess."

"I don't want guesses, Shuggie, I want facts. Stop all this nonsense and tell me the truth. Then and only then, I might be able to keep you out of prison."

"But I really don't know anything, Mister Ogston. Davie was just a mate who I was helping."

Ogston sat back and folded his arms. He then looked at Forrest, before looking back at Shuggie.

"Okay, Shuggie, I'll tell you what I'm going to do. My Superintendent is very keen for a quick outcome to this investigation and I think I'm ready to make an arrest."

Shuggie started to look worried.

"I can build a case that will confirm that you were working with Davie Milne in blackmailing a number of prominent people in this fair city of Aberdeen."

Shuggie was now looking *very* worried.

"I can further build a case of two criminals falling out. It doesn't matter why they fell out, just the fact they did. They meet, they argue and one kills the other. Nice and neat. Case solved."

Shuggie about leapt out of his chair.

"You can't do that, Mister Ogston!" he shouted.

"Oh, but I can and, more importantly, I will Shuggie. My Super's not bothered about who I put away, as long as we can stamp case solved across the file."

Shuggie sank back into his chair. "But it isn't true," he said, almost to himself.

"Oh, come on Shuggie, why let the truth get in the way of a quick conviction," Ogston said and began to stand up. As he did so, he turned to Forrest. "Formally charge Mister Gemmell with the murder of Davie Milne."

Shuggie was back on his feet again.

"You can't do that; you just can't do that!"

Ogston looked Shuggie straight in the eye. "Then start talking, Shuggie and stop wasting my time."

Shuggie now knew that he wouldn't be a free man for long unless he started telling the whole truth. No time for half-truths and lies now; he'd have to come clean. He sat down again. Ogston sat down again. Shuggie began talking.

"Back in nineteen fifty-nine, Davie was one of three men who raided H M Thompson's and made off with the money they'd had in their safe. The safe had held more money, than usual, as it had been near to Christmas and the staff were to be paid a bonus."

Ogston remembered the case. Obviously, it had never been solved. The thieves had broken in, during the night, opened the safe and made off with around three thousand, five hundred pounds. They had left few clues and certainly nothing that pointed to anyone's guilt.

At the time it had been deemed far too professional for any of the Aberdeen crooks and therefore, the assumption made that those in question had only come to the city to carry out the job.

Shuggie was still talking.

"Anyway, about a year later, I got talking to Davie in the shop. Davie used to come in sometimes and look at some of the stock. He never bought anything; he didn't need to. Davie had a way with the ladies; he could get the real thing whenever he wanted, so there was no need for him to look at pictures. One day, he asked me if I wanted to make some more money. Well. honestly, who doesn't?"

"What happened next?" said Ogston, eager to move things along.

"Davie said he had some money he wanted to keep secret. There was no way it was going anywhere near a bank, but he didn't like the idea of it being in a tin under the bed. He asked if I'd look after the cash for him. I said how much for me and when he said, I agreed on the spot. It was easy money."

"And this would have been in nineteen-sixty?" asked Ogston.

Shuggie lit another cigarette and nodded. "Latter part of sixty, I'd have thought."

So, that had to be Davie's share from the robbery, thought Ogston. *What about the blackmail money?*

"Do you still have the money?" Ogston then asked.

"Oh, aye."

"How much?"

"Nae idea, there's never been any need to count it."

"Did Davie leave any more money with you, in the last three years or so?"

"He didn't *leave* money with me; it was always delivered in those *Mitchell* envelopes. I'd take ten per cent and Davie would collect the rest."

"And you still want me to believe you knew nothing about why those people were leaving money with you?" said Ogston.

"Okay, Davie may have told me at some stage."

"Before we deal with the blackmail money, Shuggie, let's go back to the robbery in nineteen-fifty-nine. Did Davie ever tell you who else did the job with him?"

"He just said there had been three of them. Other than that, I was never told anything else."

"And did Davie ever talk about other jobs he'd pulled?"

Shuggie shook his head. "Why would he tell me stuff like that?"

"Because you seemed to be buddies."

"Nah, we were mates, but not close mates," insisted Shuggie.

Ogston felt he wasn't going to get much more out of Shuggie. One thing was intriguing him though.

"Whose idea was it to give those men a copy of one of you magazines?

Shuggie smiled. "I just thought it added a certain something. They were giving me money, the least I could do was give them something in return."

Ogston considered what best to do with Shuggie. He was happy to accept that Shuggie's shop had been no more than a drop-off point. Okay, Shuggie had known what he was doing and he'd also helped himself to ten per cent, but Ogston felt that Shuggie could be of more use to him outside of prison.

Shuggie was one of those upstanding citizens who kept his ear to the ground and picked up all manner of juicy titbits. Knowing that a prison sentence was hanging over him, were he to fail to co-operate, might just be enough to have some of those titbits find their way to Ogston's attention.

"Okay, Shuggie, I'll tell you what I'm going to do. For as long as you keep providing me with any useful snippets of information that might come your way, I'm prepared to forget about what you were up to with Davie Milne."

Shuggie relaxed visibly. "Thank you very much, Mister Ogston."

"Before all that, however, Inspector Forrest is going to escort you back to your shop where you will hand over all the money you've been keeping for Davie Milne along with your stock of hardcore porn."

Shuggie's eyes flashed a look of anger. It past in a second for there really was no place for his anger on that room. DCI Ogston had him over a barrel; there was nothing else for it, but to play things his way.

"Whatever you say, Mister Ogston," was all that Shuggie could say, under the circumstances.

Losing some of his merchandise would be costly, but it was still a small price to pay for his freedom. Shuggie knew the law would be watching him even more closely so it would be no time to take any risks.

Forrest left with Shuggie and Ogston returned to his desk. On the way, he collared one of the officers on duty and asked him to dig out all he could find on the H M Thompson robbery.

"When was that again?" the DC had asked.

"December fifty-nine," Ogston had replied.

Within half an hour, the file was delivered to his desk.

Ogston lit a cigarette and began reading.

The raid had taken place on the twenty-third of December: a Wednesday. The staff had been due to receive their wages and bonuses on Christmas Eve.

It had been a simple enough job. The back door to the property had been forced. The night watchman had been overpowered and tied up. Apart from shock, there had been nothing else found to be wrong with the old man afterwards. However, he had become something of a minor celebrity in the aftermath of the robbery, as all the daily newspapers sought to interview him.

The old man had been financially rewarded for the interviews he had given and, along the way, certain embellishments had been added to his story. It had made it more difficult for the police to ascertain what was fact and what was fiction, thus any chance of catching the crooks had been greatly reduced.

The finance office had then been entered and the safe opened. Ogston guessed that Davie Milne had not been the safe-cracker. That meant one of the accomplices had to have dealt with that. At least one of them had to be a profession criminal and he had probably been well clear of Aberdeen, long before the old boy had reported the robbery.

That would account for two of the three men who raided Thompson's that night. Who, then, had been the third man? Ogston made a note on some paper lying on his desk. It simply read: *A N Other?????*

Ogston carried on reading. It had been nearly an hour after the robbers had left before the old man had been able to work himself free of his bindings and phone for the police.

By the time the first police officers got there any leads that might have existed, were already going cold.

The old man told the police very little. His memory had only improved with the money being paid by the newspapers. He'd been able to say there had been three men, but they had kept their faces covered at all times and apart from one of them telling him to shut up, nothing else had been said.

He had been asked if the two words spoken had betrayed a dialect of any kind. The old man had said it hadn't been enough to tell.

The investigating team had then spent two weeks trying to build a picture of what had happened that night, but they got nowhere. There were no fingerprints, no footprints, no evidence to tie anyone to the crime. Three men had ghosted in, carried out the robbery and ghosted out again.

By the end of January, nineteen-sixty, the robbery had been downgraded to the sub-dormant file. No one could afford to spend any more time on the investigation, so the file was placed in a cabinet and duly forgotten about.

Until now, when DCI Ogston's interest in the case had been sparked by Shuggie Gemmell. Ogston had actually learned more in the last ten minutes than the original team had in a month. At least Ogston had some idea as to who two of the men had been.

Not that that had helped him much. One of those two men was now dead and the other still hadn't been identified and probably never would be. Maybe the third man would fall into that same category.

Ogston read the last of the entries in the file. The investigating officers had quickly come to the conclusion that the thieves had to have been working on inside information. They had known too much. Thompson's staff had all been interviewed, but no one in particular identified as a possible accomplice.

It had amounted to nothing more than another dead end.

Ogston sat back and considered what Shuggie Gemmell had told him. It had been the best part of a year between the job being carried out and the money being left with Shuggie. Where had the money been before that?

Ogston's thoughts then turned back to Ronnie Cusiter. He turned and took a file off a pile lying on a chair to his left. It contained the information already gathered on Cusiter. Ogston checked when the first shop had been opened. It turned out to be around the same time as Davie came to his arrangement with Shuggie.

Could that mean that Cusiter was the third man? A part of Ogston so wanted that to be the case and yet he still couldn't explain why he had taken such an instant dislike to the man.

In fairness to Cusiter, there was still no evidence to link him with Davie Milne, let alone a life of crime.

Ogston closed the two files and laid them both on the chair to his left. He picked up the phone and asked for an outside line. He then dialled a number and by the time he was finished talking, he had arranged to speak to Patrick Montgomery. The Councillor had agreed to come to Lodge Walk at two o'clock, the following day.

10   10

Alison had been able to get home for a proper night's sleep and arrived at her work around lunchtime on the Wednesday, feeling a lot more refreshed than she had for some time.

The figures that day did not make good reading. 248 confirmed cases and 25 suspected. The day before Doctor MacQueen had finally spoken, publicly, about which brand of corned beef might have caused the infection. He named two of them and also said that he thought it was too early to say if a third wave of the disease was on its way.

The typhoid epidemic had also been discussed in Westminster, the day before. The main topic of discussion amongst the MPs was whether, or not, the Ministry for Health had adequate procedures in place to satisfy Parliament that corned beef was going through an inspection process on entry to the country.

Michael Noble, who was the Secretary of State for Scotland, made a statement to the House. He announced the current figure for those in hospital and added that it was the worst outbreak of a disease in Britain, since 1937. He further told the House of the probable source of the infection and praised Doctor MacQueen and his team, for identifying the source so quickly.

The movement of stockpiled corned beef, from Government storage to public consumption, was also debated. MPs also had to be convinced that age, in itself, did not cause the typhoid germ to take root. They were told, quite categorically, that the germ had to have been in the tin before it arrived in this country.

The main message, from the Minister that day was that the Government could, in no way, be blamed for the events unfolding in Aberdeen. The opposition, who had appeared to be building towards a major outcry, eventually participated in what was a very low-key debate and it was later reported in the newspapers that *'the House had been mildly critical of the Government for taking so long to make a formal statement, on the subject, but that little more was said.'*

The House did ask Michael Noble where the infected corned beef had come from. The Minister did not name any names, but did say there were two possible establishments and that one of those establishments had, apparently, not used chlorinated water, while cooling the tins. He was also able to tell the House that the typhoid germ had originated outside of the United Kingdom, so no one in this country could be blamed for what had happened.

Back in Aberdeen, Doctor MacQueen was still trying to keep the Press up to date with proceedings. He had expressed his regret at naming two brands of corned beef, as only one of them could have been infected. However, he felt it was in the public interest that he made such a statement, though there was a veiled apology towards the 'innocent' brand name.

The company secretary for Fray Bentos openly criticised Doctor MacQueen, saying the medial officer for health was out of order in naming brand names, unless he was one hundred per cent certain of his facts. MacQueen, however, stuck to his guns and ordered the withdrawal of two 6-pound tins of corned beef as they had been produced from the same area of South America.

MacQueen also further reiterated his request that Aberdonians stop buying pre-cooked meat until the epidemic was over. He also took offence to a complaint that the cost of individual towels in schools was unnecessary, even though it had already been clearly proven that shared towels were a source of passing germs from one individual to another.

Amidst all this news, whether it be accurate or not, the staff at two of Aberdeen's main hospitals toiled on caring for patients as best they could.

Alison had noted that one of the patients now occupying a bed in Woodend, was a police officer. It made her think of Graeme Ogston. It made her think of happier times.

It was quite a surprise, therefore, when Matron informed Alison that there was a phone call for her from Detective Chief Inspector Ogston.

"I do hope you've done nothing wrong, Nurse Young," Matron had added, prior to heading off down the corridor.

"Hello," Alison had said, as she'd picked up the phone.

"It's Graeme. Sorry to interrupt what is bound to be another busy day, but I believe you now have one of my men amongst your list of patients."

"Gordon Jamieson?"

"Gordy to us, but yes, that's the one. I just wondered if you could tell me how he was doing?"

"Not very well, I'm afraid. He's running a temperature and prone to hallucinations at the moment. Some of the things he was saying, when they brought him in, were ludicrous."

"That's not hallucination, that's just Gordy," Graeme quipped and Alison laughed. It felt good to laugh. It felt good to find something silly in the serious mess that surrounded her. "He will get better, won't he?" Graeme then added.

"Typhoid, in itself, is not a killer, Graeme. Your colleague is young and strong; he'll get over it."

A memory caused Graeme to smile. It was Gordy, standing in the middle of the canteen just after the first newspaper headlines proclaimed typhoid was in the city.

"As long as it's nae the chuddie that's infected," Gordy had said. He always had a pack of chewing gum in his pocket. As it turned out, the chuddie had been sound, it was something else that had got him.

"And how about you, how are you holding up?" Graeme then asked, his concern more for Alison than his DC.

"I got my first decent sleep last night, since the first cases were announced, so I feel more human today."

"Do you have any idea when your next day off will be?"

"As it happens, Matron has drawn up a temporary rota, to try and give us all some proper time off. Basically, we're all getting one and a half days per week, though that might all come in half days. My next time off is from lunchtime this coming Sunday."

Graeme Ogston's heart leapt.

"Would you like to meet for a little while?"

"That would be lovely."

Graeme could sense Alison was smiling. He couldn't stop grinning either. They were like a couple of inexperienced teenagers.

"I'll pick you up at the hospital. What time will you get away?"

"I'm due to finish at one o'clock, though I can't promise to get away exactly on time."

"I'll be at the Woodend gate at one. Take your time, I'll wait for you."

Alison said she was looking forward to it already and they both put the phone down.

Detective Chief Inspector Ogston had not felt this happy in a long time. It was a rare experience, indeed, to have a girlfriend and it was even rarer to sense that Alison seemed to be feeling the same way about him, as he did about her.

There was definitely something developing between them. Graeme found himself planning ahead for Sunday. He would prepare a picnic, then they could drive into the country and enjoy some quality time together?

Even if the weather turned wet again, they could always sit in the car and enjoy their sandwiches. It was spending time together that would be important, not where that time was spent.

And, of course, there would be no cooked meat in those sandwiches.

*

At two o'clock, Patrick Montgomery walked into Lodge Walk and announced that he was there to see Detective Chief Inspector Ogston. He was shown into an interview room and Ogston was told he had arrived.

Ten minutes later, Ogston and Forrest were seated across from Montgomery who was sitting with his hands clasped on the table in front of him and eyes staring straight ahead. He was immaculately dressed, with a clean, white and ironed handkerchief protruding from the breast pocket of his expensive suit jacket.

The man positively radiated money. Although now working as a Councillor, he had come from money and had never found himself in a situation where he had not known where his next fiver would come from.

His critics strongly argued that a man of such wealth could not possibly understand the needs of the poor amongst his constituents. Montgomery had argued that it took compassion, not riches, to understand the needs of others.

Ogston paused for a second, considering the best way to approach this interview. It was really Isla Montgomery who should have been sitting in front of him. It was really the daughter who should be answering police questions, but DCI Ogston wanted to protect the girl, if at all possible.

Isla Montgomery could only have passed on information to Davie Milne, if she had heard it around the dinner table. Her father had to have been in the habit of sharing Council tittle-tattle with his family. Were that the case, then he was every bit as guilty as his daughter.

"Do you enjoy the role of a Councillor, Mister Montgomery?" was finally where Ogston chose to begin.

Montgomery seemed surprised by the question. He had already been interviewed with regard to him possibly being a blackmail victim. He'd answered all the questions, clearly stating that he had never done anything to interest a blackmailer.

What else could the police possibly want? Ogston had only said he had some follow-up questions, he never said what they might be about.

And yet he starts the proceedings with a question about him liking his role as a Councillor. Surely, the police ought to be making better use of their time than that?

"I'm still relatively new to the role, Chief Inspector, but yes, I have been enjoying it so far."

Ogston lit a cigarette and noticed the slight turn up of the Councillor's nose. He obviously disapproved of smoking, but he wasn't going to pass any comment, seeing as he was in the Chief Inspector's domain. He did sit back from the table, however.

"There must be a lot of interesting things happen, almost on a daily basis?" Ogston then asked.

"I suppose," replied Montgomery, still not clear as to where all this was heading. "I feel sure that you could say the same about your job."

Ogston ignored the comment. "Do you talk about Council business at home?"

The question was blunt and to the point. Montgomery immediately went on to the defensive.

"What, exactly, is the point of these questions, Chief Inspector?"

"Humour me for the moment, Mister Montgomery, and just answer my questions, please," said Ogston.

Montgomery harrumphed a little, but did eventually provide an answer.

"I'm not usually in the habit of discussing my work when I am at home."

"No anecdotes, or funny stories that you pass on to your wife?" prompted Ogston.

"Perhaps, the odd funny story. I'm sure you do the same with your wife."

"I'm not married, Mister Montgomery."

The Councillor sat forward again, as if he were about to go on the offensive. As it was, he simply tried to clarify a point.

"Look, am I being accused of something here?"

Ogston held up his hand. "I'm not accusing you of anything, Mister Montgomery, just gathering information."

"To what purpose?"

"I'm trying to solve a murder," Ogston then said. "A man was recently killed in his home and we are still hunting his murderer."

"But what can that possibly have to do with me?"

Montgomery sat back again, Ogston's smoke literally getting up his nose.

"You were previously interviewed by my officers with regard to you possibly being a target for a blackmailer," said Ogston.

"And I told them I wasn't a target for blackmail and that I've never done anything, to my knowledge, that would ever have attracted a blackmailer."

"The man who died was called Davie Milne. Does that name mean anything to you?"

Montgomery thought for a moment. "No."

"About six months ago, Mister Milne was going out with your daughter, Isla."

"I wouldn't know anything about that. Isla lives her own life; she doesn't need my permission in how she chooses the men in her life."

"Mister Milne was a married man, Mister Montgomery," added Ogston, as if that made all the difference in the world.

Montgomery finally looked a little concerned.

"I do admit, I would have expected better of Isla," was all he said.

"How well do you know Councillor MacLean?" Ogston then asked.

"Percy? Not all that well."

"From what I've read," Ogston added, "you don't like each other very much."

"Our dislike for each other only exists within Council chambers. Percy has a vision for the future of Aberdeen that doesn't equate with mine."

"And what might that be?"

"Percy wants to increase the size of the railway station and develop Dyce into a major airport. He argues that we need to improve the ways in which people can get to Aberdeen. My view is that, firstly, we need to provide reasons for people to want to *come* to Aberdeen. They need to have something to do if they choose to visit this city and at the moment, I don't believe we offer enough for tourists. To that end, there seems little point in spending a small fortune, on a shiny new airport and multi-tracked railway station only to find no one wants to visit in the first place."

"The two of you have had some major arguments over recent months."

It was as much a statement, as a question, but Montgomery responded anyway.

"Yes, but only in Council chambers," he stressed.

"Were you aware of Councillor MacLean's friendship with Violet Yates?"

"There was some talk in the corridors, but I never paid much attention to any of it."

"A married man and a member of staff, surely that would have elicited some response from you, Mister Montgomery?" said Ogston.

"I thought Percy was taking a risk, but nothing more."

"Did you mention any of that to your wife?" Ogston then asked.

"Not that I'm aware of."

"Nothing at all," pressed Ogston.

"Perhaps an odd comment, but nothing specific."

"You find out that one of your main Council opponents might be having an affair with a member of staff and you claim not to have spoken about it. I find that hard to believe, Mister Montgomery."

Montgomery thought for a moment. "Oh, very well, maybe I did speak about it with my wife."

"And Isla?"

"If I had mentioned it at the dinner table, then she would have been there as well, yes. Look, are you going to tell me what all this is about?"

"Blackmail, Mister Montgomery, I'm talking about blackmail and I'm talking about you providing the ammunition to fire at Councillor MacLean," Ogston replied, looking long and hard at Montgomery.

The Councillor visibly shrank back into his chair.

"But I........," he then started to say. Ogston cut him short.

"Councillor MacLean offered help and support to Violet Yates, when her husband died. There was never anything more to their relationship than that. You, however, and no doubt many more chose to put a more salacious twist on what was happening. You made comments at home, Isla heard them and passed them on to her boyfriend. That boyfriend was Davie Milne, the man we now know to have been blackmailing a number of people connected to the Council. Your daughter can't be blamed for them all, Mister Montgomery, but she can most certainly be blamed for what ultimately happened to Councillor MacLean."

"Oh my God," said Montgomery, horror etched on his face.

"We'll, obviously, need to speak with Isla as well. Do you have some idea where she'll be at the moment?"

"She has a half-day from university today, so she should be at home. She'll probably be lazing around, playing her silly records."

Forrest was sent to collect Isla. Councillor Montgomery was kept at Lodge Walk, Ogston didn't want him having any opportunity to prime his daughter. The less she knew about why the police wanted to speak with her, the better.

*

Ron Smith had been trying to get through to Graeme Ogston all day. Eventually, the switchboard operator was able to make that connection and the two men spoke briefly about the possibility of Robbie Shearer taking over the story on Davie Milne's murder.

Ogston explained that he still had no story. However, he had no problem, in principle, with Shearer being his point of contact regarding that case or any other that might arise during Ron's time of covering the typhoid.

"How's life treating you these days?" Ogston had then asked.

"Typhoid fills my every day," was the honest reply, "We've not had this big a story in Aberdeen in a very long time."

"Well at least it stops you pestering me for a crime-related story," Ogston said, also with some honesty.

"Which is why young Shearer wants to be given the crime desk. He seems to think you do have something to say, only no one's been asking," Ron then said.

"Shearer can ask all the questions he likes," replied Ogston, "but, I can assure you and him that there aren't any answers. I've never known a case to be going nowhere so quickly, but I'd thank you not to print that."

Ron was laughing as he spoke. "I'm not on the crime desk at the moment, so everything you say to me has got to be off the record."

"Tell you what," Ogston then said, "send Shearer down to see me tomorrow and I'll have a word with him. I'll have nothing to tell him, but I'll have a word none the less."

"Okay, I'll let him know. When would be best for you?"

"Five o'clock."

"Five o'clock it is then."

And with that both men hung up.

*

A little later, Forrest entered Ogston's office to tell him that Isla Montgomery was in another of the interview rooms.

Ogston led the way down and opened the door. A uniformed officer, who had been standing just inside the door, now left and the two detectives entered.

At eighteen, Isla Montgomery could be interviewed without her parents being present. As Ogston sat down, he studied the young girl closely. Her fair hair was long, parted in the middle and hanging either side of a face that was attractive, without reaching the heights of beauty. She looked younger than her eighteen years and her eyes were filled with fear.

Isla wore a coat, unbuttoned and showing a blue dress beneath. Her appearance was as immaculate as her father's and Ogston couldn't help but think that this girl ought to have been in a different league from Davie Milne.

Isla took a packet of cigarettes from her bag. They were Rothman's King Size Filter cigarettes. Nothing cheap for Councillor Montgomery's daughter. She placed a cigarette between her bright red lips and lit the end. She drew back hard on the filter and then exhaled a cloud of smoke.

Ogston began asking his questions. At first there seemed little point to what he was saying but, eventually, the penny dropped with Isla.

She admitted she'd seen Davie for a few weeks. She admitted she'd talked about some of the things her father had mentioned over dinner. Davie had always shown an interest in such things.

I bet he did, thought Ogston.

Isla insisted that it had all been meant as a joke. She and Davie had laughed about Councillor MacLean, finding it funny that an old man like him would be having an affair.

But he hadn't been, was Ogston's next thought. He fought to suppress the anger rising in him. Thanks to the stupidity of this girl and her then boyfriend, a man's career and reputation had been compromised.

And they'd thought it funny.

Isla had then gone on to say that she had never thought, for one moment, that Davie might have been a crook; that he really wanted the information from her for illegal purposes.

"Obviously, if I had had any idea at all, I'd never have said what I did," she had insisted." Davie always came across as the perfect gentleman."

"The perfect gentleman who was two-timing his wife," Ogston had then said.

"Davie was married?" Isla responded, her eyes widening with horror. "The bastard."

Not language becoming of a Councillor's daughter, thought Ogston, *but probably the correct word to use under the current circumstances.*

Ogston saw no reason in charging Isla with anything, though he did give her a severe reprimand and as he had done with Shuggie, warned that if she got involved in anything illegal over the next few years, then he'd return to her part in Davie Milne's blackmail scam and add that to the charges against her.

From the look of horror in her eyes, Ogston could tell that Isla Montgomery would probably now be a model citizen for the rest of her days.

Isla was then allowed to leave the building with her father. They both looked suitably sheepish, although the Councillor did give his daughter a rather disapproving look when they'd first met.

Once back in his office, Ogston lit a cigarette and Forrest sat opposite him. They were happy that they had uncovered one of Davie Milne's 'sources', but it was obvious there had to be more. Isla Montgomery had only known about Councillor MacLean which, in no way, covered the financial indiscretions of others.

There had to have been another accomplice working at the Council, probably in the Finance Department. On top of that, there was still the photographer to be found. Two people who had been up to their necks in a blackmail scam and yet not one shred of evidence that pointed in their direction.

As Ogston sat there, cigarette in hand, he was beginning to wonder if the Davie Milne case would ever be solved.

11   11

The typhoid figures, as Aberdeen welcomed in Thursday, 4th June, were now 275 confirmed cases and 43 suspected. MacQueen's meeting, that morning, had been even more intense than many of those that had gone before. Even he was beginning to wonder if the disease would ever show signs of abating.

Sandy Burnett had some sympathy for his boss. He was certainly glad that he didn't have to face the Press every day, even though MacQueen had brought that very much upon himself. Yes, there had been a need to keep the public informed, but to Sandy it was a tad masochistic to make it a daily grilling.

To make matters worse, for Doctor MacQueen, the vultures had really started to gather. There were many, nowhere near the coal face of course, who were complaining about the way in which Doctor MacQueen was handling the crisis.

In any major situation there are always those who think they know best. Those who find fault in others, but never go as far as popping their own head above the parapet. They complain from a safe distance. Complaining is easy, it's the doing that's difficult.

There were those who felt Doctor MacQueen had not done enough and that he had taken too long in taking the action that he had.

Others complained about the time it took to close venues where people had been gathering. MacQueen was questioned for not seeking outside help, for insisting on handling the crisis himself and keeping everything within the city of Aberdeen.

It had been argued that, if he had sought outside help, then the team seeking to beat the disease would have been considerably bigger and solutions found all the faster. Had the spread of the disease been stopped earlier then, obviously, less people would have been infected.

In the main, Doctor MacQueen had handled the criticism well. He was a man who never walked away from a fight. In his own mind, he was convinced that the crisis could not have been handled any better though, perhaps, he would not have been so open with the Press, if there was to be a next time. He sincerely hoped not.

That morning, Sandy thought Doctor MacQueen was looking tired. He usually handled pressure well, but he now looked like a man finding it difficult to sleep. In times of stress, it was always the mind that switched off last. The body can be screaming out for rest, but the brain continues to demand answers.

In the wards, the likes of Alison Young were as tired as Doctor MacQueen. It was the sheer number of patients that was now causing the problem and the fact that they were all at different stages of recovery. It meant the nurses being called upon to do an even greater variety of tasks.

Some patients, newly admitted, were terribly ill. They were the ones with the temperature and hallucinations. They were the ones in greatest pain and suffering and therefore, they were the ones demanding the most attention from the nurses.

However, those patients who had now been in hospital for over two weeks were, at least on the face of it, showing major signs of recovering. They weren't fit to be released from hospital, but they were fit to resume something closer to a normal daily routine.

These were the patients whose main battle was now against boredom. There was nothing to do in hospital and contact with families, all be it through a window, was brief and often less than satisfying.

Nothing could be brought in from outside the hospital, so children in particular found it difficult to pass the time each day. The hospital only had a few toys and, beyond them, there was nothing much to keep young minds occupied. Some of the nurses did find a little time to play with the children, inventing silly games simply to help pass the time.

It was now heading towards a month since the disease had first been reported in the city. Some were questioning whether it would ever be beaten, seeing as new patients continued to contract the disease every day.

MacQueen continued to hammer home his message about personal hygiene. The more people washed their hands and the more food continued to be better handled prior to being sold, then the quicker the spread of the disease would end.

Aberdonians were going to have to learn that the solution to the problem literally lay in their own hands.

By way of trying to illustrate that death did not walk the streets of Aberdeen, an Under-secretary, at the Scottish Office, visited the hospitals and spoke with the staff. A publicity opportunity was, of course, taken and the gentleman in question was duly photographed washing his hands.

It was a small, but much needed, nod towards Doctor MacQueen and the message he was pushing.

That morning, at MacQueen's team meeting, Peter Shepherd had once more driven home his point about the damage that had been caused to the retail industry. Many shops were reporting a drop in trade, with food outlets in particular having to constantly reassure customers that they were clear of infection and always had been.

Hotels and Bed and Breakfasts were also reporting cancellations and there was a real fear that if the disease did not show signs of abating soon, then the summer trade would be finished before it had even started.

Peter wanted more to be done, but Doctor MacQueen had nothing to offer. Until the numbers fell away to zero, he could not risk lifting any of the measures they had taken. He appreciated that livelihoods were being affected, but insisted his hands were tied.

The cycle of the disease would determine what happened next, not the actions of Doctor Ian MacQueen.

Later that morning, when MacQueen met with the Press, he told them that they had reached a critical time in the cycle of the disease.

"If, in the course of the next twenty-four hours," he said, "we have less than twenty new cases reported, then we can safely begin to think we are winning the battle against this disease. However, if there are more than twenty-five new cases, then we continue to lose that battle."

"What about the schools, Doctor MacQueen," asked one of the journalists, "will they now remain closed until after the summer?"

"Oh, I would hope to get pupils back to school before then. I have suggested that secondary schools might re-open sooner and I'm awaiting a response from the Education Authority."

"And you're still not willing to name the shop where this whole, sorry business started?" added Ron.

"I will make that announcement when I feel the time is right," was all that MacQueen would say.

No one in the room chose to press the Doctor on when that was likely to be.

However, it was without doubt the one piece of information that every journalist, in that room, hoped that he'd discover first. It was the one piece of information that all Aberdeen wanted to know and, so far, Doctor MacQueen was stubbornly keeping it close to his chest.

*

At Ogston's request, information had been sent to London, asking all police officers to be on the lookout for Caroline O'Hara. They were told that although it was part of a murder inquiry, the Aberdeen police only wanted answers concerning a party she had attended in the summer of nineteen sixty-one. To help her remember exactly which one, the London police had been told to tell her it was the party where her friend Phyllis had met the man she was to marry.

Through Caroline's parents the Aberdeen police had been able to get an address for where she had stayed, when she'd first moved to London. However, that had been back at the beginning of 1962 and the London police soon found out that she was no longer there.

There had been no one staying at the London flat in question, who remembered Caroline. It was not uncommon for people to move around a lot, when they first arrived in London. Unless they knew someone to stay with, it was often better to keep on the move.

Ogston's London contact had phoned him to say they'd drawn a blank at the address given. He had warned Ogston that if Caroline O'Hara hadn't wanted to be found then it would have been easy enough for her to lose herself in a city the size of London. Ogston had to hope that that was not the case.

However, he had by then, ascertained that Caroline and her parents had fallen out over her decision to move to London. That was why there had been no contact from her in over two years. There was always the chance that she might not even still be in London.

He had to hope, however, that London would come up trumps. Ogston's contact had suggested that Caroline would probably be sharing a flat with someone else by now. If the flat was rented in the other person's name, then it would make it that bit more difficult to find her. However, he remained upbeat in his task.

A joint operation got underway. Records were checked to ensure that Caroline had neither died, nor married. In Aberdeen, Phyllis had been asked if Caroline had any other friends, who might have stayed in touch with her. A couple of names were provided, but they too had lost contact.

It seemed as if Caroline had deliberately cut herself off from all things relating to Aberdeen, when she had moved to London. Again, this was not a surprise to the police. People move to London and then instantly regret it. Unfortunately, they can't face admitting to friends and relatives that they'd got it wrong, so they decide to stick it out in London when going home really ought to have been the answer.

It was, therefore, quite by chance that Caroline O'Hara eventually came to the attention of the police in London.

There had been a disturbance in a flat in Kilburn. A man had come home drunk and in a foul temper. He had then taken that temper out on his girlfriend, ending his tirade by throwing her down a set of stairs.

The girlfriend had been taken to hospital. She was still unconscious and the medical staff could only hazard a guess as to when she might regain consciousness. When arrested, the man had said his girlfriend's name had been Caroline Jackson, but police had found, within the woman's handbag, evidence that her name might actually be Caroline O'Hara.

Detective Chief Inspector Ogston was notified of events in London. He now knew where Caroline O'Hara was, but was still in no position to have her interviewed. The London police said they'd speak to Caroline, when she regained consciousness.

Ogston recognised it was another small step forward. However, any information he got from Caroline would not help him complete the full picture of the life and death of Davie Milne. It would just be another piece in the jigsaw, nothing more.

However, there was always a chance that Caroline's information might land Ronnie Cusiter a little deeper in the mire. There was still something about Cusiter's reaction, when first put on the spot about the party, that did not sit well with Ogston.

He still had the strongest feeling that Ronnie Cusiter was hiding something. But what?

*

Robbie Shearer had left Lodge Walk at a little before half past five. He had spent the last half hour with Detective Chief Inspector Ogston, basically being told nothing.

Ogston had welcomed the fact he was now to contact Robbie, should there be anything he wanted printed with regard to

Davie Milne's murder, or any other police investigation that might benefit from Press support.

Unfortunately, at that moment, Ogston had nothing for the young journalist.

"We have one or two lines of inquiry on the go, at the moment," Ogston had said, "but nothing worth printing."

Robbie had decided to say nothing. He already had plans of his own. If the police couldn't solve the crime, then maybe Robbie Shearer could.

With that in mind he headed for Fernhill Drive immediately after he'd left Ogston. He was armed with his usual charm and a pocket full of money. He had always felt that greasing a few palms helped immensely when gathering information.

His plan was to interview Davie Milne's neighbours. He knew the police would have already done that, probably more than once, but sometimes ordinary folk were a little reticent about talking to the police.

Maybe they'd say a bit more to a charming journalist, especially if he had money to splash about?

As it happened, he didn't have to pay out money at every stop. Some of the neighbours had nothing to tell; they'd never spoken to Davie Milne and in some cases, they'd never even *heard* of Davie Milne.

Shearer worked his way down Fernhill Drive, speaking to people living on both sides of the street. Obviously, the further he got from Milne's address, the less he expected to be told.

It was in the second last block of flats that he finally struck gold. The first door he came to was opened by a man who turned out to have known Davie Milne. However, the man then seemed reluctant to say anything more.

A crisp five-pound note soon changed all that. The man accepted the money and shoved it into his trouser pocket.

Shearer was invited in. The man gave no name and said he wanted to keep it that way. Whatever was said, his name was never to appear anywhere.

Shearer agreed.

The flat was tidy and Shearer was offered a seat on the two-seater settee. The man switched off the television and then offered Shearer a tea, or coffee.

"Coffee would be great. Milk and two sugars, please."

While the man was out of the room, Shearer wandered around, looking for clues as to who the man might be. There was nothing of any help. By the time the man returned with the coffees, Shearer was once more seated.

Shearer laid his coffee on a small table, placed to his left. He then took out his notebook and pen.

"Nae names, remember," the man said instantly.

"Of course. I still need to write down what you tell me," Shearer explained. "My memory's not that good."

"A' right," the man then said, apparently happy with the arrangement. "Ah used tae ken Davie really well. We wint tae the same school and moved tae Mastrick aboot the same time. We wid sometimes go tae the fitba the gither, but a' that stopped fin he mairriet Phyllis."

"So, what can you tell me about Davie Milne?" Shearer then said, keen to start getting his fiver's worth.

"He wis a crook. He's been a crook since we were at school. He used tae pinch money fae his schoolmates."

"You know this for a fact?" said Shearer.

"Saw it masel."

"But you never reported him?"

"Fit wid a been the point o' that? He'd jist a said the money wis his."

"Did he steal from you?" Shearer then enquired.

"Knew better than tae dae that. Ah'd a chinned him, if he'd as much as laid a finger on ony money o' mine."

"So, he stole money at school, I'm sure he wasn't alone in doing that," suggested Shearer.

"Ah heard he wis still at it," the man then said.

"Still at what?"

"Crime."

"I'm listening," said Shearer, still feeling he hadn't got anything like five pounds worth of information.

"A wee birdie telt me Davie wis intae blackmail noo. Dae onythin' for an extra penny or two, wid Davie Milne."

"Did the wee birdie tell who Davie was blackmailing?" Shearer then asked, feeling he was now getting more than his fiver's worth.

"Nae idea. Ah jist heard he wis at it."

"Who told you that?"

The man tapped the side of his nose. "Me tae ken an' you tae wonder," was all he said.

"Okay, so Davie Milne was blackmailing someone. Can you tell me anything else?"

The man lit a cigarette and then drank some coffee.

"Might ken somethin' aboot the photays he used tae blackmail fowk."

Shearer felt as if he'd finally hit the jackpot. He fought to keep his emotions in check, but deep down he was boiling with excitement.

"What might you know?" he then said.

"Might hae a name."

Shearer nearly fell off his chair at that point. He'd been edging forward with every new statement the man had made. The last movement forward had nearly taken him off the seat altogether. He regained his balance, hoping the man hadn't noticed what had just happened.

"And that name is?" prompted Shearer, almost bursting now with excitement.

The man took a moment to respond. "Ah'm thinking a fiver's nae quite enough for that kind o' information. Noo, if ye were tae gie me anither fiver, then ah reckon the name wid jist trip aff ma tongue."

Shearer knew he was being played. He could only hope that another five pounds would buy him a name that would be of some use to the police. If he could help them with their inquiries, then he'd put himself one step ahead of Ron Smith; he'd never helped the police with their inquiries.

The money was produced, grabbed and stuffed into the same pocket as the first one.

"Dougie Sim," the man then said.

Shearer's heart was pumping faster than ever. This had to be the biggest break he'd ever had in this fledgling career as a journalist. If he could just help crack the Davie Milne murder then there was no way Ron Smith was coming back to his job.

Shearer tried to keep calm as he asked his next question.

"Do you know where I could find this Dougie Sim?"

"Ye'll find him in The Starrie maist nights. He'll probably be pished, but he'll be there."

The 'Starrie' had to be The Star and Garter pub on Crown Street.

That was the last bit of information Shearer was given for his ten pounds. It might be useful, it might not. Only time would tell if the payment had been worthwhile.

Shearer finished his coffee and was then shown to the door. He thanked the man for his time.

"Dae me a favour," the man then said, "dinna come back."

Shearer just smiled and left the flat. He had no intention of going back. If the information turned out to be of some use to the police, then his visit had already been worthwhile. On the other hand, if the information proved to be worthless, then he had just wasted ten pounds of his own money and he'd have to put that down to experience.

Shearer continued down Fernhill Drive and caught the bus around the corner on the Lang Stracht. On the way into the city centre he thought over what he had just been told. The grin on his face widened as he thought about the glory coming his way if Dougie Sim really did turn out to be Davie Milne's blackmail accomplice.

Shearer was so happy, when he got off the bus on Union Street, that he decided to find the nearest pub and have a celebratory pint.

12   12

By the morning of Friday, 5th June, the figure of confirmed typhoid patients was 292, with a further 48 suspected. At his morning Press Conference, Doctor MacQueen expressed 'reasoned and sober optimism' that the tide had turned and the disease was finally on the wane.

Although that was his public message, he still wasn't totally convinced that the battle against the disease had been won. A decision was taken to check the sewers for typhoid germs. Teams were sent down to take samples and those were then sent off for testing.

If germs were found then it proved there were still carriers of the disease, somewhere in the city. However, if nothing was found then they'd know the city was now germ free. It would take a couple of days before the results of those samples were known.

Doctor MacQueen had then added that, even after the epidemic had ended, there would still be occasional checks made on the sewers for evidence of carriers. He suggested that 3% might possibly remain carriers and some of those might do so for the rest of their lives. However, he did go on to say that most of the 3% would be clear within the next few weeks.

Also, that day, Doctor MacQueen, working with Aberdeen Journals and the Corporation of the City of Aberdeen, produced a brochure entitled *How To Stamp Out Typhoid*. The message, within the brochure, was being passed on through a cartoon character called *Wee Alickie*, who was more usually seen in the *Green Final*, Aberdeen's Saturday night sports' paper.

For a change, *Wee Alickie* was educating the businesses of Aberdeen in how best to stop the spread of the disease. Usually, the cartoon character would have been passing comment on the latest performance by The Dons.

The introduction was by Doctor MacQueen himself:

The stopping of the typhoid outbreak is principally a matter of good personal hygiene by everyone, and particularly of good personal hygiene by all food handlers.

In an effort to assist every section of the community in our area, a short question and answer brochure has been hurriedly compiled, together with a Hygiene Check List, which should prove most useful to all establishments.

Members of the Aberdeen Chamber of Commerce, food wholesalers, bacteriologists, health education officers and journalists have collaborated to rush this through. This brochure is, therefore, backed by their combined knowledge and experience.

Please read it, study it and try to follow the advice that it gives.

IAN A.G. MACQUEEN

5th June 1964   Medical Officer of Health

N.B. *This brochure is being sent to 8,000 establishments in Aberdeen – to everyone except householders. For additional copies, if needed, telephone Aberdeen 29206.*

Peter Shepherd and Ron Smith had both had a hand in producing the final brochure. It contained a few pages of facts, about the disease, followed by a hygiene check list, which covered subjects such as:

The adequate supply of Soap, Nailbrushes and Towels in all toilets, likely to be used by either staff, or the general public.

The disinfecting of all toilets daily.

Ensuring that, during tea or Coffee Breaks, food was not shared and hands were thoroughly washed, before returning to work.

For the counting of bank-notes, postage and insurance stamps, all staff were to be reminded not to lick fingers and to, wherever possible, use rubber thimbles, or sponges, moistened with a little antiseptic. Again, hands were to be washed at the conclusion of jobs, such as these.

The brochure further covered the cleaning of meat slicing machines and also reminded people as to how to open a milk bottle, without risking the spread of the disease.

Sandy Burnett had not played a part in the production of the brochure. For him, however, the working day was beginning to get a little calmer. He could now, at least, get home for a decent sleep which, in itself, made everything else a lot more bearable.

He had gone to bed, the night before, and slept through from ten o'clock until the alarm went off at seven. His thoughts were no longer cartwheeling in an attempt to find solutions to a disease that, at one time, had looked as if it might have had many more cycles to go through.

Sandy could hear Winston Churchill when he said it might not be the beginning of the end but it was at least the end of the beginning.

In the hospital wards, the numbers of new patients were beginning to fall. Alison could sense the worst was now, probably, over. Perhaps, the need for eighty-hour weeks was also on the wane.

She, too, had been able to sleep better the night before. She was now looking forward to a proper date with Graeme Ogston all the more. With the chance to return to something akin to a normal working life, Alison also hoped her personal life would sort itself out as well.

Life was, generally, less frantic around the wards. Nurses were beginning to find time for other duties and although many patients were still far from well, most of them were past the worst.

In Lodge Walk, Detective Chief Inspector Ogston was still making little progress with the Davie Milne murder inquiry. He had instigated a little more digging into Ronnie Cusiter's finances, though that had offered nothing in the name of progress. There was still no clear evidence as to where Ronnie had got the money with which he'd opened the first shop.

Ogston's thoughts were interrupted by a knock at the door. It was Forrest.

"Robbie Shearer is here to see you, sir," he said.

"The journalist?" Ogston said, by way of thinking aloud, rather than actually meaning to say anything. "What does he want, I just spoke to him yesterday?"

"Just says he wants to see you," replied Forrest, "nothing more."

Ogston looked less than amused. With a case going nowhere fast the last thing he wanted was to go fifteen rounds with a journalist, especially one trying to make a name for himself.

However, much as he would have liked to have told Forrest to deal with it, his curiosity had been aroused and there was always the possibility, however slim, that Shearer might actually be there to help.

"Okay, let's see what he wants," Ogston eventually said, standing up. The two men made their way to the interview room where they found young Shearer sitting at the table, a rather smug expression on his face.

Ogston felt, more than ever, that the journalist had to be there to impart information rather than gather any. He'd probably want something in return, but Ogston was at least prepared to hear what he had to say.

Ogston thought that Shearer looked very young. He also thought he looked very scruffy, certainly not an image that sat well in Graeme Ogston's world. No police officer would ever have looked that way.

Shearer's hair had grown well over the collar of his open-neck shirt. He wore spectacles, from behind which beady eyes peered out on the world. He looked like a man who had been born to ask questions; perfect, therefore, for a journalist.

Ogston and Forrest sat down. Ogston spoke first.

"Okay, Robbie, what can I do for you?"

Shearer sat forward. "It's more what I can do for you, Chief Inspector."

Ogston glanced at Forrest, then looked back at Shearer.

"I'm listening."

"I spoke to someone last night, who wishes to remain anonymous," Shearer then said.

"It's okay, Robbie, I know all about journalists protecting their sources. Now, just tell me what you've found out."

"I now know that Davie Milne was into a spot of blackmail."

Ogston looked at Forrest again. Clearly, Robbie Shearer *had* been talking to someone. Ogston looked back at Robbie, but chose to say nothing. He wanted to know what else the young journalist had discovered.

"As part of that blackmail, Davie Milne was working with an accomplice who was a dab hand at taking photos. I think I can now offer you the name of that photographer."

Shearer was grinning like a Cheshire cat. Ogston sat forward. At last, he might be getting somewhere.

"What name can you offer me?" he then said.

"Douglas Sim."

The name meant nothing to Ogston, or Forrest.

"Do you, also, have an address for Mister Sim?"

"Not a formal address," replied Shearer, "but I do know he spends a lot of his time, care of the Star and Garter."

"Well, thank you for your help, Mister Shearer," Ogston then said, standing up again. "I'll be in touch if anything, worth printing, comes from this. In the meantime, Inspector Forrest will show you out."

Robbie Shearer found himself out on the street, but he was still smiling. He knew that Ogston would owe him one now. He could be as gruff as he liked but, deep down, he would have to show some kind of appreciation for the help he'd just been offered.

*

Later that day, two uniformed police officers entered the premises of the Star and Garter and one of them asked the barman if he knew someone by the name of Douglas Sim.

They were directed to a man, sitting in the corner of the bar, bent double over the table in front of him and clearly more unconscious than conscious.

"He gets like that a lot," the barman called over. "I was just about to phone you lot anyway."

Arrangements were made for Douglas Sim to be collected from the Star and Garter and taken to Lodge Walk, where he was offered a cell for the night to sleep off the alcohol and to, perhaps, be a little more responsive come the following morning.

Enquiries at the Star and Garter had ascertained an address for Douglas Sim so, armed with the keys they had taken off him, Ogston and Forrest set off to run an eye over Sim's residence.

The flat was small. There was a living room, bedroom, bathroom and small kitchen. It was a basement flat, at the bottom of Crown Street and little light seemed to flood the place at the best of times.

It was a typical bachelor flat. No food in the larder, just a few beers. Some unwashed dishes lay in the sink and there was also a selection of magazines, in the bedroom, which might loosely have passed as art.

However, the major find in the bedroom, were three cameras. They were all of different makes and none of them looked cheap. Other photographic equipment was found in the living room and a cupboard, in the hallway, had been converted into a makeshift darkroom. In fact, everything anyone would need to produce their own photographs.

The photographic equipment must have come at a cost. There was no way an alcoholic, like Sim, could have afforded such equipment from lawful earnings. He *had* to be up to his neck in something.

Ogston asked Forrest to arrange for a police photographer to attend at the flat and capture all that they had found, on film. He was about to turn and leave the flat, when he noticed a bundle of photographs lying on a small table just inside the door of the living room.

He moved closer and picked them up. There were eight in total and they were all of the same woman. They were all of the same, *naked*, woman. Sim had, presumably, been in the habit of looking at the photographs at every opportunity.

Nothing wrong with that, had it not been for the fact that all the photographs were of Isla Montgomery and they had clearly been taken without her knowledge.

*

Saturday morning arrived.

Douglas Sim opened his eyes and instantly regretted the amount of alcohol he'd poured down his throat the night before. Most mornings he felt that way.

He took a few seconds to focus on his surroundings. He was in a cell. How the hell had he got there? What had he done this time?

He had no memory of the night before, beyond buying another drink at the bar of the Star and Garter and returning to his favourite seat. After that there was nothing but darkness and a severe pain in his head.

He tried sitting up, but everything moved when he did that, so he lay down again and waited for the spinning to stop. For a brief moment he thought he might be sick, but even that sensation subsided.

He tried sitting up again, only this time with a little more success. His head still ached and his mouth tasted like the inside of a wrestler's jockstrap. He looked around, though there was nothing much to see. Plain walls, plain floor and a plank to sleep on. Hardly the best accommodation he'd been offered.

There was a noise at the door and eventually it opened. A young, uniformed constable came in.

"Come with me, Mister Sim," he said.

A simple enough request but, for someone like Douglas Sim, who's world wouldn't stop moving, not so easy to honour. The constable could see that his prisoner was having problems.

"You're not going to be sick, are you?" the officer asked. The last thing he wanted was to have to clean up the cell. The amount of vomit he'd cleaned up that week would have filled a bath. He really didn't want any more, especially this close to going home time.

Sim took a few deep breaths. "Dinna think so."

"Then come with me," insisted the officer.

"Gie me a minute," Sim said. "Ah need the room tae stop spinnin' first."

The officer afforded Sim the minute he'd requested and then insisted that he stood up.

"Am ah free tae go?" Sim then enquired.

The officer laughed. "At the moment, Mister Sim, you are only free to walk to the nearest interview room. Any decision on whether, or not, you are released will be made after a senior officer has spoken to you."

Sim suspected it might be a long day. He pushed down on the edge of his 'bed' and managed to get to his feet. The room was still moving, but possibly at a slightly slower pace.

"Ony chance o' a cup o' tea?" he then said.

"I'll ask," conceded the officer, "but first, you come with me."

*

The interview room was even brighter than the cell had been and the pain gripped Sim's head with an even greater intensity. He squinted at the two police officers as they came in to the room. He preferred to look down at the floor, rather than meet either of them eye to eye.

"Douglas Sim?" Ogston began.

"Fa wants to ken?" Sim replied.

"Detective Chief Inspector Ogston and Detective Inspector Forrest."

"In that case, aye, I'm Doug Sim."

Ogston confirmed Sim's address, even though he'd already been there. Sim continued to look at the floor, a grimace of pain still obvious on his face.

"Are you feeling okay, Mister Sim?" Ogston then asked.

"I'd feel a lot better if the room wid stop spinnin'," said Sim. "As it is, I feel like shite."

"The constable said you'd asked for a cup of tea?" Ogston began.

"Aye, ah did."

"I reckon, in your condition, that black coffee will be better for you, so I have some on the way."

Sim looked outraged. "Black coffee just discolours yer teeth, it does naethin' for hangovers."

"So, no coffee, then?" added Ogston.

In the absence of tea, Sim quickly deduced that *anything* would be better than nothing. At least it might sort out the disgusting taste in his mouth.

"No, I'll hae a coffee, just to be sociable, ye understand."

At that moment, the door opened and a constable came in, carrying a tray with three cups on it. He put the tray on the table and left. Ogston put a cup in front of each of them and Sim quickly took his first sip.

He really wasn't a fan of coffee, but beggars can't be choosers. Ogston then began with his line of questioning.

"Do you know a man by the name of Davie Milne?"

"Ye widnae happen to hae a cigarette, wid ye?" was the reply.

Ogston gave a cigarette to Sim and held his lighter out for him. Sim tried to line up the cigarette with the lighter, but with the room spinning even a simple act like that seemed beyond him. Eventually, he managed to light the end and sat back to inhale deeply. Ogston lit a cigarette for himself, with considerably more ease.

Sim was next to speak.

"I kent a Davie Milne at school,"

"Seen him lately?"

"Hardly, I mean, he's deid, you dae ken that?"

"Yes, Mister Sim, I know he's dead. Would you have any idea who might have killed Mister Milne?"

"Why wid ye think I might ken something like that?"

"Because you were partners in crime, weren't you, Mister Sim?"

Sim seemed to take the question on the chin, without much of a reaction.

"I've nivver committed a crime in my life, Chief Inspector with, or withoot, a partner."

"We've been to your flat, Mister Sim."

"Ye'd nae right tae dae that."

"We were concerned there might be a cat, or a budgie, needing feeding. We visited on compassionate grounds," Ogston said, the sarcasm heavy in his tone.

"If I'd kent you were going to visit, I'd have cleared up a little mair. Ma mither ayewis said ye should start every day wearin' clean underwear and wi' last night's dishes washed. Guess, I let the side doon there."

"We found the photographic equipment, Mister Sim," Ogston then said.

"It's a hobby, naethin mair."

"There were some photographs lying around."

"There usually is." Sim dragged on his cigarette and exhaled rather loudly, as if he were getting either annoyed, or fed up with the way things were going.

"I wondered why you would have photographs of Isla Montgomery? Nude photographs."

Sim finally looked up. "I've never heard o' Isla Montgomery."

"Are you really of a mind to sit there telling lies, Mister Sim?"

"Ah'm nae lyin'" insisted Sim.

"But you are, Mister Sim. I've seen the pictures myself; I know they're there."

Sim seemed to think for a moment. The effort caused him even more pain.

"Wait a minute, wid that be the bird Davie Milne wis shagging a few months back?"

"She did go out with Mister Milne for a little while," agreed Ogston.

"I nivver did ken her name. Davie asked me tae tak some pictures o' her one night when they stayed wi' me. She wis a bit oot o' it, an' probably nivver kent I was takkin' them."

"So, you took pictures of a naked girl, but you never knew her name?" said Ogston.

"Like I said, Davie winted the pictures, nae me. There wis nae need tae ken her name."

"And yet you have copies of those pictures yourself."

"Well, they were affa good, weren't there. A master needs tae enjoy his ain work at times, an' she wis an affa bonnie quine."

"Did Davie ask you to take any other pictures for him?" Ogston then enquired.

Sim lost himself in his coffee for a moment. Finally, he spoke.

"Nae that ah can mind."

"How about a few pictures in the Victoria Park, Mister Sim?" suggested Ogston. "Photos of a Councillor and a female friend?"

"Dinna ken fit you're on aboot," replied Sim, though his expression said something else. Ogston heard the words, but he was more interested in the expression. It was an expression of guilt, he felt sure of that.

"We'll be checking your bank account, Mister Sim and I feel sure we'll find more money in there than might seem right, for a person of your, how shall I put it, limited means."

"Dae fit ye like," protested Sim.

"This is a murder inquiry, Mister Sim, so I suggest you start helping us. The more you help us, the less the weight of the law will come down on top of you."

"Ah didnae kill Davie," Sim further protested.

"I never said you did, Mister Sim," said Ogston. "You didn't kill him because his death will, no doubt, have wiped out your main source of income."

Sim puffed on the last of his cigarette. "Nae sure fit ye mean, Chief Inspector."

"You and Davie Milne were making a tidy little earner out of blackmail, Mister Sim. You took the pictures and he did the rest. Once we're finished with your darkroom, I'm guessing we'll have all the evidence we'll need. You will be charged,

Mister Sim, so I suggest you keep those charges to a minimum by telling us everything that you know."

Sim pondered in silence. He asked for and received another cigarette. He finished his coffee. All the time he was thinking. All the time he was aware of the hopelessness of the situation he now found himself in.

He decided to come clean.

He provided the names of those he knew were being blackmailed and also gave up the bank account in which he had stored the money he'd been paid by Davie.

He told them everything about the blackmail, but could tell them nothing about Davie's murder. Ogston pressed Sim on the subject of the three men who had pulled off the Thompson raid, back in 1959.

Sim said he knew nothing about that either.

"So, you can't even hazard a guess as to who might have done that job with Davie?" asked Ogston.

"Davie nivver really hid ony friends. He wisnae a nice man, Chief Inspector and I feel sure there will be many more celebratin' his death, rather than mournin' it. The ladies 'ill miss him, nae the men."

"Any obvious enemies then?" said Ogston.

"Ah've nae idea fa might a' hated Davie, but ah expect the list wid a been sizeable," Sim replied.

"For example?" said Ogston.

"Ah dinna ken," insisted Sim.

Ogston, rather reluctantly, believed him. They might have been partners in crime but that hadn't, necessarily, made them bosom buddies. He left Forrest to formally charge Sim for his part in the blackmail and returned to his desk.

At least one element of the Davie Milne murder had been tidied up, but the matter of who actually killed him was no closer to being solved.

*

The papers, later that day, carried the story that Doctor MacQueen now felt the typhoid epidemic would be over by early July. He had also said, in a lighter note:

"I think Aberdeen at present is the most antiseptic resort, the cleanest resort and the one with the highest food hygiene. I have no shadow of doubt about that."

At the same time as Doctor MacQueen was suggesting an end to the epidemic, the Argentina Department of Agriculture was announcing they'd carry out a special check on canned meat, following the suggestion that the Aberdeen typhoid outbreak had started from a tin of South American corned beef. They continued to insist that the contamination may have occurred *after* the tin had been opened. They further said that there were severe controls on processing at the packing plants, which were constantly checked by both Argentinian and British experts.

Doctor MacQueen had also felt it necessary to defend his actions once more. With news of new patients starting to reduce, the Press was looking for a new angle. They were not alone in questioning MacQueen; he'd pretty much been under fire since the first day of the epidemic.

Doctor MacQueen tried to explain the enormity of the task that had faced his team, from the very beginning of the outbreak. He pointed out, that on the 21st of May there were already something like 318 people incubating the disease and around 40,000 at risk. Facing those kinds of numbers, he failed to see what more he could have done to stem the tide, other than the action that had been taken.

He further defended his decision not to bring in outside help, stating he had more confidence in working with the people he already knew. They, in turn, knew the city and its people. He would not apologise for making that decision.

13   13

Detective Chief Inspector Ogston returned to his desk on the morning of Monday, 8th June. He started by sitting back, enjoying a cigarette and thinking about what he'd done, the day before.

He had spent a very pleasurable seven hours in Alison's company. They had driven into the country and enjoyed a picnic; which Graeme had prepared ahead of meeting Alison at just after one.

They had spent the last hour together at Alison's flat. Both her flatmates had been on shifts that night, so they had the place to themselves. They had talked quite a lot, but they had also found time to introduce a little passion into their lives.

It was still early days in their relationship but there was a clear desire, from both parties, to want to spend more time together. As the pressures at work eased, they would be able to enjoy more time socially. They looked forward to spending that time together.

Just before Graeme decided to go home, he asked Alison when she'd next be off. She said she'd be off on Wednesday night and that she didn't have work again until two' o'clock on the Thursday. That meant she could be a bit later on their night out.

"How about going to the cinema?" Graeme had suggested.

"Fine by me."

"I've no idea what's on. When do you want to meet?"

"I finish at two o'clock, so I can be ready at any time."

"Good. Meet me outside the Palace Restaurant at half past five and we'll have something to eat first. I'll get a list of what's on at the cinema and we can decide which picture we'd want to see, after we've eaten?"

Alison had immediately agreed that that seemed an excellent plan. Graeme had put on his coat and made his way to the door. They had kissed again, arms tightly around each other and both of them reluctant to part.

Eventually they had separated and Graeme then left the flat and made his way home.

Sunday had left nothing but pleasant memories. Memories, which remained with Graeme Ogston, as he sat at his desk that Monday morning.

Memories that still made him smile.

*

Sandy Burnett sat in his usual place at the daily meeting. There was a slightly more upbeat feel to their meeting that morning. The hospital figures were 345 confirmed cases and 67 suspected. Still high numbers, but new patients were definitely on the decline.

Even Doctor MacQueen was looking a little happier that morning. His eyes looked brighter, no doubt from the benefit of a decent sleep. With the disease apparently on the wane, he hoped the pressure on him would start to ease as well.

There was no doubt, the worst was now in the past. However, it was likely to take some time before Aberdeen lost the tag of being the typhoid city.

Aberdonians, trying to book summer holidays, were finding their requests knocked back as soon as they gave an Aberdeen address. There still seemed a totally unfounded belief that simply being in the company of someone from Aberdeen would be enough to infect you.

The restrictions would eventually be lifted in Aberdeen, but the perception of people, living elsewhere in the country, would take a lot longer to change. Aberdeen's reputation had been seriously damaged and only time, itself, would bring about any repairs.

The city council was greatly concerned about the inevitable fall in tourism and with it the fall in revenue coming into the city. Even the most sane-minded person, who might now accept that the worst was in the past, would be unlikely to want to bring his family to a city that had been in the grip of a modern-day plague.

Doctor MacQueen knew that he would have to play his part in giving Aberdeen the clean bill of health it would need. He still hadn't received the final report on the samples taken from the sewers. The absence of typhoid germs would greatly enhance his message of optimism.

One decision Doctor MacQueen had taken, was to announce which shop had been the source of the disease. He felt safe in making the announcement as the incubation period for the disease had now passed. There was no further risk of infection from William Low.

Samuel Reynolds had been dreading the day when people would be told that it had been his shop which had sold the infected meat. The paying public were an unforgiving breed and he was deeply concerned that the reputation of the shop might never recover.

With Doctor MacQueen having now made the dreaded announcement, Reynolds would soon have a clearer picture of what the people of Aberdeen thought about his shop. He expected his profits to drop dramatically for, deep down, he would have fully understood if anyone decided never to shop with him again.

*

Detective Chief Inspector Ogston, meantime, was sitting in the canteen enjoying a coffee. It was fairly busy, but he still managed to find a table for himself. He wanted time to think.

He hadn't been sitting there very long when another man sat himself down at the table. In one hand he held a coffee and in the other, a bar of chocolate. He was a tall man, with a good head of hair and a handsome face. He was a few months shy of fifty and had been a police officer for twenty-eight years.

"Sir," said Ogston.

'Sir' was Superintendent Cameron, Ogston's immediate boss.

"Not seen you for a few days, Graeme, hope you're still keeping yourself busy," Cameron then said, his tone heavy with sarcasm.

Ogston bit his tongue. There was always a lot he'd liked to have said to Cameron but, mindful of the man's seniority, he'd always managed to keep his thoughts to himself. This would be no different.

"Always plenty to do, sir."

"How's the murder inquiry coming along?" Cameron then asked, stirring sugar into his coffee.

"Slowly, sir. We're finding out more about the victim all the time and as we uncover new information, it seems to take us down different routes."

"What do you mean?" was Cameron's next question, as he started to attack the wrapper on his bar of chocolate.

Ogston explained about the blackmail and the work involved in getting to the bottom of that. He admitted he wasn't any nearer to identifying the murderer, but he had still managed to charge one individual with regard to the blackmail. He added that others had received formal warnings, on the same subject and that all in all, it had been a pretty successful conclusion to that line of inquiry.

Superintendent Cameron seemed to brighten on hearing that. Perhaps all was not lost. At least he could tell the Chief Constable that charges had been brought without necessarily stipulating how many.

Ogston also quickly added that he had all but solved the Thompson raid, from 1959. There might never be any arrests, but at least he knew what had happened back then and that Davie Milne had been one of the robbers.

Again, Cameron seemed impressed. His initial belief that Ogston had been getting nowhere fast, was quickly dwindling.

"Good work," Cameron eventually said. He got up and left.

"Thank you, sir," Ogston said to the senior officer's back.

Ogston returned to his own thoughts. It was now time to speak with those who worked in the Council Finance Department. Milne's final accomplice had to work there; it was just a matter of deciding which one it might be.

He lit another cigarette and enjoyed the last of his coffee.

*

After lunch, Ogston made his way to the Council buildings. He had made an appointment to speak with the Supervisor of the Department; Rachel Harrison.

On announcing his arrival Ogston was shown into a large brown panelled room, in which sat six women at separate desks. They were all bent over those desks, heads down in deep concentration as if they might be punished for looking up.

At the head of the six desks, lined up in two rows of three, was a larger desk occupied by an attractive looking woman with dark hair and wearing a white blouse and black skirt. She stood up as Ogston entered the room. She announced herself as being Rachel Harrison then suggested they might go elsewhere to talk.

Ogston took one last look round the room. Down either wall was a row of fourteen-drawer cabinets and behind where Rachel had been sitting, were three four-drawer cabinets. There certainly appeared to be a lot of information stored within those four walls. A blackmailer's delight, perhaps.

Rachel led the way to a small room, next door. It was like one of the interview rooms at Lodge Walk; furnished with two chairs and a table and with no source of fresh air. They sat down. Ogston refrained from smoking.

Ogston knew that he would have to choose his words carefully. After all, there was always the possibility that Rachel Harrison could have been Davie's accomplice.

"A matter has come to our attention, Miss Harrison," Ogston began.

"Oh, please, Chief Inspector, call me Rachel."

"Very well, *Rachel*," added Ogston, "we've been informed that there may be a few Councillors who have been less than truthful with their expenses claims. I presume they are all processed through your office?"

"Yes, they are. I would add, Chief Inspector, that I'm not greatly surprised to hear that some Councillors may be fiddling their claims."

"Why do you say that?"

"Because many people view expenses as a nice little earner. They see nothing wrong in ensuring they get the maximum return from their claim, if you get my meaning?"

"But your staff must be checking for such things," said Ogston.

"We do check all the forms, but we're not always armed with enough information as to be able to identify a clear wrongful claim."

"What do you mean?"

"A Councillor could claim travel expenses for attending a meeting outside the city. He might claim for a rail journey and a hotel when, in fact, he drove and stayed with a friend."

"Don't you require receipts?"

"No, we don't, we work on trust as much as anything and before you say it, I know there's not many who would trust a Councillor."

Ogston smiled. "So, a number of false claims could have been made and your staff would be none the wiser?"

"Unless it was something truly blatant, I doubt if we would pick up on it," Rachel admitted. "We're checking more for arithmetical accuracy, than anything else."

"Might a member of your staff suspect fiddling, even though they couldn't prove it?" Ogston then asked.

"I'm sure we've all had our suspicions in the past, Chief Inspector, but without clear evidence of someone lying to us, there would always be little we could do."

Given the relative freedom of the system, Ogston was now more surprised by the fact that fiddling hadn't been rampant.

Clearly, a number of Councillors *could* be trusted. It sounded more like an open chequebook than an expenses process.

"Does everyone in your team process these expenses claims?" Ogston then asked.

"Yes. The Finance Department is split into various sections. My section deals purely with expenses and sundry payments that are made to Councillors and Council staff."

"So, no one else would process an expenses' claim?" Ogston pressed.

"No."

Ogston felt even more certain that Milne's accomplice was now either Rachel, or one of her staff. From the way Rachel was answering his questions, Ogston was fairly sure it wasn't her. That meant it had to be one of the six women sitting next door. But would he ever be able to identify which one?

"Would you know which girl had processed any particular payment?"

"Of course. They initial their work as they go along and then I carry out a ten per cent check. Anyone can clearly see who did what. We need that to please the auditors. They check our work every year."

"Would you be able to look out the claims for one, particular, Councillor?" Ogston then asked.

"Yes."

Ogston referred to his notes and gave Rachel the dates on which he knew Councillor MacCallum had been less than truthful with his returns. She left the room.

On her return, she carried a pile of paper, which she dropped on the table between them. Rachel smiled.

"This might take a little while; would you like a coffee?"

Ogston said he'd love a coffee and Rachel departed once more. Ogston started sifting through the expense claims, looking for initials as much as anything.

He could now see how he might identify who did what in processing MacCallum's claims, but he still couldn't understand how anyone would have known MacCallum was fiddling in the first place. Maybe that meant the accomplice was someone closer to the Councillor, than necessarily working in the Finance Department?

It seemed that everywhere he turned there was nothing but barriers and complications in the way. He was still looking at various sheets of paper when Rachel came back with the coffee. She also had a plate of biscuits with her.

They started to work through the claims together. Rachel called out who had processed which claim and Ogston made notes. As time progressed, Ogston could see that this was leading nowhere.

All the girls had a hand in processing the claims, at one time or another and in no instance would it have been obvious, to any of them, that the claim was bogus. No, whoever was passing information to Davie Milne, had to have been closer to the Councillors; had to be hearing them confess to fiddling.

Ogston had no idea who that could be. In fact, he was beginning to doubt if he would ever identify the source. It seemed he'd hit another brick wall.

However, it had been a pleasant time in Rachel's company. She said she'd hoped to have been of some help. Ogston thanked her for her time and the coffee.

He'd then made his way back to Lodge Walk. The first thing he did, on returning to his office, was to light a cigarette. He was in the process of enjoying his smoke when the telephone rang. It was the switchboard operator wanting to put a call through from London.

Ogston thanked her and then spoke when a man's voice appeared in his ear.

"DCI Ogston."

The voice on the other end of the phone told Ogston that Caroline O'Hara had now regained consciousness, though she was still in no position to be interviewed. The medical staff had, however, said the police could speak to her after another twenty-four hours had gone by.

Ogston hoped that Caroline might be able to help him fit yet another piece to his jigsaw puzzle.

*

News finally came through from London at two o'clock on the Tuesday afternoon.

The day had started with the papers announcing that there was now 358 confirmed cases and 58 suspected cases in hospital. The good news, however, was that only 4 new patients had been admitted in the previous twenty-four hours, which had been the lowest admission figure since the epidemic had commenced.

There was a real sense amongst Doctor MacQueen's team, that the corner had been well and truly turned. Some semblance of sanity was returning to the hospitals; the war had been won.

Alison was doing less training and more hands-on work again. She felt a lot happier for that. She had become a nurse to help sick people, not wander about checking on how *others* were helping sick people.

Graeme Ogston, meantime, was receiving a name from London. A name that might finally open some doors in a case that continued to remain stubbornly difficult to crack.

The name he received was Gerry Craig and a very interesting name it was too. Ogston called Forrest through and told him the news.

"And neither Mrs Milne, nor Ronnie Cusiter could remember being at Gerry Craig's house?" Forrest said, the disbelief evident in his voice.

"Hard to believe, isn't it?" said Ogston with a smile. "I just had a niggle in the gut about *Ranald* Cusiter. I'm sure he's been up to no good, it's just a matter of whether or not we can prove it."

"Do you want him brought in?" asked Forrest.

"Bring in both Cusiter and Phyllis and put them in separate rooms," answered Ogston. "We'll have a chat with them later, but first we'll let them sweat it out for a little while. In the meantime, we'll go and have a chat with Gerry Craig, I'm sure he'll be delighted to see us."

*

Gerald McKenzie Craig was well known to the police.

He had fingers in pies and pies everywhere. Some were legal, many were not. If there was ever anything close to a Mister Big in Aberdeen, then it would have been Gerry Craig. Anything dodgy and he was probably involved, only at a level where he would never be caught.

Gerry was far too clever for that. A lot was done in his name and yet his name would never come up, no matter who the police interviewed. Either through payment, or fear, Gerry ensured he was protected from any accusation.

No one would ever have crossed Gerry Craig. The consequences were just too severe.

Basically, that left the police with nothing more than suspicion. There was never any evidence to link Gerry Craig with anything even remotely illegal. On the face of it, he was the very model of a successful businessman and pillar of the community.

Craig was sixty years old. He had been born and bred in Aberdeen. He had been too young to get actively involved in the First World War and slightly too old for the Second World War. During the second conflict he had played his part in helping to feed the good people of Aberdeen, but always at a price that suited him better than his customers.

Craig had made a profit from the Second World War, which many found repulsive. However, he had done so, in such a way as to not attract a great deal of attention. Everything Gerry Craig did was under the radar; everything conducted well away from the prying eyes of the law.

It had helped Craig's cause, however, to retain one or two police officers on his payroll. They had mainly been senior officers, men of authority who could quickly quash any possibility of a junior officer causing any problems for him. It had allowed Gerry Craig to remain one step ahead of anyone intent on investigating him.

However, today would not be a day when Gerry's police contacts could be of any help to him. Only Ogston and Forrest knew about Caroline O'Hara and what she might say about Craig's parties. There was no one to help Gerry now.

He lived well. He had a house on Rubislaw Den North, where he lived with his wife Agnes. His first business had been a small butcher's shop on St Andrew Street. One shop had quickly become half a dozen, just in time for Britain declaring war on Herr Hitler. Craig had quickly taken over other businesses, until he had nearer to twenty shops across the north-east of Scotland.

He also acquired farming land and was able to supply his own shops from those farms. Cutting out the middle man saved time and money. His profits began to rise markedly.

Craig involved himself in anything that might make him money, caring little for whether, or not, it might be legal. He built walls around himself, barriers to prying eyes and ears.

He made a lot of money in a short space of time. He constantly attracted the attention of the police. No one could believe he'd made his money without breaking the law at some point. At various stages of his life, he had been hauled in for questioning but, through a mixture of a lack of evidence and a smart lawyer, he had always been released.

Just after the war, a major investigation had been instigated, all be it controlled by one of the officers on Craig's payroll. Nothing of any consequence had been found and the Chief Constable, himself, had issued a decree that Gerry Craig was to no longer be hounded.

Successive detectives had all wondered about Gerry Craig and how many crimes he'd been involved with. They had all dreamed of bringing Craig down, of being that one successful officer who had finally dug the dirt and been able to put him away.

It had never been more than a dream.

So, it was with mixed emotions that Ogston walked from the car to Craig's front door that day. He had met the man twice before, both times at formal events and on both occasions, Ogston had come away with a bad taste in his mouth.

Gerry Craig was arrogant, smug and very, very confident that he was fireproof when it came to police investigations. His wife, Agnes, dripped with jewellery and wore furs that positively screamed affluence. Even at the age of fifty-six she was a handsome woman, who carried herself with the bearing of royalty. All her married life she had been accustomed to the best.

Ogston rang the bell and glanced at Forrest. His Detective Inspector was looking nervous. He had never met Craig before, but he'd heard all the stories.

Ogston then looked around the driveway. The house was huge and set well back from the road, affording a great deal of privacy to the residents.

The door was opened by a man; a very tall man, broad of shoulder and with a mean expression on his face. He looked anything but the butler type.

"Yes?" he almost snarled at the two men.

Ogston showed his identification and announced both his own name and that of Forrest, as he did so.

"We'd like to speak with Mister Craig," Ogston had then added.

"He's busy," said the man.

Ogston took a step closer. The man, blocking the doorway, was a good three inches taller and clearly spent a lot of time in the gym. Ogston was pretty sure that one punch from this gorilla and he'd be knocked out cold, but he wasn't going to be intimidated by him.

Ogston looked up into the man's face. "We're investigating a murder, which means the work I do trumps anything Mister Craig might be doing. Now, if you don't want to be charged with obstructing a police inquiry, I suggest you not only let us in to the house, but also tell Mister Craig that we're here."

There was a stand-off for a few seconds. Nothing was said, but both men stared hard at each other, neither showing any sign of giving ground.

Eventually, the gorilla stood back and allowed Ogston and Forrest to enter a large and ornate hallway. The décor was so over the top it made Ogston physically cringe. No doubt, this was the hand of Agnes Craig as it seemed unlikely that Gerry would have given much thought to colour schemes and artwork.

They were shown through to the drawing-room, which was situated at the back of the house. There were patio doors, leading out to a large and well-maintained garden.

"I'll tell Mister Craig that you are here," the man then said and left the room, closing the door behind him.

Ogston went to the window and looked out on to the garden.

"Some place," said Forrest.

"And all paid for legitimately," added Ogston, the sarcasm shining through.

A moment or two later, the door opened and Gerry Craig came in. He was dressed in grey trousers, with a light blue, open-necked shirt. He immediately went over to a table, where a number of spirit bottles were laid out. He poured himself a whisky and took an ice cube, from an ice-bucket sitting beside the bottles.

"Can I offer you a drink, Chief Inspector?" he then said.

"Yes, thank you," Ogston replied. "I'll have a whisky and soda."

"Ice?"

"No, thank you."

"Inspector?" Craig then said, holding up a bottle in the process.

"No, thank you, sir, I'm driving."

"Too bad," said Craig.

He poured a whisky and added a dash of soda. He then turned and crossed the room to where Ogston was standing.

"Please, sit down both of you," he then said, waving an arm in the general direction of a three-piece suite, which occupied the centre of the room.

Craig sat down last and reached for a box, lying on the table beside his chair. He took out a cigar and then offered one to his 'guests'. Both declined, though Ogston did take the opportunity to light a cigarette.

Craig lit his cigar, then sat back in his chair; cigar in one hand, drink in the other.

He looked very relaxed, but then he would be, the man had no need to fear the police. He knew they would never have anything on him.

Craig still looked mean. He was solidly built, clearly a man in good physical shape. His hair was cropped close to his head and apart from the odd grey hair, still holding its colour.

Craig's eyes were bright and his mind sharp. He had had a few verbal duels with the police, over the years, and had come to enjoy them. He remembered having met Ogston before and had at that time, made a point of finding out more about him. He knew, therefore, that Ogston was not to be taken lightly.

"What can I do for you, Chief Inspector?"

Ogston flicked some ash into the ashtray and took a sip of his drink. It was extremely strong. He guessed it was meant to be; Craig was endeavouring to get a police officer drunk whilst on duty.

"I'm here to test your memory, Mister Craig," Ogston began. Craig's left eyebrow rose in a questioning manner, as if to say *'I'll do my best.'* "What can you tell me about Ronnie Cusiter, whom I now believe likes to go by the name of Ranald?"

Craig considered the question for a moment. "Ranald Cusiter? Doesn't he sell clothes, or something?"

"He does, Mister Craig. What else can you tell me about him?"

Craig shook his head. "Thought I was doing well knowing he sold clothes," he then added, with a smile.

"He's been here, at one of you parties," added Ogston.

"Good heavens, Chief Inspector, half of Aberdeen has been at one of my parties, at some point of the last ten years."

"How about Davie Milne?" Ogston then said.

Craig shook his head. "Another name that means nothing to me. I assume, however, that he has been at one of my parties as well."

Ogston could sense that Craig was toying with him. He wasn't going to let the man get under his skin, however.

"The same party, as it happens," said Ogston.

"Did these men know each other?" Craig enquired.

"I believe they did, Mister Craig. And I believe they knew you as well."

"Really?" said Craig, He puffed on his cigar, took a drink from his glass and then spoke again. "I honestly can't bring either name to mind, Chief Inspector, so I'm guessing they were nothing more than extras when they came to my party."

"Extras?" queried Ogston.

"Yes, people invited to make up the numbers. They're usually local businessmen, successful in their own little world, but totally inconsequential in mine. I rarely even speak to the extras, I'm far too busy talking to the *real* guests."

"So, you don't know Ranald Cusiter at all?" pressed Ogston.

"As I said, I know he sells clothes and I believe he is reasonably successful at it. I expect that was why he was invited to one of my parties in the first place. Look, Chief Inspector, are you able to give me some idea as to when these men might have been at one of my parties?"

"The summer of sixty-one," replied Ogston.

"Oh, come now, Chief Inspector, I struggle to remember who I met last week, let alone who I may have crossed paths with nearly three years ago."

"But Davie Milne and Ronnie Cusiter weren't just party guests, were they, Mister Craig?" Ogston then said.

Ogston didn't actually know what Davie and Ronnie were to Gerry Craig, he was just probing at the moment.

"Weren't they?" said Craig, sounded suitably vague.

Ogston ignored the reply and moved on.

"Do you have much say in who gets invited to your own parties?"

Craig smiled. "Agnes plays a major part in who gets invited. I also employ a party organiser; she deals with the actual inviting."

"Could I have a name for this party organiser?" asked Ogston.

"I can't actually remember who was doing that job three years ago, Chief Inspector so, no, I can't give you a name."

"Convenient," said Ogston.

Craig smiled again. "It would only be convenient if I had something to hide."

Which, of course, you have, thought Ogston.

"What is the purpose of your parties, Mister Craig?"

"To have fun, Chief Inspector. You do know what fun is?"

Craig's grinning face was beginning to annoy Ogston. His anger was simmering under the surface and it was becoming a constant fight to keep it there.

"Is that why the girls get invited," Ogston then said, "to allow your male guests to have fun?"

"I'm not sure I like what you are implying, Chief Inspector. I have attractive, young women at my parties for the same reason I have the extras. A party goes better with a lot of people attending especially if the right mix is achieved."

"And what do you term as a good mix?" enquired Ogston.

"Put it this way, Chief Inspector, if I went to a party and found only one, single woman amongst thirty-five single men, then I'd feel somewhat cheated. A mix of the sexes makes everything go that little bit better."

"Where do you get the attractive, young women from?"

"I have no idea, that is all down to my party organiser."

"Who currently organises your parties?"

"A lovely, young woman by the name of Susan. I, honestly, can't remember her second name."

"How can we contact this Susan?"

"I'll get a contact address for her, before you go."

"Thank you," added Ogston, feeling this conversation, like the murder inquiry, was going nowhere. He decided to change the subject and see what reaction he got. "What can you tell me about Christmas, nineteen fifty-nine?"

Craig thought for a moment. "I seem to remember having a stinking cold that year, completely spoiled Christmas."

"It was the Christmas when three men pulled off a raid at the offices of H M Thompson and made off with a sizeable sum of money which had been destined for the pay packets of the employees."

Craig sat, waiting for more to be said. When it wasn't, he felt obliged to say something.

"Did they now?"

"Yes, they did, Mister Craig and not a year and a half later, it seems that two of the three to carry out that raid, were here at one of your parties."

It was a statement that wasn't wholly accurate. Only Davie Milne could be placed at that raid. It was only in Ogston's mind that Cusiter found himself there. Craig thought the statement might turn into a question but, when it didn't, he thought it best to say something.

"I'm sorry, Chief Inspector, but are you implying that I *too,* had something to do with that raid?"

"I think you knew about it and I think, through that, you also knew Milne and Cusiter. The real reason for them being at one of your parties, was they were friends of yours."

Craig laughed. "What a warped mind you have, Chief Inspector. Whether you choose to believe me, or not, I do not know Ranald Cusiter and I do not know Davie Milne. If they were both at one of my parties then it was nothing more than pure coincidence."

Craig drained his glass and went over to re-fill it. This time Ogston was not offered anything. Craig returned to his chair and sat back again.

"What about Caroline O'Hara, does that name mean anything to you?" Ogston then asked.

"Let me guess, Chief Inspector, she was at the same party?" Craig replied with some sarcasm.

"She was," agreed Ogston, "and she brought a friend with her; Phyllis Duncan. Phyllis isn't that common a name and she also happened to be extremely attractive. Perhaps you remember her?"

"At my parties, Chief Inspector, I am surrounded by pretty faces, none of which mean anything to me. I am a happily married man who likes looking, but nothing more. I do not remember names, at the best of times, whether they be common or not. Now, if you have nothing other than meaningless statements to make, I suggest we part company while I am still of a mind to let you walk out the door of your own volition."

"Is that a threat, Mister Craig?"

"It is just a statement confirming how tired I have become of your questions if, indeed, I can truly call them questions."

Craig began to stand up. Ogston knew he had nothing more to say that would make any difference to Craig's mood. He had been outmanoeuvred, plain and simple.

He fired one last salvo.

"Davie Milne is now dead, he was murdered."

Craig paused. "I'm very sad to hear that, Chief Inspector, but the name still means nothing to me."

"And you still insist Ranald Cusiter means nothing to you, beyond knowing he sells clothes?"

"I do," replied Craig. "Now, if you would just follow me into the hall, I'll arrange for you to get Susan's contact details."

The gorilla was dispatched for Susan's details and a piece of paper handed to Ogston at the door. Ogston thanked Craig for his time and suggested they'd probably speak again, sometime.

"Always enjoy my little chats with the local police, Chief Inspector," Craig said, as he held the door open. He watched the two officers walk to their car.

He then closed the door and hurried through to the room he used for business purposes only.

It was time for action.

14   14

14

Ranald Cusiter was beside himself with anger, by the time Ogston got back to Lodge Walk. He had been shouting and swearing for more than half an hour, insisting, in no uncertain terms, that no one had any right to keep him there against his will.

Ogston left him to boil for another half an hour, while he went to speak with Phyllis first.

"I now know whose party you were attending, when you met Davie," was the first thing Ogston said to Phyllis.

She was looking nervous, as if she were unsure of what to say. When she did reply, her voice was weak.

"It was Gerry Craig," she said.

"You knew all the time?"

Phyllis nodded.

"Then why lie?"

"Because I know Gerry Craig has a reputation and I didn't want to be tarnished by it."

"How did you get the invite?"

"Oh, that part was true. I went with my friend Caroline. She was the one with the contacts. She told me there would be rich men at the party and if I played my cards right, I might get a present, or two, from some of them."

"In return for what?" asked Ogston and got a stare that could have killed in return.

"Certainly not what you might be thinking, Chief Inspector. I am a respectable woman with personal standards that I wouldn't lower for anyone."

"And instead of meeting some rich man, you met Davie?" added Ogston, not even trying to hide the disappointment in his voice.

Phyllis actually smiled. "He was a breath of fresh air at that party. He was the only one who acted anything like normal, even if he was trying to chat me up all the time."

"Can you remember anyone else who was there?"

"I didn't know anyone in the first place," Phyllis replied, "so there were no names to remember."

"Where did Mister Cusiter fit in to the evening?"

At that point, Phyllis grew more nervous. She asked for a cigarette, explaining she didn't usually smoke, but she'd like one at that moment.

Ogston offered her one from his packet. She placed it between her lips and lit it from Ogston's lighter. He lit one for himself at the same time.

Phyllis took a moment before speaking.

"Ranald was just another guest."

"Who happened to know Davie," prompted Ogston.

"He might have known of Davie, but I don't think they knew each other, as such."

"But Cusiter remained friends with you," added Ogston.

"Ranald fancied me, that was all. As soon as Davie and I started having problems, Ranald was there to provide a shoulder to cry on. In every respect, he has been the perfect gentleman. How many more times do you need to be told that before you'll finally believe it?"

"Did you speak to Gerry Craig when you were at the party?" Ogston then asked, choosing to ignore the question.

"I shouldn't have thought so. Craig wouldn't waste time with the likes of me."

"Do you remember if Craig spoke to Ranald, or Davie, that night?"

"I don't remember, Chief Inspector," replied Phyllis, "but I wouldn't have thought so, they were as unimportant as I was."

"Did Davie ever mention Craig's name after you were married?"

"Good heavens, no," came the somewhat horrified reply. "Why ever would you think Davie would have had anything to do with a nasty piece of work like Gerry Craig?"

"We now know that your ex-husband was not only a blackmailer, but had once been part of a gang who pulled off a robbery in nineteen fifty-nine."

"A robbery?" repeated Phyllis, sounding as if there was no way she could believe that of Davie.

"Yes."

"So, if Davie was this master criminal, where was all the money going, because I never saw any of it?"

"The money is there, Miss Duncan, but there appears to be no evidence of him wanting to spend it."

"Then why have it?" asked Phyllis.

"Plans for the future, perhaps?" suggested Ogston. "Plans in which you played no part."

Those last words stung Phyllis deeply. No wonder Davie was so keen on getting a divorce. She began to wonder who he had made plans with; it had to be another woman, that rather went without saying.

Ogston continued. "Miss Duncan, I have to ask you this again; why did you put up with your husband's womanising?"

"I've already told you. I didn't feel as if I had any other option. Much as he spent all his time with other women, I never thought it would lead to a divorce. I ought to have seen the writing on the wall when he eventually offered to provide evidence for just such a thing."

"And had you got divorced, you would have received half of very little, while he walked away with thousands," added Ogston.

That stung even more. Had Davie cared so little for her? If so, why get married in the first place? Had it all been about getting her into bed? Had it all come down to the fact she'd made him wait?

It didn't seem much of a reason for getting married, especially when he hardly struggled to attract other women. Phyllis couldn't see what had been so special about her. Why would someone like Davie go as far as marrying anyone?

Nothing made sense anymore.

Ogston offered Phyllis a coffee, which she accepted. Forrest went to make the beverages while Ogston kept the flow of questions coming.

"Did you ever suspect, at any time, that Davie might be involved in something illegal?"

Phyllis shook her head. "There was never any reason to suspect him of anything other than his constant need to chat up every woman who crossed his line of vision."

Ogston heard the answer, but he wasn't totally convinced of its honesty.

"We now also know that Davie kept his blackmail material in your kitchen," Ogston then said, his eyes studying Phyllis's face even closer. "There was every chance you might have come across it, quite by chance of course. Do you still maintain that you knew nothing about your husband's illegal activities?"

Phyllis took the last drag from her cigarette and squashed it into the ashtray. She then looked up, her eyes fixing on Ogston's.

"Very well," she then said, "I did come across his hiding place, though I never spoke to him about it and I never knew, for certain, what he was doing with those pictures."

"Did you remove the items?" asked Ogston.

"No."

"Did you talk to Cusiter about what you'd found?"

"I may have mentioned it, not that Ranald showed any interest in what Davie was doing."

Ogston changed the subject again.

"Has Ranald Cusiter ever spoken to you about where he got the money from, to start his business?"

"No. That would be none of my business, Chief Inspector."

"So, you've no idea how he suddenly became wealthy enough as to be able to open a shop and stock it with items brought up from London?" added Ogston.

"He did mention a silent partner, whatever that is."

"But he never said who?"

"That would also be none of my business, Chief Inspector and I'm guessing it would be none of yours, either," came the rather blunt reply.

"That still remains to be seen, Miss Duncan," said Ogston, as Forrest came back into the room, carrying a tray on which three mugs had been placed.

"Missed anything?" Forrest said, as he sat down.

"Miss Duncan was just telling me she knew about her ex-husband's photograph collection, but she maintains she had no idea why he had them. Hard to believe, I know, but that's what she's saying."

Ogston studied Phyllis's face closely, as he said those words. He could see the flash of anger in her eyes, but he could also see something else. She had that look of guilt; the look that everyone passing through those police interview rooms always tried to hide.

Phyllis Duncan was not that good a liar. Her voice may have spoken false words, but her face gave her away every time. Her eyes were too honest.

Ogston drank some coffee and then leaned further across the table, bringing his head closer to Phyllis.

"I'll be honest with you, Miss Duncan; I don't believe you when you say you had no idea what Davie's photograph collection might be for. I think you had a pretty good idea of what he was doing and that that was the final straw for you. It was the real reason you left him, wasn't it?"

Phyllis drank her coffee and seemed unwilling to respond to the question. Eventually, however, she did speak.

"I spoke to Davie about what I'd found. He laughed and said it was nothing, just a little hobby. I challenged the fact it had to be illegal, but he just told me not to worry. I could just about live with the women in his life, but not the fact I'd married a crook."

"But he never mentioned the robbery in fifty-nine?" said Ogston.

"No, I knew nothing about that, until you mentioned it earlier."

"We now know three men pulled off that robbery. Would you offer any guesses as to who, amongst Davie's few male friends, might have been on that job with him?"

Phyllis thought for a moment. "I can tell you who brought Davie to that party at Craig's. Maybe he was the crook and Davie just tagged along?"

"Who might that be?"

"Joe Traynor; I'm sure you'll know him."

Ogston smiled. "Oh yes, we know Joe alright," he then said, glancing at Forrest in the process. "My thanks for your help, Miss Duncan. You'll need to give us a formal statement, along the lines of what you've said here today. I'll send a constable through and once we have your statement, I'll arrange to have you taken home."

"What about Ranald?"

"We'll speak to him now," was all that Ogston would say. He and Forrest left the room and a uniformed constable was sent in to take Phyllis's statement.

Ogston instructed Forrest to arrange for Joe Traynor to be picked up and taken to Lodge Walk. They were to make sure that Cusiter didn't see Traynor, just in case there had been history between them.

Ogston then went through to speak with Ronnie Cusiter. As he entered the room, an empty mug flew past his head and bounced off the wall.

Ogston deduced that Ronnie was none too pleased to see him.

*

At the very moment Ronnie Cusiter was throwing mugs around at Lodge Walk, Gerry Craig was receiving a phone call.

The caller was a man known only as Simpson. He was Gerry Craig's go to, whenever problems needed ironing out.

Simpson was not a nice man; he'd never tried to be. He had learned, at an early age, that brute force and ignorance could go a long way.

He'd hired out his muscle to the highest bidder. For the last five years that had been Gerry Craig. Simpson was now thirty-three years old and rich. Many in Aberdeen had met him and many had the scars to prove it.

The man took no prisoners and that was what Gerry Craig liked about him.

"I've got news for you, boss," Simpson said.

Gerry Craig stopped writing and sat back in his chair. He could tell from Simpson's tone that the news probably wouldn't be good.

"I'm listening."

"Ronnie Cusiter is at Lodge Walk as we speak."

"What the hell for?"

"No idea, as yet. He was taken to Lodge Walk along with that bird he's got living with him now."

"That *bird*, as you so quaintly put it, is Davie Milne's widow," Craig said.

"Davie Milne, the guy whose murderer I'm trying to find?"

"The very same."

"Why all the interest in him, boss, did he mean something to you?"

"Davie meant nothing to me. He was just another low-life who tried his hand at crime and didn't do too well out of it."

"Then why be so keen to find out who killed him?" Simpson said, still struggling to understand his boss's motivation.

"Because I usually know who kills people in Aberdeen," Craig replied, "especially crooks. In this case, however, there seems to have been nothing but silence and that worries me. I don't know why, it just does."

"Fair enough, boss."

"Anyway, why would the police want to speak to Ronnie?"

"I've not been able to find out."

"Is Ronnie still refusing to play ball with us?" Craig then asked.

"Hasn't budged these last few years. Have to say I have some respect for the guy, he doesn't scare easily."

Craig thought for a moment. He was trying to work out if Ronnie Cusiter could possibly know anything that would cause damage to the world around Gerry Craig. Cusiter had been a thorn in Craig's flesh for the last three years, maybe this was to be his way of fighting back.

But, if that were the case, what could he possibly know that would be of use to the police? And what of Phyllis Milne, how had she ended up with Ronnie, so quickly after leaving her husband.

The other matter troubling Craig deeply was why his payroll police officers hadn't phoned to tell him Cusiter was at Lodge Walk. He paid them enough, they were supposed to tell him things at times like that.

"Is there still no word on the street about Davie Milne's murder?" Craig then asked.

"Not a peep, boss. The last I heard; the police investigation was going nowhere as well."

"And *no one* can even hazard a guess as to who killed Davie?"

Craig found it hard to believe that there was no one in Aberdeen who seemed to know the identity of the murderer. There was usually always someone willing to talk, either out of fear or need for financial gain.

"As I say, boss, not a peep."

Craig thought some more. Eventually, he came to a decision.

"Okay, this is what I want you to do. I want Ronnie reminded of who really runs this city. I want him brought into line, once and for all. In short, I want you to deal with Ronnie Cusiter; I want you to make sure he says nothing of any consequence to anyone. Do I make myself clear?"

"Crystal, boss. What about that bird he's shacked up with?"

"What about her?"

"Do we pay her a visit?"

"No, you do not," Craig said, rather emphatically.

"But we at least pay the shops another visit?" Simpson then said.

"Not at the moment. Let's see why there is all this police activity first."

"You sound worried boss," Simpson then said.

"DCI Ogston paid me a visit earlier. He was asking about what I might know about Ronnie and Davie Milne. The next thing I'm hearing is that Ronnie is at Lodge Walk speaking to the police. Too bloody right I'm worried, so you deal with this and you deal with it quickly."

"Sure thing, boss," said Simpson and the line went dead.

Gerry Craig put the phone down. For the first time he was concerned that the police might be getting a little too close for comfort. So much activity and not a word from anyone at Lodge Walk. His people were being kept out of something so did that mean their cover had been blown? Gerry poured himself a drink and tried to set his mind on other problems. For now, Ronnie Cusiter would be placed in the *come back to that later* box.

*

Back at Lodge Walk, Ogston finally got Cusiter to sit down. He was still shouting for a solicitor, but Ogston denied his request on the grounds that they were simply having a chat. There was no need for legal representation.

Cusiter finally accepted the offer of a coffee and Ogston, once more, sent Forrest to organise something for the three of them. Ogston kept his questions and comments general, until Forrest returned.

Ogston sipped some coffee and then began.

"I suggest you make yourself comfortable, Ronnie, because I'm going to tell you a story."

"It's *Ranald,*" snapped Cusiter, his anger flooding to the surface again.

"As I said, *Ronnie,*" Ogston then said, "I'm going to talk about events in the past; events which I believe involved you. Just before Christmas, nineteen fifty-nine, three men entered the premises of H M Thompson and emptied the safe. They made good their getaway and took the money to a pre-arranged location, where they hid it until the immediate interest in its whereabouts died down.

Once it was felt safe to do so, the money was finally split three ways. Davie Milne had made arrangements with a local shop owner, to have his share looked after. You invested much of your money in opening your first shop and the third man, Joe Traynor, probably pissed his against a wall somewhere, because the man has a drink problem.

You decided, on the back of your new-found wealth, to become a respectable businessman and I have every faith in the fact that you have done nothing illegal since.

Davie Milne, however, was not so fastidious. Keeping to the straight and narrow was not Davie's way, so he started a little blackmail on the side. It was lapsing back to his criminal ways that provided the final straw for Phyllis. She could just about accept his womanising, but not his criminal ways.

Phyllis contacted you; seeing you as the only friend who might be able to help her in her hour of need. You'd wanted Phyllis in your bed ever since you'd first seen her so, presented with the chance to take a step closer to that final objective, you drove over as fast as you could."

Cusiter sat forward, as if about to say something. Ogston silenced him, with a wave of his hand and then continued speaking himself.

"Phyllis told you about Davie's side line and it worried you. After all, you had secrets of your own, so what if your pal turned against you. What if, in knowing you wanted Phyllis for yourself, he threatened to tell her everything unless you paid up. There in, Ronnie, lies a motive for murder."

Cusiter nearly leapt out of his seat at that moment. His eyes flashed with anger and Ogston thought, for a few seconds, that Cusiter might actually try to swing a punch.

"Don't even try to pin Davie's murder on me, Chief Inspector!" he practically shouted. "I know nothing about Davie Milne's murder and contrary to that wonderful piece of fiction you just told me, I know *nothing* about Davie, full stop."

"But you weren't complete strangers, were you?" prompted Ogston.

Cusiter drank some coffee. He appeared to be thinking. Finally, he spoke.

"Davie Milne and I were acquaintances, nothing more. We used to both go to the Pittodrie Bar, before home matches. We'd talk football, nothing else. Outside of those Saturday afternoon meetings, we meant nothing to each other. It was pure coincidence that we were at that party at the same time."

"Ah, yes, the party," Ogston then said, lighting a cigarette. "Maybe you've now remembered which party that was?"

Cusiter realised, in that instant, that the police now knew where he, Davie and Phyllis had been, that summer evening back in 1961. There seemed no reason to lie anymore.

"We were at Gerry Craig's house."

"Gerry Craig," repeated Ogston, "that great pillar of the community. I mean, Gerry's never been involved in anything illegal, has he?"

Again, the sarcasm dripped from Ogston's tongue.

"I wouldn't know, Chief Inspector, I don't know Gerry Craig."

"And yet you got invited to one of his parties?"

"Because I'm a successful local businessman, nothing more!" Cusiter, again, almost shouted. He calmed down a little and continued speaking. "Gerry Craig likes to surround himself with pretty girls and successful men. He likes to act as if he's better than everyone else. I only met him that once and took an instant dislike to the man. Had it not been for the fact that Phyllis was there, I would have left long before the end."

For the first time, since he'd met Ronnie Cusiter, Ogston finally began to wonder if he'd judged him wrongly. Ogston had interviewed a lot of people. He had learned, over the years, to read people, as they answered his questions.

The way he now read Cusiter, told a different story from the one he'd expected.

"So, you'll know nothing about the Thompson job?" he then said.

Cusiter drank some coffee and shook his head. "I read about it in the papers but no, Chief Inspector, I know nothing about that, or any other job."

"You do know Joe Traynor though?" Ogston added.

"Not really. Joe was more a mate of Davie's. He'd sometimes be with Davie at the Pittodrie Bar. I never really liked him, there was something sleekit about him that I couldn't accept."

"How about Davie, did you like him?"

"Initially; when it was just about football. Once Phyllis came on the scene, all that changed however. I learned about his womanising and hated him for the way he treated Phyllis. She deserved better than that."

"Phyllis did tell you about Davie's hiding place, didn't she?" Ogston then asked.

"Yes, she did."

"Did you investigate the contents of that hiding place?"

There was a silence for a moment. More coffee was drunk, before anything further was said.

"It was me who emptied it. I was so bloody annoyed with Davie that I thought if I destroyed all his evidence, he wouldn't be able to carry on with his little side line."

"Did you look at any of the material?" was the next question.

"A quick glance, nothing more. As soon as I saw the content of the first few photographs, I had a pretty good idea of what Davie had been up to. Destroying it all seemed the right thing to do. I took them home with me and burned them in the back garden."

"Maybe you then went back to kill Davie, such was your anger regarding the way he'd treated Phyllis?" Ogston suggested.

"Chief Inspector, if I had wanted Davie out of the way, so that I could be with Phyllis, then I'd have killed him a long time ago. There was nothing in the photographs I destroyed to harm me. I was simply protecting others."

"Did Davie contact Phyllis with regard to the photographs going missing?"

"Not as far as I know."

"Did he contact you?"

"No. Look, most of the material was photographs. Burning them would only have held him up for so long. He'd have had copies printed from the negatives and continued on his merry way. I knew it would be no more than a delaying tactic."

Ogston was beginning to believe everything that Cusiter was saying, much to his annoyance. He had so wanted Cusiter to be guilty of the robbery and of knowing Gerry Craig. However, it now looked as if neither was the case.

"Going back to Gerry Craig," Ogston then said.

Cusiter looked exasperated. "I've already said, I didn't know the man. Gerry moves in higher circles than I do, Chief Inspector."

"Let's talk about the party itself for a moment," Ogston then said. "You said Gerry liked to surround himself with pretty girls, where do you think those girls came from?"

"Someone told me they were, in the main, acquired through some agency for actors. Their Head Office is in Edinburgh."

"Do you have a name for that agency?"

"No, it wasn't something I ever needed to know. Obviously, Phyllis had no connections to the agency, she was simply there with a friend."

"We've spoken to Gerry Craig and he claims the girls were only there to create an equal mix of the sexes. Would you agree with that?"

"What do you mean?" enquired Cusiter, finishing his coffee.

"Did you witness anything untoward involving the girls attending that party?"

"Untoward?" repeated Cusiter.

Ogston felt sure that he was now being deliberately obtuse.

"Anything *sexual*?" explained Ogston.

"Are you now looking for your very own Profumo Affair, Chief Inspector?" Cusiter replied.

"I'm not looking for anything in particular, Ronnie, I'm just gathering evidence and see where it leads me. Now, what were the girls *really* doing at Gerry Craig's party?"

Cusiter sighed heavily. He seemed reluctant to speak, at first, but soon grew tired of the silence he was creating.

"The girls were being friendly, nothing more."

"Phyllis said her friend had told her that she might get a present from one of the men at party, if she was lucky. Now, Phyllis took offence to my suggestion that she should do anything untoward in return, but the impression given was that there was more than just friendship on offer at those parties."

"Obviously some of the men paired off with the girls, but that is what happens at parties," Cusiter then said.

"Paired off as in left the party?" prompted Ogston.

"No, paired off as in went upstairs."

"So, there was sexual activity at the party?" said Ogston.

Cusiter laughed. "Chief Inspector, there is some level of sexual activity at most parties, particularly where the rich and successful meet. Many of the girls go there with the sole intention of finding a sugar daddy. Now, they may not have been offering sex at those parties, but I'm sure some of them might have done anything to help pay the bills."

"Did you recognise the other men at the party you attended?"

"A high proportion of them, yes."

"And would I be right in assuming that most of them were married?"

"Yes."

"And that none of them had their wives with them, at the party?"

"Correct again."

"So, the girls wouldn't have been needed, to balance the sexes, if those dirty old men had taken their wives in the first place," Ogston now suggested.

"Correct again, Chief Inspector."

Ogston sat back. Finally, he had possibly found a chink in Gerry Craig's armour. This could be the one way of throwing Craig in a cell and losing the key. If Ogston could tie Craig's parties to prostitution and the acquiring of call girls, then he could build a case that might finally stick.

"Would you be prepared to make a formal statement about what went on at Gerry Craig's party?" was Ogston's next question.

Cusiter looked horrified.

"No. I'm not going to incur the wrath of Gerry Craig by making half-statements that would only land me in serious trouble and probably get you nowhere. He is a man who does not like his reputation being tarnished and he is a man who tends to react against those who say too much. I have already said too much, Chief Inspector and without a solicitor, I won't be saying anything more."

Ogston knew he would get nothing more from Cusiter, but he was happy with what he'd been told already. It didn't help him in his search for Davie Milne's murderer, but it might just help him put Gerry Craig away and that would be a far bigger achievement.

Ogston drew the interview to a close and arranged for a car to take both Cusiter and Phyllis, home. He went back to his office to collect another pack of cigarettes, then met up with Forrest again and went to interview Joe Traynor.

*

Traynor was sitting in an office, with a uniformed constable for company. He was short, insignificant looking man, with a mop of black hair and the makings of a beard on his chin. He was smoking and looked calm enough, considering they had kept him waiting with no explanation as to why he was there.

Traynor looked towards the door as Ogston and Forrest walked in.

"Hello, Mister Ogston, it's been a while," he said, with a smile.

Joe Traynor had crossed paths with Detective Chief Inspector Ogston on many occasions. He was well known around Aberdeen, both to the police and the other petty crooks.

"I believe you know Ronnie Cusiter," Ogston said, beginning by testing what Cusiter had already told him.

"I know a lot of people," said Traynor, finishing one cigarette and lighting another.

Ogston smiled. "I'm sure you do, but can you confirm that one of them *is* Ronnie Cusiter?"

"I believe he wants to be called Ranald these days. God knows why."

"But you *do* know him?" prompted Ogston again.

"I don't really *know* him, Chief Inspector. We used to cross paths ahead of some of the Dons' matches, but it was only over a pint or two and a chat about how the game might go. If we both hadn't gone to the Pittodrie Bar then I wouldn't have known him at all."

"Did Cusiter know Davie Milne?" was Ogston's next question.

"In the same way he knew me. We talked football, that was all."

"And, how about Gerry Craig, do you know him?"

"As far as I know, he never went to the Pittodrie Bar," came the reply.

"But you knew Craig from somewhere else?" pressed Ogston.

"Look, Chief Inspector, you're better off *not* knowing Gerry Craig, he's a nasty piece of work."

"Really?" was all that Ogston said. He was keen to see where this might be leading.

Traynor dragged hard on his cigarette and let the smoke filter out through his nose. It took a minute for him to speak again, perhaps regretting his previous statement.

"You'll know as well as I do, Chief Inspector, that Gerry Craig has a reputation. You don't want to be too close to someone like that."

"And yet you went to one of his parties, Mister Traynor."

"Did I?"

"Yes, you did. Around three years ago, you went to a party that was also attended by Ronnie Cusiter and Davie Milne."

"If you say so," came the rather non-committal response.

"I do say so, Mister Traynor. We have witness statements to the effect that you were there, now why would you get an invite to a Gerry Craig party?"

Traynor thought for a moment. "When was I at that party?"

"Summer of Sixty-One."

"Summer of Sixty-One," Traynor repeated as he thought back to why he might have been there. It suddenly came to him. "Ah yes, that was the summer I drove a delivery van for one of Gerry Craig's shops. Sometimes he invited his staff to a party, by way of saying thanks for all our hard work."

Bollocks, thought Ogston.

"What was in your delivery van?" Ogston then asked.

"Meat of course, Chief Inspector. What else would I be collecting from a butcher's shop?"

What else indeed? thought Ogston. *Knowing Gerry Craig, it could have been anything.*

"Okay, so as a trusted member of his staff, Gerry arranged for you to attend a party at his house?" Ogston asked, his tone betraying the fact he didn't believe a word of what he was being told.

"Got it in one," replied Traynor. "I'd have taken Davie as my guest, us being mates and all that."

"Were you a close mate?"

"As close as anyone not wearing a skirt could ever be to Davie."

"Close enough as to commit crimes together?" added Ogston, his eyes watching Traynor even more closely.

He detected surprise, rather than shock. Maybe he was getting somewhere after all.

"Look, Chief Inspector, I'm no angel myself, but I never did anything dishonest with Davie Milne."

Ogston went over the raid at H M Thompson's again and asked Traynor if he knew anything about it. Traynor, at first, shook his head. Ogston pressed some more, playing on the fact that Traynor's criminal record was as long as Union Street; no one would ever believe that Traynor had no knowledge of the other crimes committed in Aberdeen.

Eventually, he began to talk more openly.

"Okay, Chief Inspector, maybe I did know about Davie pulling that job at Thompson's all those years ago, but that was because he told me, not because I was there. You know me, Chief Inspector, I might thieve from the odd house, but I've never been involved in big league stuff like the Thompson job. As far as I know, Davie was only along for the ride. He provided the local knowledge and a bit of muscle. The other two were up from Glasgow. I never heard any names and to be quite honest, I never *wanted* to know their names. Davie got a payment from the job, but it wasn't as much as the others walked away with."

Ogston's initial theory, on the Thompson job, was rapidly falling apart, He'd been wrong about Ronnie Cusiter and now, it seemed, he was wrong about Joe Traynor as well. Had the planning for the job been done outside of Aberdeen then it would certainly explain why the investigating team had been unable to find a solid line of inquiry.

A couple of professionals had been sent up to carry out the job. Davie Milne had been paid as hired help and nothing more.

Ogston moved on. "Did you know that Davie had also been into blackmail?"

A look of genuine surprise crossed Traynor's face.

"Now, that, I didn't know about."

"Did Davie talk much about the women he'd been seeing?"

"All the bloody time. You practically got their vital statistics from him."

"Did he ever mention knowing someone who worked for the Council?" Ogston then asked.

Traynor thought for a moment.

"He went out with an Isla Montgomery for a little while. Her dad's a Councillor."

"We know about her, but I'm thinking more about someone who actually *worked* for the Council?"

Traynor thought for a moment. He seemed about to say he couldn't think of anyone when, suddenly, his expression changed.

"Wait a minute," he said, "Davie did speak about some bird who worked in the Council offices."

"Can you remember her name?" Ogston said.

Traynor gave the matter some thought.

"I'm sure Davie called her Grace," he eventually said. "He said she was a real looker and was apparently madly in love with him."

"Can you remember in which part of the Council this Grace worked?" Ogston then asked.

"She worked everywhere, Chief Inspector. Grace was one of their tea ladies."

Ogston almost laughed out loud. Of course, who could be better placed to hear the tittle-tattle going around offices?

People would gather around the tea trolley and gossip. No one pays any attention to the tea lady, she's just there to serve the tea and keep her mouth shut.

Ogston was annoyed with himself, he should really have thought of that earlier.

15 15

As of Wednesday, 10th June, the confirmed cases of typhoid were 376, with another 55 suspected. The numbers of new patients being admitted to hospital was down to single figures.

Although Doctor MacQueen was still holding his daily meetings and also his daily news conferences, the Press were beginning to lose interest now that patient numbers were dropping and the epidemic appeared to be under control.

The Press were a fickle mob. They ran with a story for only as long as there was a sensational element attached. They liked to write stories which they claimed were in the public interest, but the real reason behind any story was to sell papers. The local papers in Aberdeen were no exception. To them the typhoid epidemic had been manna from heaven.

People would buy papers to find out the latest news. For as long as the epidemic lasted, they would buy those papers, no matter what. The daily newspaper was the best and often only way to keep abreast of events. The Press would, therefore, want to keep the story going for as long as possible.

The problem was, however, that with numbers of new patients now dropping and the fear level dropping with them, there was no longer the same reason for people to buy papers, at least not in the numbers that editors would prefer.

Not that anyone would ever have admitted it, but the Press, collectively, would have been disappointed with the lack of deaths. Modern news was all about death, the more people who died in an incident, the bigger the coverage.

The sad fact, for them at any rate, was that there had only been the one death and that hadn't been through typhoid alone.

News from the check of the sewers had finally come through as well and Doctor MacQueen had been delighted to read nothing but good news. It had been a last worry for him and he was relieved to know that the findings had not set them back in any way.

It was yet another sign that the corner had been well and truly turned. The Press would have to look elsewhere for sensationalism.

Ron Smith was certainly losing interest in the job he was still being asked to do. He had lived and breathed the subject of typhoid for nearly a month, but there was less and less to write about now. The worst of the crisis had past, so maybe it was time for Ron to go back to his crime stories and leave typhoid for someone else to mop up.

Unfortunately, for Ron, his editor did not agree. He wanted his best man on the typhoid story until there was no story left to tell. There was always the, distant, chance that another wave of the disease could hit the city.

Ron did not think that was the case, but his editor could not be shifted in his opinion. Ron had returned to his desk feeling nothing but anger mixed with a large dose of frustration.

Ron had noticed Shearer's eyes following him back to his desk. He also noted the slight smile on the young man's face. Ron knew that look; he had once been prone to look that way himself; back in the day when ambition still burned inside.

Ron knew that the quicker he got his old job back, the better. The day would come when Robbie Shearer would have to be put in his place but that day was still some way off. After the typhoid, however, the gloves would be off and the thought that went through Ron's mind was: *Let battle commence.*

Across the room, Robbie Shearer was thinking plenty himself. He, too, was frustrated but for totally different reasons. Here he was, covering the crime desk yet there was no crime to write about, other than the petty nonsense passing through the Sheriff Court.

He still hoped that a major story would come out of the Davie Milne investigation. He still hoped that the help he'd offered the police would bring him something in return. However, as each day went by, Robbie Shearer was left wondering if his big chance would ever come.

*

Ranald Cusiter kissed Phyllis and left the house at just after lunchtime.

He walked to his car and got in. He started the engine and engaged first gear. He moved the car away from the kerb, and made his way down to the lights on Westburn Road. He was visiting one of his shops; it was time to put in an appearance and check the books.

Most of what happened in the business world of Ranald Cusiter was now left to others. In truth, Cusiter had never really had a business head at all. On those early trips to London, he had relied on others to guide him in regard to what he bought. He worked on the principle that what was good for London was even better for Aberdeen.

It had worked.

Cusiter was to be visiting his outlet, which was situated at Holburn Junction. As per a prior agreement, he was able to park his car in the car park of the Prince Regent Hotel. He would return there for some lunch later but, for the moment, there was work to be done.

He visited his outlets every fortnight, though neither on the same day, nor the same time. His managers had to be surprised by his visit, so as to prevent them preparing for him coming by hiding anything they had not wanted him to see.

Cusiter trusted his managers, but only to a point. Everyone was capable of double-crossing, in the name of greed.

Cusiter got out of the car and locked the door. There was a slight drizzle in the air and he wore a coat and hat. As he turned away from the car, he paid little attention to a Ford Cortina parked across the street.

He should have paid attention to it, the car had been no more than two car lengths away from him, since he'd left home.

He pulled up his collar and walked through to Albyn Place. He turned left and started to make his way down to the junction.

He was almost the shop when the dark Cortina started to speed up. The car mounted the pavement, drove straight through Ronnie Cusiter, sending him into the air. It then sped off, through the lights at the junction and right down Holburn Street.

It had all happened in the blink of an eye, leaving behind shocked witnesses and a seriously injured Ronnie Cusiter.

Someone, in one of the shops, phoned both for an ambulance and the police. Some people hurried to see if they could help the victim, others hurried in the opposite direction, keen to put as much space between themselves and a police investigation as was possible.

*

Ogston received the news an hour later when he returned to Lodge Walk. He had been out interviewing the mysterious Susan, who currently arranged Gerry Craig's parties. She had turned out to be a young, trendy woman who seemed to constantly have pop music playing in the background, from a small record player plugged in in the corner of what passed for an office.

She had only been doing the job for the last two years, so could be of no help to Ogston with regard to the party back in nineteen sixty-one. She did, however, confirm that she kept a list of Aberdeen's most successful men and made a point of inviting them to one of Gerry's parties. She also confirmed that, occasionally, staff members were invited, particularly if they had done something special for the company.

And what about the girls?

They were acquired through the Bon Accord Acting Agency which, in turn, was part of the Saltire Acting Agency; the Head Office of which was in Edinburgh. Susan provided an address and telephone number.

Ogston had not liked Susan, nor the manner in which she spoke to him. Clearly, she felt that she worked under the protection of Gerry Craig and as such she was free to speak to anyone in any way she chose. Her manner was brusque and often, downright rude.

Ogston looked forward to the day when Susan would be caught doing something illegal. He would take pleasure in charging her.

Back at Lodge Walk, Ogston was brought up to speed with what had happened to Ronnie Cusiter. He had been run down, by a hit and run driver and was now in a serious condition in hospital.

Ogston pulled on his coat and headed for the door.

When he arrived at Foresterhill, he found Phyllis Duncan already there. She explained that one of the staff in the shop had phoned to let her know what had happened. She had made her way straight to Accident and Emergency.

Phyllis was crying and looking extremely distressed. "They won't let me see him," she then said, "I'm not family."

Ogston said he'd try to find out what he could. He managed to find a doctor, but there was little to be said, beyond the fact that Cusiter was in a very serious condition and the chances of him surviving were slim at best.

Ogston chose not to tell Phyllis how bad things were but, instead, simply said the doctors were doing all that they could.

Ogston then found Sergeant Alan Sangster, who had attended the scene and arranged for statements to be taken by those witnesses who had stayed to see the police.

Sangster explained, that as far as he could ascertain, the car was deliberately driven at Cusiter and at a speed, which seemed to show an intent to kill.

"So, someone wanted poor Ronnie dead," commented Ogston.

"It certainly looks that way, sir."

"Any news on the car that hit him?" was Ogston's next question.

"Dark Ford Cortina. No one got the registration. Couple of witnesses said there were two men in the car. It sped off down Holburn Street."

"No doubt to the nearest garage, where the colour will have been changed, along with the registration plate. I'm guessing that car won't look anything like it did an hour ago."

Sangster nodded.

Ogston went back to be with Phyllis. He took a couple of coffees with him, which he'd been able to get from one of the nurses.

It seemed pretty obvious who was behind this attempt on Ronnie Cusiter's life. The police speak to Gerry Craig and then to Ronnie. Within no time at all Ronnie is lying at death's door. If he had ever had anything to say against Gerry Craig then he was unlikely to say it now.

Yet again, Craig would walk away smelling of roses. Yet again, Ogston's blood boiled. More than ever he wanted to get the necessary evidence to put Craig away.

Ogston was still sitting with Phyllis when a doctor came out to speak to them. Ogston had already explained to the medical staff that Phyllis was as close to Ronnie as family, probably closer. They had agreed to keep her informed.

The doctor arrived with bad news. Ronnie had died having never regained consciousness. Phyllis was inconsolable. Ogston put his arm around her shoulder and she wept into his shoulder for a few minutes.

Eventually, Ogston arranged for Phyllis to be driven home and for a WPC to stay with her until a friend could be contacted.

Only then did Ogston go back to the office.

*

Gerry Craig received the call at the same time as Ogston got back to his office. Simpson had decided not to waste any time on Cusiter. He had decided on action and he was now phoning to tell Craig that that action had been successfully taken.

"I never told you to kill him," Craig had said.

"You told me to take care of him, boss and that's what I did," said Simpson. In his simple world *taking care of someone* could mean only one thing. "Anyway, boss, he's not dead yet."

"But is he likely to survive?" asked Craig.

"Probably not," admitted Simpson.

The call had ended there, but Craig was to find out later that day that Cusiter had died. He couldn't decide it he was happy or not. Maybe having Ronnie out of the way was for the best, at least he'd stop being that thorn in Gerry's flesh.

Later that evening, the doorbell rang and Gerry let Simpson into the house. They went to the study where Craig took an envelope from his desk drawer and handed it over.

"Want a drink?" he'd then asked.

"No thanks, boss," Simpson had replied, "I have a young lady keeping it warm for me, if you know what I mean?

Simpson was still grinning as Craig showed him out the front door.

16   16

The City and Woodend hospitals were still filled with typhoid patients come Thursday, 11th June. Only 8 new patients had been admitted, but the other 431 confirmed, or suspected, cases were still occupying beds and ward space.

No one had been allowed home.

Alison Young had the day off, but on her return to work on the Friday, she would be back at the City Hospital. Her work at Woodend was over.

Alison had woken that morning with happy memories of the night before. She had been out with Graeme and they'd had a lovely time.

They had gone to the cinema. There was still a ban on anyone under eighteen being allowed into a cinema, without being accompanied by an adult, and it had meant fewer people choosing to go in the first place.

They had gone to the Queen's Cinema, to see *The Man Who Shot Liberty Valance,* starring John Wayne and James Stewart. Both Graeme and Alison liked westerns and they'd sat in the back row, Graeme's arm around Alison's shoulder, and enjoyed every minute of the unfolding story.

After the film, they'd gone to a café on Union Street for a coffee and to talked some more. They'd then gone back to Alison's flat, where they had been required to spend some time in her own room, seeing as both her flatmates were in the living room, watching the television.

They had spent an hour talking.

They were finding that they had so much in common, which seemed to be bringing them closer together all the quicker.

When the time came for Graeme to go home, he didn't really want to. However, it would not have done Alison's reputation much good if he had been found in her bedroom come the morning.

They would have to have known each other a lot longer before anyone would be staying all night.

*

Whilst Alison was wandering around the flat that morning, Detective Chief Inspector Ogston was pulling together everything that was known, concerning the murder inquiry.

It was still a very slim file.

In light of Ronnie Cusiter's death Ogston now re-visited the evidence, only this time he was looking for anything that might be tied to Gerry Craig or any of the goons known to be working for him.

Was it possible that Craig had ordered Davie Milne's murder? If so, why? Ogston had uncovered nothing that linked the two men, other than that one party nearly three years ago.

It seemed highly unlikely, therefore, that Craig would have had any reason to be displeased with Davie Milne.

Ogston made some notes, hoping that writing things down might, in some way, sharpen his mind.

Davie Milne - blackmailer. The remaining accomplice likely to be Grace the tea lady. Need to check with the Council Staff Section for full details on Grace. We know, thanks to Doug Sim, many of those who were being blackmailed. Thankfully, the list isn't that long.

The fact that Davie Milne, Ronnie Cusiter and Joe Traynor were all at the party at Gerry Craig's on the same night, seems nothing more than coincidence. There may have been connections, but unlikely to find them now.

On the murder itself:

No sign of forced entry, so Davie Milne knew his killer.

No fingerprints, so killer had to be wearing gloves. Was that a sign of coming prepared to commit murder, it wouldn't have normally been cold enough for wearing gloves?

Murder weapon, nearest heavy object at hand. Sign of temper, but maybe not of being prepared for murder. Heat of the moment? Might it have been a woman? Height factor might preclude a woman. Would have had to have been quite tall.

Was Davie Milne being a blackmailer, the motive for the murder?

And as for Ronnie Cusiter – sorry.

*

By late afternoon, Ogston knew all he needed to know about Grace Holmes. She was one of four tea ladies who pushed their trolleys around the Council building, bringing cups of tea and coffee to the workers and thus preventing them from having to leave their desks.

It was a twice-daily ritual to meet in the corridor and get your cup filled. Staff would gather around, chatting in those few moments it took to collect their beverage. Things were said and more importantly, things were heard.

Grace had finished work for the day, so Ogston and Forrest decided to pay the lady a visit at home. She lived in a flat on Wallfield Place, in Rosemount. As far as her colleagues knew she wasn't in a relationship at the moment, though few confessed to knowing her that well and, therefore, anything was possible.

The two detectives climbed the stairs and knocked on the door that had the word *Holmes* stuck to it. The door was opened almost at once and the police officers were greeted by a highly attractive young woman, with long dark hair and big blue eyes. She wore a black dress and slippers.

Her expression asked the question: *Who are you?*

Ogston showed her his identification card.

He then introduced Forrest and asked to be let in. Grace stepped back and the two police officers entered the flat.

It was a two-roomed affair. The bedroom was to the front and the living room to the back. They were shown into the living room and offered a seat. Grace sat down herself and sought the reason for the police calling on her.

"Did you know a man by the name of Davie Milne?"

"Yes."

"Were you in a romantic relationship with him?"

"He was married but, yes, we had some fun together."

"Whose idea was the blackmail?" Ogston then asked. The bluntness had been deliberate.

Grace sank back into her chair. So, that was why they'd come to see her? Obviously, she had read about Davie's murder and wondered if blackmail might have provided the motive. Maybe this visit would confirm her suspicions.

"Davie's idea, though I spoke about it first. I meant it as a joke, but Davie immediately jumped on the idea and could see pound signs flash in front of his face. I'd mentioned how the staff seemed to forget I was there when they started gossiping. They really can be so indiscreet sometimes."

"So, you provided the information and Davie did the rest?"

Grace nodded. "We didn't see it as doing any harm. It wasn't as if the Councillors couldn't afford it."

"Blackmail is illegal, no matter whose moral code you apply, Miss Holmes," Ogston said. He then asked, "How did Davie pay you?"

"In cash. I put it into my bank account in small amounts so as not to attract attention to myself."

"So, you knew you were doing wrong?" added Ogston.

"I never really thought about it. I gave Davie information and he gave me money. I never gave much thought to the bit in the middle."

"Okay, you picked up on the general gossiping that went on in the corridors," Ogston then said, "but how did you get the actual evidence you'd need to present to your victims?"

"How d'you mean?" said Grace.

"You hear that a Councillor is fiddling his expenses, but how did you get the evidence of those fiddles? How did you get your hands on their claim forms?"

"I didn't," answered Grace. "We played on the fact all those Councillors were feeling guilty as hell about what they were doing. The mere fact that someone *claimed* to know what they were up to was enough. Davie just threw a few dates at them and said we knew they were fiddling. Guilt did the rest."

Ogston almost smiled. He'd spent all that time trying to discover how Davie Milne had got his blackmail evidence and here he was now being told there hadn't been any. In short, Davie Milne had bluffed his way to a small fortune.

"And what about those Councillors who weren't fiddling their expenses?" Ogston then asked.

"Oh, they were the ones we liked catching out the most. We knew they'd pay better money, seeing as they had a bigger secret to keep."

"So, you'd hear comments about some Councillor or other, having an affair and you'd pass that on to Davie."

"Yes."

"And what did Davie do with that information?"

"He got some mate to take photographs, then he'd send copies of the photos along with a veiled threat that we'd go public if payments weren't made."

Ogston decided to come back to the subject of payments later. For now, he changed the subject homing in on the relationship Grace may have felt she was having with Davie Milne.

"Were you in love with Davie?" Ogston then asked.

"Hadn't thought about it; we were just having fun."

"You did know that Davie was a womaniser, Grace and you were *never* the only woman in his life?"

Grace smiled. "I knew he was married, Chief Inspector, so the fact he was spending so much time with me made it crystal clear what a shit he was, especially when it came to women. I was under no illusions, if that's what you're thinking."

"Did Davie ever tell you about the information he received from other sources?" Ogston enquired.

Grace's expression changed. Maybe she was hearing this for the first time?

"What do you mean?"

"Just what I say. Davie didn't just depend on your information in picking his blackmail victims. There were other women."

Actually, Ogston only knew about Isla Montgomery, but he felt that if he painted the picture as black as possible then he might get a reaction from Grace.

"You telling me that Davie was blackmailing people I knew nothing about?"

"Probably" replied Ogston. "What kind of money was Davie asking from his victims?"

"We agreed we'd only ask for the money that was being fiddled. As I said, it was done more in fun than anything else. We just felt the money would be better off in our accounts than anyone else's."

"And what about those victims who were having affairs?" prompted Ogston.

"Much the same, as far as I knew. Look, it was just a bit of fun."

"You keep saying that Miss Holmes and, in your mind, it might have seemed like nothing but fun. However, to Davie Milne it meant much more."

Grace looked concerned. Was she missing something?

"What do you mean?"

"I'm sorry to have to tell you, Miss Holmes, but Davie Milne was stringing you along," Ogston then said. He told Grace the amount of money Milne had put in his Mitchell and Co account. He also told her that a large sum of money had been recovered from another source. Ogston concluded:

"So, you see Miss Holmes, your boyfriend was a very rich man indeed and yet you were never going to see much of it."

"The bastard," Grace announced to the world.

"Still think he cared for you?" added Ogston.

Grace considered the matter for a few seconds. Clearly, she had been conned as much as everyone else. In return for pocket money, she had provided Davie with information that had made him rich.

She felt betrayed. The tears flowed and Ogston left her to find a handkerchief in the handbag lying on the floor beside her.

Grace then provided a full confession, in which she filled in some of the gaps left by Doug Sim. As she spoke, she had felt more and more betrayed by a man she had thought, at least on occasions, to have loved her. She ought to have known better. After all, if a man can cheat on his wife, he can cheat on anyone.

Grace was formally arrested and they drove her down to Lodge Walk, where she was booked in and put in a cell, awaiting a brief court appearance the following morning.

Ogston went back to his office. He felt some sympathy for Grace. It was a case of a life destroyed through misplaced love. A young woman, destined to spend some time behind bars, simply because she fell under the spell of the wrong man.

17 17

It was now Friday, 12th June. A decision was announced in the newspapers that day. Senior pupils would be returning to school from the 16th of June, but for morning classes only. There was still to be no school dinners offered to pupils.

It was good news for everyone but the senior pupils, who had no doubt been enjoying their extended holiday. As for the primary schools, they would remain closed in the meantime.

It had also been announced, the day before, that William Low's had closed and would remain that way until the 22nd of June. No reason was given, though the company did say that the staff had been retained and would be carrying out work on the premises.

What hadn't been printed was that Samuel Reynolds had asked his Head Office for a transfer. He felt it would be in the best interests of everyone if he moved on and another manager could then have the job of rebuilding confidence in the public of Aberdeen.

In Lodge Walk, Detective Chief Inspector Ogston had spent the morning working on matters other than the Davie Milne murder. There were reports to sign off and opinions to be offered regarding other inquiries.

For Ogston, it made a refreshing change to talk about cases that just might be solved. He was still lost in other, more general matters when the phone rang. He picked up the receiver.

"Chief Inspector Ogston?" he said. A woman's voice started to speak in his ear.

"My name is Felicity Gardiner, I'm a junior partner at Edmonds and Ledingham. We have been dealing with the estate of Ronald Cusiter and I'm phoning to tell you that Mister Cusiter left a parcel in our possession, which has your name on it."

"Do you want me to come and collect it?" asked Ogston.

"If you would be so kind. We'll need to get you to sign for it, I hope you don't mind."

"Not at all. I'll be up as soon as I can."

"Very good. Just ask for me at reception," the voice said and the phone went dead.

Ogston put his receiver down and pondered for a moment on what Ronnie Cusiter might have left for him. He wondered *when* the parcel had been left with Edmonds and Ledingham. It had to have been relatively recently, as Cusiter hadn't know of Ogston's existence until he'd paid them a visit in the immediate aftermath of Davie Milne's death.

Ogston decided to waste no more time. He put on his coat and left the building.

*

Ogston arrived at the offices of Edmonds and Ledingham, which were situated at 1, Golden Square. The interior was mainly of dark, highly polished wood. Corridors ran, in both directions from the reception area. There seemed to be a number of offices, which probably meant a large number of staff. Those who were visible to Ogston had head bowed and seemed lost in whatever they were doing.

A young girl greeted him at reception and within a few minutes he was being asked, by Felicity Gardiner, to follow her through to what Ogston assumed was *her* office.

Ogston sat down as Felicity made her way over to a cabinet situated in the corner of the office. She was a young woman, probably not that long out of university. She had dark, short hair and a pixie-like countenance. She wore a black skirt and white blouse. There was a matching jacket hanging over the back of her chair.

All the time she was in Ogston's company her expression never veered from the serious. Felicity was obviously of the opinion that solicitors should never look happy.

She took a parcel, the size of a shoe box, from the cabinet and brought it over to her desk. She laid it down and then turned her attention to a pile of papers that were lying beside the telephone, which sat to the right of her desk. She took a sheet from the pile and slid it across to Ogston.

"If you could just sign and date that at the bottom," she said.

The policeman in Ogston made him read the content of the sheet of paper, before he came even close to putting pen to paper. It was simply an acknowledgement of receipt; he was not signing his life away. He put pen to paper.

Felicity then gave him the parcel. Written on the front, in large black letters, was:

For the attention of Chief Inspector Ogston (and no one else)

Ogston looked across at Felicity as she sat down. "When was this left in your possession?"

Felicity opened a folder in front of her and ran her finger down what appeared to be a list of dates and events. Her finger stopped its travels, presumably at the line referring to the parcel.

"The morning of the tenth of June."

The morning after he'd been interviewed at Lodge Walk, thought Ogston. *He must have been concerned that something might happen to him.*

Ogston had no more questions. He was keen to get back to his desk and find out what, exactly, was in the parcel. He thanked Felicity for her time and she showed him to the door. He tucked the parcel under his arm and set off towards Union Street. The journey back to Lodge Walk was a little quicker than usual.

Once back in his office, he took off his coat, hung his jacket over the back of his chair and started to rip the paper off the parcel. It was a shoe box. Inside were mainly photographs. He quickly deduced that these must be the photographs that Ronnie Cusiter had taken from Davie Milne's secret spot in the kitchen. So, he hadn't destroyed them after all.

Accompanying the photographs was a letter. Ogston lit a cigarette and sat back to read the contents.

Chief Inspector, if you are reading this, then I am dead; as I thought I would be, if I'm being honest.

You will already have deduced that these photographs were being used by Davie to blackmail a number of people. Telling you that I had destroyed them was the only real lie I told you.

Maybe someone in the photographs is your killer. All I can say is, it wasn't me. I hated Davie with a passion, but only for what he did to Phyllis. I have never loved anyone more than I loved Phyllis. Keep an eye on her for me. Please.

I have to tell you, Chief Inspector, that I am no crook. I know you didn't believe me, but I really did start the business with help from a third party. I can now tell you that that third party was my uncle in Canada, who leant me enough to open my first shop. I didn't tell you before because, quite frankly, it really was none of your business.

Davie pulled the H M Thompson job with two heavies from Glasgow one of whom was the safe-cracker. Can't give you any names. Sorry. Only knew because he blurted it out one day in the Pittodrie Bar. He was pished at the time and probably hadn't realised what he was saying.

As well as the photographs you should find a sheet of paper on which I have provided you with details that will, hopefully, allow you to lock Gerry Craig away for a very long time. I'm guessing Gerry ordered my death. God knows why, I was never going to be a threat to him and yet he'd always assumed, for some reason, that I was.

However, now that I'm dead he can't harm me anymore, can he? That being the case, I can tell you everything I know and provide you with what little evidence I have managed to piece together.

Gerry lives in a cesspit world and yet never gets himself covered in shit in the process. He likes to think he's protected on all sides. He likes to think the police will never build a case against him. He likes to think he's God's gift to the planet, but with complacency comes mistakes.

In fact, Gerry's made two of them.

Firstly, he tried to involve me in his city centre protection racket.

That was the reason I was invited to a party at Gerry's house. I was there twice. Both times I found myself in the company of a lovely girl called Karen. Her details are on the other sheet of paper, along with a brief statement she agreed to give me. But more about that later.

Anyway, whilst at that first party I was approached by a large scary looking man who answered only to Simpson. He tried to talk me into making monthly payments to him. He said that if I didn't then he couldn't guarantee the safety of my business and my staff. I knew I would be paying to be protected from Simpson himself, so I told him to get lost.

He did not take kindly to my attitude.

I was then invited to a second party. That was the party at which I met Phyllis. As you know, Davie was there as well. Nothing more than coincidence, I can assure you.

I was pressurised at that party as well. Simpson warned me again of what might lie ahead, if I didn't pay.

Once more, I told him to get lost, only using language a little stronger than that.

From that moment I knew my days might be numbered. In telling Simpson to get lost, I was really telling Gerry Craig to get lost and Gerry does not take kindly to anyone standing up to him.

Since that night there have been a couple of incidents in my shops, but nothing that I couldn't handle.

I would hope that if you quietly ask around other city centre shops, you'll find someone prepared to support what I'm telling you here. If you can get Craig for the protection racket then make sure you get Simpson as well. Craig just issues the orders it's Simpson who breaks bones.

And drives hit and run cars I bet, thought Ogston. He continued reading.

His second mistake was the girls.

The girls were acquired through the Bon Accord Acting Agency, which is a bona-fide agency, working out of offices on Union Terrace. However, beneath the surface of respectability, is a layer that is not so savoury.

Some of the girls are prepared to make their money anyway that they can. They get paid good money to attend Gerry's parties and for that kind of cash it goes without saying that they are expected to 'entertain' Gerry's guests. Some do, some don't. The ones who do, tend to be invited back again and again.

I'm sure you're getting my drift here.

The girls are collected and brought to Gerry's house. They are paid for being there and they are driven home afterwards. I spoke to Karen and one of her friends. They weren't too willing to tell me much at first. However, since my first meeting with Karen I've been putting a little money her way. I suppose I was trying to get her away from Gerry Craig, in my own small way.

Karen's gratitude for what I'd done for her, finally manifested itself in the statement you now have in your possession. She also managed to get her friend to make a statement, though it doesn't include much at present.

Karen's cost me a few bob these last three years, but if it ends up putting Gerry Craig behind bars, then every penny will have been worth spending.

The Agency pays the girls and Gerry pays the Agency. I expect the link won't be obvious but hopefully if you dig deep enough, you'll find something.

By the way, don't bother talking to anyone at their Head Office in Edinburgh, they know nothing about Gerry Craig or his parties.

Speak only to the man in charge in Aberdeen. His name is Corbett Alsop. He'll try to sound stupid, but he isn't, believe me.

If you can guarantee protection for Karen and her friend then I think you'll find they'll be very co-operative, especially if Craig and Simpson are on their way to prison.

Sorry you thought so badly of me, Chief Inspector. Maybe, as a result of what you've just read, you'll change your opinion of me ever so slightly.

I wish you every success in knocking Gerry Craig off his perch and wiping that smug expression off his face in the process.

If the Metropolitan Police could build a case against Stephen Ward (and he wasn't a criminal) then hopefully the Aberdeen Police can build a better one against Gerry who, everyone knows, hasn't got an honest bone in his body.

Once again, Chief Inspector, all I ask in return is that you keep an eye on Phyllis, at least until she meets someone else. I should also tell you that I changed my Will recently. I have left everything to Phyllis; the house, the shops, all my money. She won't want the half of it, but that's her problem now.

Anyway, I hope she finds the happiness she deserves.

Ronnie Cusiter

P.S. I never thought the Ranald idea would ever catch on.

Ogston sat back in his chair and lit a cigarette. The reference to Stephen Ward harked back to the Profumo Affair. Many believed that Stephen Ward had been innocent of all charges brought against him, even though the court saw fit to find him guilty in his absence. He had taken an overdose, from which he never recovered. Even at a time like that, the Establishment chose to close ranks and blacken a man's name even further.

Ogston now pondered for a moment on how best to move forward against Gerry Craig. Every step would have to be taken carefully. One whiff of police involvement wafting around Gerry's nose and he'd have had an expensive lawyer hot footing it to Lodge Walk before anyone could say *nearly got you.*

Ogston still had his suspicions about some of his colleagues. For the moment, all he had heard were rumours, but some of those rumours had been pretty strong and spread by officers he respected and who, he believed, would not have passed on such rumours unless they, themselves, believed them.

The problem was that without knowing names, it meant he had to pretty much mistrust everyone and that might have to include his own Superintendent. However, he couldn't see any way of keeping Cameron out of what he was doing. There would be certain requests, which would require his authority before they could make their way up the chain of command.

There was no way that Ogston could get around his immediate superior officer. He had no other option but to trust him. Without Cameron's help nothing that Ogston did would ever find its way to the Chief Constable and without the Chief getting involved, Gerry Craig would never see the inside of a cell.

Whatever went up the line it would have to be cast iron. There could be no mistakes in going after Gerry Craig. One more police cock-up and Craig could enjoy the Chief Constable's protection for years to come.

Ogston knew he would have to tread carefully, but he was more than ready to do just that.

*

The next day was the 13th of June. It was a Saturday but it still found Ogston at his desk. He had spent much of the previous evening pondering on matters pertaining to nailing Gerry Craig. It had meant that, when he'd gone to bed, he'd found sleeping almost impossible. At six o'clock he had given in and climbed out of bed. He'd had some breakfast and then made his way to work.

There were two lines of inquiry requiring careful planning. Firstly, there was the possibility of a major protection racket being conducted right under Ogston's nose, in the city centre of Aberdeen. Protection rackets were distasteful at the best of times, but Ogston found it even more annoying that it was happening all around him and he'd never been made aware of it.

He had come around to thinking about Ronnie Cusiter's shops. The heavies had been keen to pull Ronnie in to their racket for nearly three years. Ronnie had, single-handedly, kept them at bay. However, now that Ronnie was no longer there to stand up to anyone, would that open the door for the heavies to return? Was Phyllis now in some danger as a result?

She probably wouldn't want the responsibility of running three shops but, until she managed to sell them, she would have to accept that people would now come to her for decisions to be made.

Ogston's concern for Phyllis had led to him phoning her earlier and arranging for him to go and see her. Until he had spoken to Phyllis there was nothing further that he could do with regard to the protection racket.

There was, however, something he could do about Karen and her friend. They had to be contacted and told that the police were now investigating events that may have occurred at Gerry Craig's house, on the nights he'd thrown a party.

Ogston was also concerned that any action he now took at Lodge Walk would, in some way, become known to Gerry Craig's payroll police officers. The last thing he wanted was for Karen and her friend to be 'got at' before police officers could interview them formally.

To that end, Ogston called a couple of Detective Constables through to his office. He briefed them on what Ronnie Cusiter had told him and gave them the contact details for both Karen and her friend.

Ogston then told the officers to collect both girls.

"Get them to pack a bag and then take them to this address," Ogston then said.

One of the DCs recognised the address, which was in the Ferryhill area, as being a safe-house which had occasionally been used to keep high-powered witnesses, prior to commencement of the trial they were to give evidence at. Ogston gave them the keys and told them to stay with the girls until a protection rota could be drawn up.

"There's a phone in the house," Ogston had then said. "Phone me once you have them safe. Only talk to me, however. If I'm not at my desk don't leave a message; wait until you can speak to me in person."

"Okay boss," said one of the DCs, immediately picking up on the gravity of what he was getting involved in.

They both left Ogston's office, picked up their coats and made their way to a car parked out the back.

Ogston, meanwhile, put on his own coat and made his way up to Argyll Place. It was time to talk to Phyllis once more.

Half an hour later, Ogston was seated in the front room of Argyll Place, a cup of tea in one hand and a ginger biscuit in the other. Phyllis sat across from him; her eyes still dark from crying. The loss of Ronnie had obviously hit her hard.

Before Ogston could say anything, Phyllis told him that she now knew that the man she'd always called Ranald, should actually have been Ronnie. She was happy to refer to him as Ronnie from now on, after all that had been the name on all the documents she'd inherited.

Ogston began by explain that Ronnie had left a parcel for him. He said that the contents of the parcel had not only included the photographs from Davie's blackmail scam, but also a letter in which information had been provided on other matters. He, of course, was not prepared to say what those matters might be.

"He had mentioned he'd left something for you," Phyllis conceded.

"Did you notice any change in Ronnie, in the days leading up to his death?" Ogston asked.

"In what way?"

"Did he seem worried about something, for example?"

Phyllis smiled. "Ronnie was always worried about something. He was a caring man, no matter what you might have thought of him."

Ogston knew that he deserved that jibe. He'd never hidden his belief that Ronnie was crooked in some way. How wrong he had been.

"I totally mis-read him, Miss Duncan and for that I can only apologise. He *was* a good man; I can see that now."

Phyllis wondered what Ronnie had left for Ogston, to change his mind so radically.

"Anyway," Ogston then continued, "I came here to talk about something specific to the shops."

"I don't want them," Phyllis responded immediately. "I don't really want anything; I feel such a fraud."

The tears returned. Phyllis produced a handkerchief again and dabbed at her eyes and nose.

"You're no fraud, Miss Duncan. Ronnie loved you very much. It seems only right that you should inherit all that he worked so hard to build up."

"But I have no head for business, Chief Inspector. Left to my own devices I'd bankrupt the business in a matter of months."

"Then arrange to sell the shops," suggested Ogston. "Let someone else worry about them."

It seemed the only course of action open to Phyllis. She said she'd have a word with the solicitors at the first opportunity.

"Meantime, however," Ogston had then begun, "I need your permission, while you are still the legal owner of those shops."

"Permission? What for?"

Ogston explained about the protection racket and the fact Ronnie had been keeping trouble at bay for the best part of three years. Phyllis instantly looked worried.

"Am I in any danger?" she asked.

"I shouldn't think so," Ogston had replied. Not the strongest endorsement for Phyllis's safety, but probably the best she could expect.

Ogston then went on to explain how he intended to deal with the possibility of heavies returning to the shops demanding they become part of the racket. Once he had finished, he asked Phyllis to give him the green light to proceed.

"Do whatever is necessary, Chief Inspector," she had then said. "I know it's what Ronnie would have wanted."

Ogston thanked her and then asked if she had any information regarding the shops. He was looking for staff details, points of contact, that sort of thing. Phyllis had left the room, returning moments later with buff folder, which she gave to Ogston.

He'd laid down his cup and popped the last of his biscuit into his mouth. He then opened the folder and scanned through the contents. It seemed to contain everything he wanted. He did, however, quickly identify a problem for himself.

Ogston was hoping to put undercover police officers into each of the shops, along with cameras if at all possible. The hope was that a photograph could be taken of any heavy who came to the shop uttering threats and menaces. His problem, however, was that all the staff in the shops were women. His undercover officers, in that case, would have to be women as well.

Only, WPCs didn't get involved in front-line policing. If he was to get the help, he needed then he not only required the permission of the Woman Police Sergeant, responsible for the small team of WPCs, but also the agreement of each of the officers asked to go undercover.

No one could order them; they would have to volunteer.

But that was a problem for later. In the meantime, Ogston thanked Phyllis for her time, her permission and the folder she'd provided. He then made his way to the door, shook her hand, then turned and walked out on to the pavement. He paused and looked back. Phyllis looked so vulnerable standing there.

Keep an eye on her, Ronnie had asked. In that brief second Ogston could see no way that he'd be able to do that and it brought a great sadness upon him.

He then set off up the hill, hearing the door shut behind him.

*

On his return to Lodge Walk, Ogston enquired at the front desk if Superintendent Cameron happened to be in that day. Usually Saturdays took Cameron on to the golf course, though there were occasions when he'd come in at the weekend, usually when the Chief Constable had requested something.

Today was to be one of those occasions when he was at his desk. Ogston had hurried to his own office, put the finishing touches to information and requests he'd aim to pass across Cameron's desk and then made his way to the Superintendent's office.

As he knocked on the door, he still felt a sense of trepidation; after all he wasn't entirely sure that Cameron could be trusted.

Ogston was told to enter. He opened the door and walked into the room. Superintendent Cameron sat behind a desk covered in paper. He had a pen in his hand and appeared to be struggling with a report of some kind.

Clearly, the Chief Constable had requested something and Cameron was struggling in the delivery. He looked up; his anger evident in his expression. He had not liked being interrupted.

"Yes, Ogston, what is it?"

"I need to speak to you, sir."

"Have you solved that bloody murder yet?"

"No, sir, but I may be about to land a bigger fish that that."

Cameron's expression changed to one of interest. He laid his pen down and waved a hand in the general direction of a chair on the other side of his desk.

"Sit down."

Ogston told his superior officer everything, including his plan to catch the heavies involved in the protection racket.

"Gerry Craig, eh?" Cameron had said, sitting back in his chair and smiling. "I've been after that bastard since I first joined the Force. He's a slippery character, are you sure you can get enough on him?"

"That's what I'm working on at the moment, sir," Ogston said, getting the feeling that he *could* trust Cameron after all.

Cameron sat forward again as Ogston slid his search warrant request across the desk. Cameron asked why the warrant was being sought. Ogston explained about the agency and the fact it could well be a front for prostitution.

Cameron smiled all the more.

"If you can put Gerry away, Graeme, they'll give you a bloody medal, you do know that?"

And you'll bask in my glory, thought Ogston.

"Will you take this to the Chief Constable, sir?"

Cameron nodded. "I'll speak to the Chief on Monday. He'll be on-board, don't you worry. However, I ought to warn you that the Chief suspects we may have one or two Craig moles here at Lodge Walk. To that end, let's keep this between ourselves and the Chief, at least until we can make a move of some kind."

"I've heard the rumours as well, sir."

"Bet you thought twice about coming to me," Cameron then commented. He was smiling.

"I'd be lying if it hadn't crossed my mind, sir," said Ogston.

"Good man, Graeme, you'll go far. Now, leave this with me and I'll leave it up to you as to when you speak to Woman Police Sergeant Keddie about getting three of her girls for the undercover work. It won't be too dangerous for them, will it?"

"I think the danger will lie more with the manageress of each shop, sir. They're most likely to be threatened."

Cameron nodded. "I hope to God you're right, Graeme. Now get out there and nail the bastard."

"I'll do my best," Ogston said, as he made his way out of the office. He was already feeling a lot better now that he knew his secrets were safe from Craig's moles.

Just before Ogston left the office that day he received a call from one of the DCs currently holed up with Karen and her friend. All had gone well and both girls were now under police protection.

Ogston had drawn up a brief rota to allow that protection to continue. He had wanted to keep the numbers knowing about the girls, to a minimum. To that end the rota was short. Two officers would cover midnight to midday and a further two officers would cover the remainder of the day.

They were to speak to no one, other than DCI Ogston and DI Forrest. They were, however, informed that Superintendent Cameron was aware of what they were doing, just in case he had made contact for any reason.

18   18

It was now Monday, 15th June; a full month since the first typhoid victims had come to the attention of the medical profession in Aberdeen,

449 people were still in hospital, 394 of them confirmed cases of typhoid. However, thoughts were now turning to when patients could be discharged, rather than admitted.

Doctor MacQueen had little to tell the Press and, in turn, the Press had little to tell their readers. Ron Smith, once more asked to be taken off the typhoid story and once more his editor suggested they leave things as they were. Ron could no longer understand why his editor continued to think that way.

Ogston, on the other hand, had the bit between his teeth. All thought of Davie Milne had now gone, his focus was now entirely on putting Gerry Craig away.

Ogston had got to work early that morning. He had visited WPS Keddie before she had even had time to get her coat off.

Ogston had been of the mind that getting three women officers to volunteer for undercover work, was likely to be the most difficult part of his plan.

Women had only come in to the police in Aberdeen during the Second World War. Back then it had been as part of an auxiliary service. It had been 1947 before the first women police officers had been formally employed and initially, there were only three of them.

Policing was still seen as a man's world. Women officers were used for issues involving women and children, but there was never any thought of them dealing with front-line activities. The only women officers, currently working for Aberdeen City Police, were all in uniform and both the Chief Constable and Superintendent were concerned for their welfare were they to ever be put in harm's way.

As the women's section of the Police Force was essentially run separately from the men, the final decision, on whether or not the constables could even be approached, would lie with WPS Keddie. She was a formidable woman, who protected her charges at all times.

As it turned out, rather than put up barriers, WPS Keddie had been delighted that her girls were finally getting the opportunity to do some real police work. She had said, she felt sure she'd get three volunteers easily enough and she had been right.

Ogston had his three names by nine o'clock that morning.

He then went to speak with the small team of boffins, who dealt with all the technical matters that arose within the Force. He wanted three cameras, all of which could be activated remotely.

Obviously, if the WPCs were under threat, they would hardly have time to pick up a camera and take a picture, especially without being noticed. No, the photograph had to be taken, without the knowledge of anyone else in the shop.

Later that morning, one of the technicians went, with Ogston, on a tour of the three shops. One was situated at the point where Union Street became Albyn Place. Ronnie Cusiter had been just outside the front door when he'd been killed.

The other two outlets were in George Street and Market Street.

On their arrival, Ogston had explained what was planned and that Miss Duncan had given her permission. However, he still checked that the staff in each shop hadn't wanted to raise concerns of their own. Nothing had been forthcoming. In fact, all the staff seemed keen to see off the bullies once and for all.

The technician was then left to set up his equipment in each of the shops. He had been delighted to find that all three shops had been designed in exactly the same way, which meant it was possible to situate a camera in exactly the same place in each location. It was equally easy to run a wire from the camera to the counter, allowing the camera to be triggered without anyone at the counter having to move.

The cameras were positioned with all but their lenses covered so that any noise that was made in the taking of the pictures, would be deadened as much as possible.

By early afternoon there was a WPC in each of the shops. The technician had then gone to each location and briefed them in the operation of the camera. By the end of that day, the WPCs felt ready for anything.

Ogston had only been given permission to run an undercover operation for one week. He had to hope that the heavies would visit sooner rather than later. In the meantime, he had sent a couple of uniformed officers around the city centre shops to enquire if anyone knew anything about a possible protection racket that was being run by person, or persons, unknown.

Ogston hadn't expected much of a response, but he lived in hope anyway.

*

Rather than going straight home that night, Ogston decided to pay the safe-house a visit and check on how things were going.

He found the two girls watching television and the two police officers in the kitchen. Ogston was brought up to date with the fact that both girls were prepared to give evidence, were Gerry Craig ever taken to court. However, they were not prepared to live the rest of their lives cooped up in a police house, safe or otherwise.

If Craig wasn't in custody within a matter of weeks, then they'd withdraw that offer of help and take their chances back in the big, bad world. Ogston could understand their point. He didn't want things to drag on any more than was necessary either.

However, it did present him with another problem. He couldn't be sure that he could afford four detectives to be tied up with the girls for weeks on end. Even with Craig in custody it would be some time before he would appear in court. That meant the girls remaining under protection for possibly months, rather than weeks.

As Ogston left the house that night, he knew that he would have to come up with another solution. However, he already felt that he might have that solution, though it would require the arranging of a meeting before it could be put into action.

Ogston had checked his watch. It was just after six. He used the phone at the safe-house to dial a number. He was delighted that the number was answered and a brief conversation followed. Ogston then replaced the receiver and left the house.

*

Half an hour later and DCI Ogston was sitting in the Prince of Wales Bar. It was busy, but then the Prince of Wales always was busy. Ogston was pleased that he didn't recognise any faces as he'd entered the bar. He'd then bought himself a pint and sought a seat towards the back of the premises.

Moments later he saw Robbie Shearer stopping at the bar and ordering a drink for himself. He then came over and sat down beside Ogston. Ogston spoke first.

"I finally have a story for you, Mister Shearer, but it's not one you'll be able to write just yet."

Shearer wondered what game was being played.

"Is this about Davie Milne?"

"No, this is about a much bigger fish, possibly the biggest," said Ogston, taking a cigarette from his packet and lighting it.

Shearer twigged immediately as to who Ogston was probably talking about. There only was one truly big fish in Aberdeen.

"Gerry Craig?" he said.

Ogston nodded. Shearer's excitement levels rose instantly. He could feel his heart racing, as was his mind. He could already see that piece on the front page of the Evening Express with his name at the top of it. He could already see the editor elbowing Ron Smith aside and offering the crime desk to Shearer on a permanent basis.

He was pulled from his reverie by Ogston speaking again.

"I need your help."

Shearer sat forward. "I'm listening."

Ogston explained about the two girls who were prepared to give evidence against Craig. Shearer could already see the Nationals throwing a fit at missing out on a story of this magnitude. He would get the scoop on it; it would be the name of Robbie Shearer that would be attached to it.

"Just think of the story those girls could give you," Ogston then said, "if they live," he then added with chilling honesty.

Shearer knew exactly what Ogston was talking about.

"You want us to protect them?" he then asked.

"You'd be protecting your story as well," said Ogston. "Once they've had their day in court, we can arrange a new life for them somewhere outside of Aberdeen. In the meantime, we need them safe, but ready to testify when the court case comes around."

"*If* the court case comes around," added Shearer. He'd heard the stories about Gerry Craig and also how good his lawyer was. Money can buy anything, including freedom.

"Oh, we'll get him into court, don't you worry about that," said Ogston.

Shearer presumed the police had to have already gathered a great deal of evidence against Craig if Ogston was as confident as he was. His excitement level rose even higher.

"I'll need to run this past my editor," Shearer then said.

"I understand, but I don't have much time. You'll need to get back to me tomorrow."

"I can do that," said Shearer, eagerly.

Ogston took some papers from his pocket and handed them to Shearer. The papers were duly shoved into the inside pocket of the journalist's jacket.

Shearer finished his pint and hurried back to his desk. He had to get his thoughts together before he spoke to the editor. But that discussion would have to wait for the morning.

Ogston went home. He would have a lot of work to get through, over the next few days, and he wanted to get all the rest he could.

*

The next morning, Corbett Alsop arrived at the offices of the Bon Accord Acting Agency and unlocked the main door. The time was a quarter to eight.

For him, it would be anything but a normal day.

He had no sooner taken a step into the office space, when a group of men rushed him from behind and he was pushed across the floor and into a chair.

He was about to protest, when the leading man thrust an identification card in his face.

"I am DCI Ogston and I have a warrant to search these premises. I also have a number of questions to ask you, so if you'd just remain seated, I'll get back to you as soon as I can."

Ogston then barked out some instructions to the rest of the team with him. They then began a thorough search of the premises, while Ogston made arrangements to have Alsop taken down to Lodge Walk.

Before he was taken away, Ogston asked Alsop about the other staff who worked there.

"There's only Tracy and she won't be in until nine."

Ogston told the others to expect Tracy around nine and then left with Alsop.

*

Alsop said very little. He denied any knowledge of wrongdoing at Gerry Craig's parties, claiming that he only sent the girls to make up the numbers and balance the sexes. The money he paid the girls was by way of a retaining fee; he didn't want them going to another agency.

"Do you ever get these girls an actual acting job?" Ogston had eventually asked.

"They're not that easy to come by, especially in the north-east of Scotland. That's the main reason I send them to the parties; it gives me an excuse to pay them something."

"Are they paid out of agency funds?" Ogston enquired.

"Of course, where else would the money come from?"

"A third party," suggested Ogston. "Someone with an interest in making those parties a success."

"No idea what you mean," said Alsop.

Corbett Alsop was not what Ogston would have described as very masculine looking. He came across as being rather effeminate in his actions and seemed to constantly overplay being offended by whatever the DCI might suggest.

Alsop wore very brightly coloured clothing and Ogston put him down as being a bit of a peacock, always preening himself to ensure he always looked at his best.

"Do girls get booked for other parties, or are we just talking about Gerry Craig?" Ogston then asked.

"Mister Craig is the only one to make use of our agency for that purpose."

"And does Mister Craig pay anything to the agency for those girls?"

"Well, of course there are expenses to be met."

"By Mister Craig?"

"Not directly, no. Mister Craig pays the agency a standard fee and from that, we pay the girls whatever they are due."

Ogston made notes of everything Mr Alsop said. He kept Alsop occupied until lunchtime, by which time some of the team had returned from their search of the agency. They had come up trumps.

Tracy had arrived at nine and made them all a cup of tea. She'd thought it all very exciting to have her workplace overrun with police officers. She had even flirted with a couple of them, before sitting down to file her nails while police officers continued to swarm all over the premises.

Around mid-morning, a key had been found in Alsop's office that didn't seem to fit anything. By that time Tracy was sitting at her desk reading the morning paper. She had been asked if she'd any idea where the key might fit. She had happily told them that there was another room, which the agency rented, in the basement. Two officers had gone down to that other room and found a number of items, which were to prove of great interest to all those involved in the investigation.

They had gathered up books, papers and other random notes and brought them back to Lodge Walk so that the DCI, himself, could run an eye over them.

Alsop was to be kept in an interview room until Ogston said he could be released. He was to be denied any phone calls, but they could provide him with some food should he request it.

Ogston did not want Alsop tipping off Gerry Craig that a police investigation of any kind, was underway.

The information, found in the basement room, was better than anything Ogston could have wished for. Alsop had kept detailed records of all the transactions connected with the girls and by association, the parties. Each girl had been listed along with any payments made to her. More importantly, he had written notes beside some of the entries, explaining why some girls had paid more than others. The words 'services rendered' appeared at regular intervals.

In terms of bringing Gerry Craig down, it was dynamite. He might try to argue that he hadn't known what was going on at his own parties, but Ogston felt sure a half-decent jury would see though that in a heartbeat.

Ogston went back to speak with Alsop. Confronted with the fact that the police had his unofficial finance records, Alsop was quick to seek a deal.

"I can give you the final piece of the jigsaw that will see Gerry going away for a long time."

"And what would that be?" enquired Ogston.

Alsop sat forward. "First, I need your assurance that I will walk away from all this. Once I give you Craig, I need time to disappear, otherwise my life won't be worth anything."

"It depends on what you are offering, Mister Alsop," said Ogston.

"I have tapes," Alsop replied, a slight smile crossing his face. "I have Gerry talking about his parties. In fact, I have Gerry *bragging* about his parties. In short, Chief Inspector, I have Gerry talking himself into prison."

Ogston could not believe his luck. The finance records had been worth having in themselves, but if there really was taped evidence of Craig incriminating himself, then there wouldn't be a need for *any* jury, his guilt would be beyond doubt.

"Okay, once we've heard your tapes Mister Alsop maybe then we'll discuss deals," Ogston said.

Alsop sat back in his chair. "No way, Chief Inspector. I want that deal agreed, written and signed off, before you get anything more out of me."

"But the tapes might be worthless to us," insisted Ogston.

Alsop smiled again. "Look, Chief Inspector, most of the girls I sent to Gerry's parties called themselves actresses, only very few of them had ever acted in their lives. Not unless you call faking it during sex as acting. I have Gerry on tape talking about the type of girl he wanted at his parties and his reasons for having them there. He completed business deals, but only after the girls had entertained Gerry's guests. It was sex that got him those deals, Chief Inspector, not Gerry's dazzling business acumen.

Ogston did not need to consider the matter any further. Clearly, Alsop had evidence that would be the end of Gerry Craig. After all these years chasing him, they finally had the evidence to put him away and lose the key. Ogston agreed to Alsop walking away, after the tapes had been heard. A loose agreement was drawn up and both parties signed it. Ogston was pretty sure that both Cameron and the Chief Constable would have agreed with his actions, had he bothered to involve them.

After all, putting Craig away would be a major feather in everyone's cap. The Chief would dine out on that story for some time to come.

*

While Ogston was coming to his agreement with Alsop, Robbie Shearer was leaving his editor's office.

The editor agreed that Shearer was on the verge of one of the biggest stories to reach the pages of the Aberdeen Journals in many a year.

However, he had also told Shearer that Aberdeen Journals did not have the kind of money that would be needed to keep two witnesses in protection, for any length of time. Only the national newspapers could cover that kind of cost and not miss it.

Much as it had pained the editor to say it, but he'd told Shearer that he'd have to go a national paper and give them the scoop.

Shearer's heart sank. He hadn't been totally surprised by what his editor had said to him. He'd rather worked it all out for himself. That didn't diminish the way he felt, in any way. He would have to give away his biggest story, someone else would write it first; someone else would have their name on the front page.

"But, remember," the editor had then said, "you'll still write the local version. Your name will still be at the head of our story and for those readers who missed the morning papers, it'll seem like a scoop to them."

Shearer had brightened hearing those words. It mightn't be so bad after all. There would only be a matter of hours between the national story and his.

It was with that in mind that Robbie Shearer left the Aberdeen Journals offices in Broad Street and made his way up to Belmont Street. He paid a visit to the local editor of the Scottish Daily Express.

Shearer pitched his story. The editor was instantly interested. He had access to a budget that could cover the cost of keeping two witnesses safe for as long as it might take to get Gerry Craig to court. In the meantime, those two girls would be providing his paper with the biggest story they'd had in a while.

Shearer agreed to the Express leading with the story, when the time came to do so. Shearer would then write the local version. The Scottish Daily Express would print in the morning and Shearer would write his piece for the Evening Express that same day. It might no longer be a scoop, but it was still a bigger story than Ron Smith had ever written. That was good enough for Robbie Shearer.

Shearer told the Daily Express editor that he'd now phone his contact at Aberdeen City Police and arrange for how the girls could be collected. Shearer would then contact the Express with that information.

Within two hours, all contacts had been made and the girls moved from the police house. The Daily Express had arranged for them to be taken out of Aberdeen, but even the police weren't being told exactly where they would be housed. Ogston could see them whenever he wanted, but there was still concern for Craig's moles, so secrecy was of the essence.

As DCI Ogston sat at his desk that evening, he couldn't help but smile. Everything had finally come together nicely. Alsop's tapes had been retrieved and listened to. There was no way Gerry Craig's lawyer was going to get him out of this mess.

Alsop had been released, mid-afternoon, and was already on his way to London, where he intended re-inventing himself and hoping that he never crossed paths with anyone even remotely connected to Gerry Craig.

Graeme Ogston went home happy that night. He was looking forward to the morning. He was looking forward to Gerry Craig's expression when all the evidence was presented to him.

Sometimes, life just couldn't get any better.

19   19

Tuesday, 16th June, arrived with bright sunshine in the sky and real warmth in the air.

Ogston almost floated into work that morning, such was his joy at being able to finally knock Gerry Craig off his perch. He took time to enjoy a cigarette and cup of coffee before collecting Forrest, along with two uniformed officers and heading off to Gerry Craig's house.

It was eight o'clock and Aberdeen was just beginning to wake up. The roads were getting busier, as people made their way to work. It was a happy car that drove out Queens Road, up Forest Road and on to Rubislaw Den North.

On arrival at the house, the four police officers almost marched to the door and Ogston rang the bell. It took a few moments but eventually the door was opened, only this time by a petite young woman, wearing a maid's uniform.

"We're here to see Mister Craig," Ogston said, pushing past the woman and heading into the hallway. "Where is he?" he then said, looking back at the somewhat concerned, maid.

"I'll need to......," she began to say.

"Okay, we'll find him ourselves then," interrupted Ogston, as he set off towards various open doors.

He found Gerry and Agnes Craig in the dining room. They were having breakfast and Gerry was reading the paper.

"What the......," Gerry Craig began to say, as Ogston entered the room.

"Charge him, Inspector," Ogston said, cutting Craig short.

Forrest began to formally charge Craig on a number of counts. Craig wasn't listening. He was too busy telling Agnes to contact their solicitor. Agnes put her tea cup back in the saucer and said she would make the call as soon as she'd found the number.

By the time Ogston got back to Lodge Walk Craig's solicitor, Harry Fulton, was already waiting for them. Fulton was a typical defence solicitor; slimy in the extreme, immaculately dressed and keen to get his extremely rich clients off, no matter what it might take.

Harry Fulton usually worked on technicalities. He'd got many a guilty client off simply because the police paperwork hadn't added up. Ogston would make sure he'd not get his client off this time.

Ogston had never liked Harry Fulton. The man had no scruples, he would cheerfully have watched a serial killer walk free rather than lose a fee.

Craig was led to an interview room and allowed a few moments with his solicitor, before they were joined by Ogston and Forrest. Graeme Ogston had never looked forward to an interview as much as he was looking forward to this one.

Ogston found Gerry Craig looking as smug as usual. He had, obviously, had his head filled with the usual bravado from Harry Fulton. Ogston could almost hear Harry's booming voice:

"Just give me half an hour and I'll have you home before your coffee's gone cold."

Ogston laid the papers he'd brought with him on the table. Forrest was carrying a small tape recorder, which he also placed on the table. Ogston then lit a cigarette and deliberately blew smoke into the faces of Gerry Craig and his solicitor.

Fulton glowered at him, but Craig continued to smile. He was so sure that he'd be released soon.

Ogston eventually took a sheet of paper from near the top of the bundle he'd brought in to the room and slid it across the table towards Harry Fulton.

"The list of charges we've brought against your client, just in case he forgot any of them."

Fulton looked down at the sheet of paper and then he, too, smiled.

"This is nonsense, Chief Inspector, and you know it."

"Which charge in particular is nonsense, Mister Fulton?" Ogston then asked.

"Well, all of them of course. There can't possibly be any evidence to substantiate any of this."

"Listen to Mister Fulton, Inspector Forrest," Ogston then said, a note of sarcasm in his voice. "There, apparently, can't *possibly* be any evidence."

"That *is* what he appears to think, sir," added Forrest.

Both police officers continued to stare at Gerry Craig, with only the occasional glance at Fulton. For the first time, Craig's expression began to change. Smug was giving way to concern and the glances between client and solicitor were becoming more noticeable.

"Come on then, Chief Inspector, take your best shot and then we can all get out of this stuffy room and get on with our lives," Craig then said.

It was now Ogston's turn to smile. He puffed on his cigarette for a moment, then placed it in the ashtray and reached for the tape recorder. Next, he produced the first of the small reels he had been given by Alsop.

Both Craig and Fulton watched, with growing concern, as the tape was placed on the spool and pulled through to attach to the empty reel on the other spool. Ogston then pushed the play button and watched Craig's face closely. The words coming from the machine could be clearly heard by everyone in the room.

Of course, they weren't just any words; these were Gerry Craig's words and delivered by Gerry Craig himself. They were damning words, they were words that confirmed guilt and the fact they were in his own voice, made it next to impossible for him to deny anything.

Fulton glared at his client. His expression said:

What the hell have you done?

On the tapes (for all three were played to Craig), he spoke of the need for the girls at his parties and what he expected of them when they attended. He admitted he would pay the agency extra, if the girls provided extra. Alsop had been right, on the tapes Craig was bragging.

He wanted Alsop to know what a powerful man he was and what his money could buy. In the process, of course, he was admitting to all manner of criminality.

Harry Fulton looked back at Ogston. He wasn't looking so confident now.

Gerry Craig, meanwhile, sat in silence his face turning various shades of red as his anger levels rose.

When the last of the tapes finished Ogston sat forward and, this time, looked straight at Harry Fulton.

"Still reckon we have no evidence?"

"I wish to have some time with my client," Harry Fulton then said.

"Not yet," replied Ogston. "We're not finished."

Ogston then talked both Craig and Fulton through the fact they had witness statements as to what went on at the parties. Those statements provided eye witness accounts of events at the parties that seemed to support the very thing Craig had been heard asking for on the tapes.

During the parties his home was, effectively, being used as a brothel and the girls attending his parties were expected to prostitute themselves, all in the name of entertaining his guests and winning him kudos in the business world.

The financial records, from the Bon Accord Acting Agency, further proved that Gerry Craig had paid for services that, on so many levels, broke the law.

Ogston chose not to mention the possibility of the protection racket. He didn't want Craig calling off his heavies; he wanted photographic evidence of their existence and then, that too, could be waved under Craig's nose.

Gerry Craig was going away for a long time and his incarceration would begin immediately. He would be kept in one of the cells until the court case could be arranged. The police would strongly argue that, were he released, Gerry Craig would do a runner.

The man had the money to go anywhere he chose. He wouldn't hang around to defend himself in court; he knew how guilty he was. There was no doubt he'd run and there wasn't a judge in the country who would have disagreed with the case being put forward by the police.

Harry Fulton left Lodge Walk knowing that the best he could now achieve would be damage limitation. No matter what Harry Fulton said now, his client was going to prison. All Harry could do was prepare Agnes for the inevitable time apart from her husband.

Ogston went back to his office, sat back in his chair and laughed out loud.

"At last, at long last, we can put that bastard behind bars and watch him rot."

"What about the protection racket, sir?" Forrest then asked.

"We've only got the week to see if anything happens," replied Ogston. "But even if that goes nowhere, we've still got him, the protection racket would just have been the icing on the cake."

*

Tuesday had brought good news to the Aberdeen City Police. It had also brought good news to Doctor MacQueen and his team. Only one new patient had been admitted to hospital and there were no reports of any other suspected cases.

There were still 450 people in hospital. Doctors would now need to decide on when at least some of those people could be discharged. That decision would be entirely up to the hospital authorities. Patients would need to be clinically well before they'd be tested to ensure they were not still carrying the disease. Only then would they be considered for release.

Normality was returning everywhere. Alison Young was back doing her usual duties at the City Hospital. Sandy Burnett no longer needed to meet with Doctor MacQueen every day and his daily routine no longer centred around typhoid.

Ron Smith, meantime, had been told by the editor that he would be back on the crime desk as from Monday, 29th June. He had also been told about the Gerry Craig story and the fact it would have to go to young Shearer. The editor then said he was of a mind to have two dealing with the crime desk. Ron was getting a partner, whether he wanted one or not.

Ron would have to come to terms with working with Robbie Shearer and also with the fact that he'd missed out on the biggest crime story Aberdeen had read about in many a year.

The fact that Robbie had had to miss out on the scoop had rather lessened the blow, at least in Ron's own mind.

*

The following day Graeme had telephoned Alison's work and been quite surprised to find that she was on duty and he could speak to her. They had arranged to go out that night.

Not long after talking to Alison, Ogston was called to one of the interview rooms. A woman had called asking to speak to the officer in charge of the Davie Milne murder. She had some information, but would only speak with the officer in charge.

Ogston met up with Forrest and they went in to the room together. They had been given the name Yvonne Rigby and, as they sat down, Ogston found himself studying the woman more closely.

She looked to be in her mid-thirties. She had dyed blonde hair, styled in a perm that made her look older than her years. She was dressed in rather drab clothing and there seemed to be a haunted look in her eyes.

Yvonne Rigby was there to tell a story. She spoke about her husband; her abusive husband. She spoke of having lived with the man through ten years of marriage and how, in that time, he had occasionally beaten her, especially after a drinking session.

She then spoke about Davie Milne. He had flirted with her when she'd been in buying her cold meat at William Low's. He'd then bumped into her, quite by chance, when she was on Union Street one day. They'd gone for a coffee and got talking. They had then started meeting on a Sunday afternoon.

Up until a couple of weeks before Davie Milne's death she had been meeting him nearly every Sunday. She would drive to the Mastrick Shopping Centre, pick him up and then drive to Countesswells, where they'd park in a quiet spot and have sex.

She'd found it all very exciting. It made her feel young again.

But around the last time she'd met with Davie, she had begun to suspect that her husband might have known about what was going on. He'd accused her of being different in some way and demanded to know what had changed. She'd played it down, but felt sure he hadn't believed her.

Yvonne Rigby was now of the opinion that her husband had killed Davie Milne.

However, when pressed for details she hadn't been able to provide any. There was no evidence to connect Yvonne Rigby's husband to Davie Milne and even Yvonne couldn't explain how her husband would ever have found out where Davie lived.

It seemed like another dead end to Ogston, so he'd asked Forrest to deal with interviewing Mr Rigby. That interview had taken place later that day. Forrest quickly deduced that Rigby knew nothing specifically about his wife, he merely suspected that she was having an affair as her manner towards him had changed.

He had admitted to sometimes losing his temper with her, mainly when he had a drink in, but as Yvonne had not wished to press charges, Forrest could do no more than warn Rigby that his actions could land him in court one day.

All that was reported back to Ogston and the matter closed.

20 20

It was now Thursday, 18th June.

The night before Graeme and Alison had enjoyed more time in each other's company. They had gone to the Majestic Cinema where they'd sat through *Under The Yum Yum Tree,* starring Jack Lemmon and *Women Of The World,* an Italian-made B-movie.

There had been little choice, the cinemas still seemed awash with X-rated films. Graeme and Alison had presumed that, although *Under The Yum Yum Tree* was also an X, it might at least carry some humour, if Jack Lemmon was in it.

Women Of The World had turned out to be a series of short, travelogue-style films, that had been cut together to make something suitable, at least in length, for cinema release.

Unfortunately, at least for Graeme Ogston's embarrassment levels, the film had spent more time appreciating the female form than ever exploring the geography of any particular country. He couldn't begin to think what must have been going through Alison's mind.

Probably, *why's he brought me to this?*

The balcony of the Majestic was split into two distinct areas with a corridor running between them, off of which came the stairs down to the entrance. Graeme and Alison had found a seat in the back row of the front section. There was no one else there.

Given how bad the Italian film had been, Graeme was beginning to understand why. It had nothing to do with the typhoid, it was just the standard of the films that was keeping everyone away.

Graeme had hoped Jack Lemmon would save the day.

Between films, Graeme took the chance to apologise to Alison for some of the content of the Italian film. As it was, she laughed and told him she wasn't *that* easily offended. She then added that it hadn't just been the abundant flesh that had made it a bad film.

The main feature didn't prove to be much better. Again, sex was at the core of the story, although Hollywood's idea of sex did differ considerably to that of the Italians. There were a few laughs, but as a film it was a crashing disappointment.

The film had finished and the few patrons still left in the cinema had stood for the national anthem. They'd then made their way out of the building.

Alison had invited Graeme back to her flat. This time, she had bought a half bottle of wine and it, along with two glasses, were sitting in her bedroom, when they arrived back. Again, both flatmates were glued to the last television programmes of the day, so Alison had been happy to be able to close the bedroom door on them.

She and Graeme had spent a pleasurable hour in which they had gone as far, sexually, as either was prepared to go at this stage of their relationship.

Thoughts of the night before were still in Ogston's mind as he sat as his desk, that morning, reflecting on all that had happened over the previous month. Amidst all the turmoil of a typhoid epidemic, a murder inquiry had taken him down many roads, none of which had actually led to a murderer's name.

He may not have solved a murder, but he had solved a raft of other crimes, all related in some way to Davie Milne.

Gerry Craig was going to prison, probably for a very long time. That had been something Ogston had never thought possible.

He had solved a five-year-old robbery and even though two of the three men were still at large, the file in Lodge Walk could now be closed.

He had two people in custody awaiting their punishment for the part they'd played in Davie Milne's blackmail scheme. He also hoped that all the local Councillors would consider being a little more truthful when completing their expenses claims.

His only regret, regarding his actions over the last month, was the fact he'd been so wrong about Ronnie Cusiter. He wished he'd had the chance to tell Ronnie that. However, that was never going to happen now thanks to the mindless actions of one of Gerry Craig's gorillas.

On that subject, Ogston still had men looking for Simpson, but so far to no avail. He had obviously heard his boss had been arrested and done a runner. Ogston felt sure that a thug like Simpson would surface again somewhere, providing muscle for some other kingpin of crime.

Hopefully he'd do something stupid and be lifted for it.

Yes, all in all, it had been a successful time for solving every crime but the murder that had started it all.

Ogston gave everything one last sweep within his mind and then came to a decision. He pushed back his chair and stood up. He went to see Superintendent Cameron. He went to tell him that he was closing the Davie Milne murder inquiry, at least for the foreseeable future. Maybe, one day, new evidence would come to their attention and the case could be re-opened again.

Cameron had seen no reason to question Ogston's decision. He was still celebrating the fact Gerry Craig would no longer lord over the city of Aberdeen. He still had the mental picture of the Chief's face when he'd been told that the evidence against Craig was solid. That would keep him going for long enough.

Ogston returned to his desk and picked up on a file that had been left on his desk.

Within a matter of hours, all thoughts of Davie Milne had been well and truly banished from his mind.

*

The following morning was Friday, 19th June. It was a bright and sunny morning. Evelyn Gauld, a twenty-three-year old assistant librarian, became the first typhoid patient to be discharged from hospital. There hadn't exactly been a fanfare of trumpets, but her departure from hospital had been acknowledged as being quite a milestone and a sure sign that the disease had been beaten,

Over the following month all the patients would be discharged from hospital.

The main legacy left by the typhoid epidemic, would be that Aberdeen would remain one of the top spots in Britain for good personal hygiene. Food was never to be handled in the same way again as more stringent measures were introduced to ensure that something like typhoid never raised its ugly head again.

Outside of Aberdeen changes were being made as well. The government was taking steps to ensure that the corned beef stock no longer contained tins that had been lying around for years. People had to have faith in what they were buying and the habits of old simply had to change.

The Queen visited Aberdeen on the 27th of June and in doing so, sent out a message far and wide that Aberdeen was as safe a place to visit as anywhere. Thankfully, over time, more and more people formed the opinion that if it was safe enough for the Queen, then it was safe enough for them.

Normality slowly returned to the city of Aberdeen.

Aberdonians had come through dark days, days in which some businesses had gone under and others would take months before recovering. But recover they would, both the businesses and the people who had been infected by the disease.

In the years to come fewer and fewer people would remember those darks days. The events of 1964 would cease to have any real meaning, simply being consigned to words in a newspaper or history book.

It would take another medical crisis, this time world-wide, to bring meaning back to the actions taken all those years ago.

EPILOGUE

You might like to know what happened to the people you've just been reading about.

Doctor Ian MacQueen died in 1992, at the age of 82. His role as Medical Officer of Health had ended in 1974 when the posts were removed from the National Health Service. In his time as MOH he had promoted contraceptive counselling for teenagers – controversial at the time – and Aberdeen had been the first city to introduce the service.

Gerry Craig went to prison. There had been no success in photographing anyone involved in the protection racket. However, when the papers reported Gerry Craig as being off the street, shop owners came forward in their numbers, including one photographic outlet who brought evidence with them of the men involved.

As a result, some of Gerry Craig's employees also found themselves going to prison. Simpson was finally caught and charged with the murder of Ronnie Cusiter. At his trial, little more than circumstantial evidence was produced but Simpson looked a thug and the jury clearly agreed. He was found guilty and sentenced.

Ogston had added that to his list of successes.

Gerry Craig's prison sentence turned out to be a lot longer than his body's ability to survive it. He died in 1969.

On the second last day of January, 1965; the same day as Winston Churchill's funeral, Graeme Ogston and Alison Young got engaged. They were married at the end of November the same year. They would have two children, one of whom would join the police and rise to the rank of Superintendent, something his father had never aspired to.

Sandy Burnett's role also changed in 1974 when the Department he worked in was closed down. Having carved out a career that was, essentially, administration driven Sandy played a major part in the formation of regional health services after the advent of the Grampian Region in 1975. Health services went through a never-ending series of changes in the years after 1975 and Sandy was involved in many of them, in one way or another. He eventually retired in 1994.

Inspector Forrest remained an Inspector until the day he retired, which was in 1975. He had been happy doing what he did and for the last few years had spent most of his time working with the new recruits. He had enjoyed his time working with DCI Ogston and felt that he learned a lot.

Gordy Jamieson fully recovered from typhoid and went on to reach the rank of Inspector. There had been no one more surprised than Gordy that he'd managed that. There were still, however, many around the police office who understood little of what he said.

Phyllis sold both the house and shops and left Aberdeen. She moved to Glasgow, where she met and married her second husband. She never spoke of her first husband, or of the man she'd really loved but had never been given the time to build a life with.

Ron Smith eventually became editor of the *Evening Express* in 1970, a job he only held for two years as he died young, succumbing to cancer long before his time.

Robbie Shearer never got the break that would take him away from Aberdeen. The Gerry Craig story had been the pinnacle of his career and that had only lasted a few weeks. After that, it had all been downhill. He had eventually moved from crime to become the sports' journalist for the *Press and Journal*. He had a unique way of writing about Aberdeen's home games. He'd settle himself in the Pittodrie Bar, twenty minutes before the game was due to end and wait for the fans who had been at the match to arrive. Robbie's report would then be an amalgam of various opinions gathered from the Pittodrie Bar clientele. As a result, Robbie's account of a game might not always have been as accurate as it should have been. He'd even got the score wrong in one report, though a colleague had managed to correct the error before going to press.

In 1967, William Low closed their shop in Aberdeen. The customers had never returned in suitable numbers. The company never tried trading in Aberdeen again.

In 1994, William Low ceased to exist as a separate trading name, when it was bought over by Tesco.

Also, in late September of 1994, a group of volunteers were clearing out a house in Carnoustie, hoping to find some valuable items to sell on behalf of the charity for which they worked.

In a bedside drawer, one of the volunteers found a dairy. It had 1964 on the front and was filled with neat, though very small, writing. The volunteer thought the contents might be of interest, so she put the diary in her pocket and went about her business.

The same night she had finally got around to reading the contents of the diary. Most of it was quite boring. Just the daily routine of the individual who had initially owned it.

That was until the month of May.

The entry for the 20th May, made the reader stop and gasp. It simply read:

Killed Davie Milne last night. Didn't mean to, just lost my temper. He'd tried to blackmail me and I could never have allowed that.

For the rest of May and into June, the entries were mainly about the typhoid epidemic. The reader had never heard about typhoid in Aberdeen and had found those entries really interesting.

All the more interesting for the fact the owner of the diary had been the manager of the very shop where the disease had started. How cool was that?

But, of course, it wasn't the typhoid entries that now played on the reader's mind. She had uncovered a confession to murder. What should she do about that now?

Would it be worth going to the police? Surely, they'd not be interested after all these years. The owner of the diary, Samuel Reynolds, was dead as would many of the other people involved in the case all those years ago.

The reader made a decision. She tore out the page on which the confession had been written but kept the rest as a social history document. She, herself, was only twenty-one and therefore had no memories of the sixties at all.

She would keep the fact that Samuel Reynolds had been a murderer to herself. No one else need ever know.

And she stuck to that decision.

Safe to say, that in late 1994, a seventy-three-old Graeme Ogston would have cared little to be told about who had actually killed Davie Milne. He had long forgotten the case, simply putting it down to one that got away.

He had retired from the police in 1970 and he and Alison were still happily married all those years later.

Graeme Ogston was a man content with the way his life had panned out. He had long accepted that, in his time as a police officer, there had never been any divine right to solve every crime that came his way.

He had retired happy with his record and content in the knowledge that you can never win them all.

As for the Summer Cup Final of 1964. The match, which had been due to be played in June, was finally played during August and September. It took three matches to decide a winner. The games were as follows:

1st August – Pittodrie – Aberdeen 3 Hibs 2

5th August – Easter Road – Hibs 2 Aberdeen 1

Aberdeen then won the right, by toss of a coin, to have home advantage in the deciding replay. Two days before the Forth Road Bridge was opened, Hibs travelled to Aberdeen. They were managed, at that time, by Jock Stein.

2nd September – Pittodrie – Aberdeen 1 Hibs 3

Hibs twice won the Summer Cup and it currently lies in the trophy room of Easter Road.

Aberdeen were never to win the Summer Cup but, then again, Aberdeen rarely won any trophies until Alex Ferguson arrived.

But that was another story entirely.